Tom

The Next Chapter

by Lisa M Billingham

1

WARNING

This book contains scenes that some readers may find disturbing. If you are affected by anything contained within, please seek help. Professional contacts can be found at the back of this book.

This book or any portion thereof may not be reproduced or used in any manner whatsoever without the express written permission of the copyright holder except for the use of brief quotations in a book review.

This book is a work of fiction. Names, characters, places and incidents either are products of the author's imagination or are used fictitiously. Any resemblance to actual events, locales or persons, living or dead, is entirely coincidental. Any errors are entirely at the hand of the author.

First published in the UK in 2022

ISBN - 978-1-8382929-2-8 (Paperback)
ISBN – 978-1-8382929-3-5 (eBook)

Dedication

This book is dedicated to the abundance of people who helped to make it happen and supported me through the process. (You know who you are.) I am truly grateful to you all.

My heartfelt thanks and sincere gratitude go to the following people who helped with the research for this book: Andy Bate, Brian Mills, Lee Baker, Sergeant Dan Mills, Gareth Keyte, Steve 'Lobby' Thornton, Karl 'Don' Francesco, John Mayfield, The Royal Engineers Museum, The Ministry of Defence, plus those who wish to remain anonymous. Without them, this book would not be in existence.

PREFACE

Tom is balancing precariously on a Combat Engineer Tractor in the middle of the desert, attempting to free the camouflage net currently trapped on the driver's hatch. Dressed in full combat gear, the added weight of the NBC suit makes it difficult for Tom to manoeuvre his body safely. With the threat of chemical warfare all too real, Tom has no wish to remain on top of the vehicle for longer than is absolutely necessary. The dust is wreaking more havoc than he initially expected. Fine grains of sand coupled with spilt oil and the clumsiness of the heavy over boots make it even harder for Tom to gain purchase on the net. Swearing profusely under his breath, moving his body around slightly to lock his knees, he tugs even harder. The net refuses to budge. "Come on, you bugger. Shift."

Tom puts his full 13 stone body weight behind the net, he yanks again.

Desperate to release it so that he can cover the vehicle and climb down. Somewhat glad he now has a shaved head; the sweat still drips into his eyes, but at least it isn't clinging to his hair. The heat of the desert is going to take some getting used to. Finally, after another couple of tugs, the net unfortunately rips, but at least it's free, and he's able to pull it over the remainder of the vehicle. The bang from a missile attack sounds in the distance; he needs to get down off here. And fast.

Grabbing the end of the net to secure it, Tom turns around, ready to climb off the vehicle and out of the firing line. For now.

His brain is trying to work out the best way to get down. Jump? Or maybe not. He isn't very high off the ground, but he doesn't want to risk injury. Placing his hand on the driver's hatch, he prepares to slide his foot over the side to

7

reach for the track, wondering whether it will be wide enough to balance on. The tread on his clumsy over boot catches in the hole in the netting as he bends down to grab it to secure it over the side. His foot slips, in a panic, he reaches out for something to grab hold of. There is nothing.

Feeling like he's the star in a slow-motion movie, he summersaults backwards, trying to throw himself away from the vehicle and any protruding pieces of metal, aiming for a soft landing on the sand. Catching his foot on the headlight as he gambols over, he twists and bounces awkwardly onto the sand. A loud snap resonates in his ear, and a wave of nausea overtakes him as he lands.

Lying in repose, his right knee angled awkwardly beneath him. The pain, not registering at first, intensifies until he passes out.

Two of the lads from the troop are working at the rear of the vehicle, digging shell scrapes. The sergeant is studying plans leaning on the wall to the side of the vehicle.
"Where's Gold?" The sergeant shouts, looking up from the documents for a moment and seeing an empty space where Tom was previously standing.

"He's on top of the vehicle, Sarge," came the only reply.
"No, he ain't. Shit." Crawling around the side of the vehicle, enemy fire resounding in the distance. The sounds like thunder, the sky lit up like lightning, the sergeant calls for help as he discovers Tom's inert body lying at odd angles on the sand.

Placing his hand on Tom's neck, feeling for a pulse, "Gold, can you hear me?"
Murmuring incoherently, Tom knows his mouth is moving, but he has no idea what he's saying.
"What was that, Gold?"

8

"Knee, crack, sick," is all he can mumble before he passes out again.

In and out of consciousness, Tom barely knows what's happening as the other members of his troop pick him up to place him in the back of the Land Rover and evacuate him to the makeshift field hospital tent, erected scarcely an hour ago.

The tent is only a few hundred yards away, the sergeant travels on the side of the vehicle and jumps off upon arrival. Diving into the tent he calls out, "Small, where are you?"

"Here, Sergeant."

She follows the sergeant out to the vehicle and between them, they manage to get Tom off the Land Rover and place him onto a thin mattress on a poorly constructed metal frame.

"What happened, Sergeant?

"Who knows? He mumbled something about his knee, and it was in a funny position when I found him."

Small, who lives up to her name in height, but is quite the reverse in personality, looks worried.

Have they done more damage by moving him, she wonders?

As if reading her mind, the sergeant answers, "I know moving him wasn't the best course of action, but we need to cover the vehicle before the sun fully sets, without casualties holding us back."

Nodding her understanding, Small answers, "I'll look him over now."

Checking his vital signs and his stats as best as she can with the scant amount of equipment issued to them, the swelling in his knee is apparent even through his combat trousers and over suit. The only way to examine it is it cut the trouser legs off. As soon as she does, the knee swells even more. Jesus. He needs proper medical attention, possibly surgery. And quickly.

Murmuring, Tom begins to come round. "What happened? Where am I...?" he manages to croak out as he feels the medic taking his pulse.

"You've had an accident, Gold. Try not to move."

"Mmm."

"I'm giving you some morphine for the pain. It may make you feel sick, but I need to examine your knee properly." Feeling around the swelling, she knows it's too bad for her to make a proper diagnosis. "Something cold," Small says to herself. "I need something cold." Looking around, she realises there is nothing. With no X-ray equipment or proper operating facilities, Tom's options are limited.

February 1980

Blazing Rows and Home Truths

Thursday 14th February

"For crying out loud, Son, what is wrong with you? Get out of bed. NOW!"

Jolting him, his brain in a fog, Tom gingerly opens one eye to see his mother towering over him.

"What time is it?" Tom asks as he rolls onto his side, his almost athletic torso barely visible under the winter sheets.

"You may well bloody ask; it's 11:30. How many more jobs are you going to lose before you wake up to yourself?" Sylvie shouts, her voice almost at a screech, her blood boiling. "Your grandfather has bent over backwards for you." *Lord only knows why; you waste of air.*

"What was that, Mom?"

"Do you realise how many good people he turned down just to get you out of the shit? Again! Quit bloody dossing and get yourself to work."

"Why are you here, mother? Why aren't you at the shop?"

"I would have thought that was blindingly obvious? As you clearly aren't at work and your grandfather can't get hold of you, he's telephoned the shop four times already. Now get up, you lazy, useless piece of shit and get to work."

Yanking the sheets off his bed, almost pulling him out of it with the force she uses, Tom should have realised; today was not the day to answer her back.

Clearly, she had more to drink last night than I did by the temper on her. Stand your ground, Tom. Stand your ground. He mutters to himself.

13

Never one to be embarrassed, he stands up towering over his mother, butt naked and not caring, staring at her, both their eyes blazing, itching for an argument.

"Can't you for once in my 17-year, shitty life be fucking nice to me? Every day there's something I haven't done or I've failed at. Every. Single. Day.

Immediately, she turns on him. "You've brought nothing but trouble to our front door and…" she screeches.

"I brought nothing but trouble?! Me?! That's rich, coming from you."

"You're not too big for a slap even now, Son. Watch your mouth."

"No, Mom, you watch yours. Have you ever wondered why I'm the way I am?"

"What's that, Son? Lazy, pig-headed, slovenly, a useless failure... need I go on?"

"No, Mom, you've made it quite clear how you feel about me. Maybe I should leave and never come back..."

"Just get to bloody work and apologise to your grandfather, he's worried sick, and it's all your fault."

Storming out and slamming all the doors on her way, Sylvie leaves Tom standing there. Dumbfounded, he grabs hold of his pillow and pounds it until he's exhausted, years of pent-up heartache, bullying, and anger bury themselves in the helpless bedding.

"What did I do to deserve such a vile mother?" He mumbles to himself.

Happy birthday to me.

Pulling himself together, amazed at how much better he now feels, he realises he should get to work. He loves his grandfather more than life itself and hates to think he's upset him, although he isn't altogether surprised.

Quickly grabbing his work clothes, he dresses as fast as he can, races down the stairs and dives into his brand new, white Audi Coupe, courtesy of his grandfather.

Still over the limit, he races through the narrow streets of Birch Tree Town, through Rose Bush Village and into Malthaven; the beautiful scenery whizzes passed. Arriving at the factory just in time for lunch, his grandfather is waiting for him at the gates, his arms folded across his chest.

Oh no, this doesn't bode well; he looks angrier than mother.

Putting his best foot forward, he trots over to the gate, "hey, Gramps, how's it going?"

"Come up to the office, Son; we need to talk."

Nonchalantly Tom follows his grandfather to his office on the first floor overlooking the production line. Tom stops for a moment to admire the Airbus wings currently being born in their factory. He sticks his chest out, proud that his grandfather has won such a lucrative contract but not showing one ounce of gratitude for the car he got out of it.

"Right, Son, sit yourself down."

Tom does as he's bid; his grandfather's look brooks no argument.

"You have two choices, Tom. Pull your finger out, or get out. You're my grandson, and I love you, but I'm running a business, not a charity. I spoil you because your mother was and still is a useless article, but you've gone too far now."

Gobsmacked at the lecture, which is unusual for Maurice but not entirely unexpected. Tom sits in stunned silence.

"I've been thinking, maybe a stint in the Army would be good for you. I can't do anything with you. You won't listen to me when I try and train you. This will all be yours one day. What are you going to do with it?"

Stunned and feeling very hurt, Tom can only hang his head in shame as he nods his ascent that his grandfather is right.

"You lost your tongue, Son?"

"No, Gramps, I'm sorry. I won't let it happen again."

"I took the liberty of obtaining an application form for you. I suggest you fill it in now and get it posted."

Tom swallows his words. *I guess I'm not going to wheedle my way out of it this time.*

Application Outcome
Monday 16th June

"Tom, you're up early, Son. What's happened?"

Waving an envelope at his grandfather, Tom slowly looks up from his toast and coffee, too nervous to say anything.

"You haven't opened it. Is it from the Army?"

Tom nods slowly, almost choking on his toast as his mouth is so dry and his hands are shaking.

About time, Maurice thinks to himself.

"Are you going to open it?"

Shaking his head, "I don't think I can, Gramps, you do it."

"Why are you shaking so much, Son? Another night on the pop, eh?"

The sound of disgust he could hear in his grandfather's voice prevents Tom from answering. *Why bother? He won't believe me anyway.*

Maurice glances down at Tom, notices how scared he seems. *Not so brash now, are you, young man? Good, maybe this will teach you a lesson.* Maurice prays to himself.

"I thought you were up for this, Son."

"I didn't really have much choice, did I? I would have been out on my ear.' Neither you nor mom and dad want me here. What was I supposed to do?"

"Now, Tom, that's not fair; we agreed you would try, and if you got in, you'd give it a go. You know I'm happy to have you here," *not so sure about Jack and Sylvie, but hopefully, they'll get a new place of their own too. Soon.* "It will all be yours one day anyway."

"Don't talk like that, Gramps."

"Why not? It's true, no one else in the family wants this big house, but you need to do something, you're wasting your life, and I didn't know what else to do. I thought it might help you get back on your feet. Plus, you might just enjoy it. You're fit enough, lad, and I can't see why you wouldn't do well."

"I haven't come off my feet, so why do I need to get back on them?"

"Tom, you want for nothing, absolutely nothing, but you've been spoiled all your life, mainly by me, so I take some responsibility for the way you've turned out..."

"What?"

Holding his hand up to stop Tom interrupting, "no, Son, it has to be said, you have a brand-new car outside that most folks round here would give their eye teeth for, but you don't appreciate it. You never even said thank you when you were given the keys, and whilst it will all come to you one day, I'm dammed if I'm going to let you throw away everything I've worked my whole life for like you throw your wages away on the booze and horses. When you have a job, that is. You're getting as bad as your mother."

At the reference to his mother, Tom's blood boils. *How can he compare me to her!* Before he can say something he will regret, Tom walks away, muttering under his breath, "I'm sorry, Gramps." As if that alone would be enough to get him off the hook.

Maurice, who's slightly deaf, doesn't hear him and waves his hand for the letter. "Come on then, let's have it."

Using a bread knife to slice open the envelope, Maurice quickly removes the letter, keener than Tom, to learn the outcome.

Please, God, he's got in; he needs all the help he can get.

"What does it say, Gramps? I haven't got in, have I?"

Forlorn and feeling dejected, Tom slouches in his chair, his arms on the table. "What now then?"

"What makes you think you haven't got in, Son?"

"The look on your face."

"This is my normal look, and you have got in. It says they want you to report to Freedom Hall, Peace Hampton, on Monday 30th June, ready to begin basic training on the 7th July, so you'd better get yourself sorted. There's a list of instructions for you, which I'm sure even you can cope with"

Handing the letter back to Tom, "I need to go and place a job advert in the paper. Well done, Son. This is the start of something new for you. Don't blow it."

Leaving Tom dumbstruck, Maurice grabs his coat and makes his way to the back door. "See you at work," he shouts over his shoulder as he climbs into his black Jaguar mark two, a Christmas present to himself.

Still in shock, Tom opens the letter to read himself, not quite believing what's happening. *It's real then, what the hell...*

Monday 16th June - Evening

"You don't normally eat with me, Son; why now?"

"Dunno, guess I thought I'd best make an effort being as I won't be here much longer."

Never one to mince his words, his grandfather almost chokes on his soup, responds, "you've left it a bit late, Tom; there's no backing out now. You made your choice with your actions. You do understand that don't you?"

Christ, I'm not a child.

"Yeah, Gramps, I know, but…"

"But nothing, Son, now eat your dinner.

Desperately scared but putting on a brave face, Tom stares down at his soup. *What am I going to do? Why the hell did I even apply? I'm not disciplined enough for Army life or courageous enough to bloody fight.*

"Gramps."

"Yes, Son."

"What happens if I don't get through training. Will I be able to come back here?"

"We'll see. You have lessons to learn. Being grateful for what you have for starters."

Drowning His Sorrows
Saturday 28th June

Tom props up the bar of *The Frog and Snail* in Malthaven. Listening to *Kenny Rogers, Coward of the County*, number one a few months ago, makes him feel worse than he already does. *That's me. Coward.*

"Jees, Reg, can't you put something a bit more cheerful on the jukebox."

"Hey, what's up, Mr grumpy? This was your favourite song not long ago. What's eating you?"

"I know, I'm just…"

"Drowning your sorrows? It looks like, what's happened?"

"Army, mate. Next week. Can't wait to get away from… them but scared as hell."

"What. You joined up?"

"I know! It was Gramps's idea. Apparently, I need discipline and order in my life. Who knew?" Tom harumphs.

"Well, he does have a point; old Maurice ain't as stupid as you think."

"Gee, thanks, Reg. I thought you were on my side."

"No one's side, mate, but you do need to sort yourself out; I'll agree with him there."

Staring into his pint, *mmm maybe I do, if Reg is saying it too. Why the Army though? I'll never know.*

"What was that Tom, I didn't quite catch it?"

"Oh, nothing, just thinking out loud."

"Ah well, look at ya, half pissed, underage, and you haven't even been here an hour yet. Lost more money today too, I bet."

"Mmm, yup."

"I rest my case then."

"You've made your point, Reg; I'm off now." Tom slurs as he grabs his car keys from the mat on the bar beside him.

"Not so fast, young man." Reg, his reflexes faster than lightning, despite his rotund frame, catches Tom's hand and relieves him of the keys. "I think you'd better walk."

"What! It's four bloody miles, don't be ridiculous." Tom hollers, attempting to grab the keys back but unsure which of the two Regs he should aim for.

"You can't even see straight. How the hell do you propose to drive?"

"It wouldn't be the first time, Reg."

"Aye, it may well not be, but it isn't going to be this time. Have no fear. Come back tomorrow to fetch it."

Realising Reg won't back down, Tom stumbles off to the gents to relieve himself before walking home.

"Anyway," Reg hollers to his retreating back. "Good practice for the Army." *You'll have more than four miles to walk then.* Reg says to himself. *What a shock that lads got coming to him.*

"Ha, ha, ever the comedian, Reg, see ya round."

Day One – Basic Training
Monday 7th July

Roll call over, Tom waits in line for his kit to be issued. Hopping from foot to fit a mixture of nerves and excitement for his new life. Once the kit is issued, each trainee from training party 80/6 makes their way to the designated meeting point for their team during training. Tom spots a youth, slightly older than him, 18 already, he guesses, looks slightly overweight although he looks as tall, his shaved head shimmying in the early morning sunlight of daybreak looking down at his feet. *Wow, I'm not the only nervous one here then, by the look on his face. Wonder what happened to him.* Tom ponders to himself, pleased he may finally have found someone he can relate to. *Great, it looks like he's on my team too, winner. This should be fun.*

"Right, you lot. First things first," Corporal Daily, a short bald man with a gruff voice and a steely stare, shouts. "You will now learn how to make your bed."

Stifling a laugh, Tom stares in amazement. *I already know how to make a bed. Not that I bother very often though.*

The group of recruits follow the corporal to their billets and gawp in disbelief as he pulls the sheets off the first bed. Tom, always in the wrong place at the wrong time, catches the corporal's eye and is therefore allocated that first bed.

"You." Corporal Daily says, staring at Tom, making him feel uncomfortable under his gaze. "Come here."

"Yes, Sir."

"What's your name?"

"Tom Gold, Sir."

"You will address me as Corporal, I will address you as Gold. Is that understood?"

"Yes, Corporal."

"Get a move on, lad."

Speeding up his step Tom crosses the room and stands to attention at the side of the bed.

Corporal Daily talks Tom through making his bed, picking him up on the slightest error. Once Tom has finished his first attempt, the corporal seems suitably impressed but still expects a higher standard. Addressing the rest of the recruits, he tells them to pick a bed and make it. Pulling Tom's bed apart at the same time.

"Redo that, Gold. Better this time."

"Yes, Corporal."

Shaking his head as the corporal walks away, Tom mutters under his breath. *Learn how to make a bed. How ridiculous.*

"What was that, mate?" A voice behind him asks.

Turning sharply, Tom sees the youth he spotted earlier making the bed behind him. "I didn't realise I'd said that out loud. I can't believe I'm being taught how to make a bed!"

The youth laughs at him, "this is the easy bit. Wait until you get a few weeks into training."

"Why, what happens then?"

"You'll see. What's your name by the way? I'm Phil."

"Tom, good to meet you." He answers as the two young men shake hands.

Having made their beds, the corporal inspects them and pulls them apart.

"Again. Both of you. You will not continue with further training until you can make your beds properly. Understood?"

"Yes, Corporal," both of the lads respond in unison as they set about doing the task again. Both are deep in concentration.

Finally, having made a good enough effort for the corporal to send them on to the next task, they head for lunch in the mess hall. Tom and Phil walk over together, chatting away like two long lost buddies.

"You want to hit the town on Saturday, Phil?" Tom asks as they enter the mess hall, glancing around to get their bearings.

"You are kidding, right?" Phil laughs. "You do know we aren't allowed out until halfway through training?"

The colour drains from Tom's face, "what! Not at all?"

"You really didn't know. Did you not read all your paperwork?"

Tom harumphs, "guess not." Still in shock, he follows Phil to the serving hatch to collect his meal. In a bad mood now, knowing he won't get his dose of biting snakes, his favourite tipple, Tom takes it out on the young lad serving the food.

"What's this?" Tom grunts as the food is slopped onto his plate.

"What's it look like?" responds the chef, a tall, muscular lad who has the kindest face here Tom has seen so far. Realising it isn't the lad's fault he hadn't read his paperwork properly, Tom softens his voice, feeling a little more at ease with him than most of the others, "I've really no idea, what is it?"

"Liver, onions and mash. Good for you, keep your strength up," he answers. "God knows you're going to need it."

"What was that?" Tom asks.

"Nothing mate, enjoy your dinner."

27

"Thanks, I will." *Not. But beggars can't be choosers.*

The Hill
Monday 18th August

"Right, you lot, first up is a warm-up," Corporal Daily shouts. "Split into two teams, and we are starting today with orienteering for six miles with your kit on your back then running back to base, for the idiots among you, that's here. Last one back does the exercise again. Got it?"

"Yes, Corporal," the team shout in unison.

Giving the instructions, the corporal shouts. "You have your maps; get to it."

Jesus, this looks hard, Tom mutters under his breath.

"What was that, mate?"

"This looks bloody impossible, Phil."

"You think this is bad? It gets worse."

Worse, God, what am I doing here? "How can it be any worse than the last six weeks? I already feel like I'm out of my depth."

"Me too." While they prepare for the task ahead, Phil caries on talking. "He's serious, by the way," Phil nods at Tom, "about the last one doing it again."

"How do you know?"

"He's my Uncle."

"Really. I didn't know that. He'll go easy on you if you're last then."

"Why would you know? And no chance, it will be worse for me; come on, I for one ain't risking it."

Kits on their backs, they jog to catch up with the rest of the party at the starting point, following them out of the gates and onto the main training ground. Miles and miles of gorgeous field stretch as far as the eye can see. Abandoned buildings and obstacles dotted about all around them.

Picking up the pace as the rest of the group gain further momentum and begin to move out of their sightline, Tom realises he has his work cut out if he's going to get through the rest of the training.

Struggling to keep up, panting and now panicking, Tom realises he is, in fact, last. Stopping to take a few deep breaths, he glances out over the fields in front of him. Straight ahead, standing out amongst the weeds, is a single Sunflower, tall and straight and completely isolated amongst the blades of grass. *That's just how I feel.* Tom thinks, lonely in a crowd of 50. *How can that be?*

"Gold! Quit dawdling and get a move on. Do you really want to do this again?" The corporal bellows down his ear, scaring the wits out of him. He hadn't heard him jogging behind him.

"No," Tom whispers.

"Pardon."

"No, Corporal." Tom almost yells back, managing to refrain himself and keep a civil tone.

Tom picks up his pace, and follows the well-trodden path round to the right and begins his ascent up the hill, praying he can catch up with others who are no longer in his line of vision.

A couple of miles later, Tom spots Phil's back at the top of the hill, stopping to check his map. *Thank goodness, at least I won't be last on my own if I can catch him up.*

Just as he reaches the peak of the hill, he picks up his pace and makes the descent down the other side, his kit bag straps chaffing his arms and back, the weight increasing with each step.

Tom glances up at the sky; the clouds look heavy, just like his kit bag. Losing sight of the team again, he stops to check his map; unsure whether he has it the right way up, he struggles to decipher where he actually is. There are so many crossroads on the map and so few landmarks over this side of the training ground.

Left or right? Make a decision, man.

Feeling the corporal descending on him again, he abandons the map reading. He turns right, passing a dilapidated metal wilding, a prefabricated remnant of the first world war, a building that will haunt his dreams for years to come. Without checking his map now that he has a landmark, he continues on the path. Seeing the back of his team mate's camouflage jackets a short way in front, Tom breathes a sigh of relief. *Thank god I turned right!*

Breaking into a faster jog, he catches up with them. It isn't Phil who is last though, he doesn't recognise the fella from the back, although with a team of 50, why would he? *Phil must have got a wriggle on.* He thinks out loud.

Jogging even faster, seeing the halfway point a few yards in front of him, he overtakes four of this team mates.

Thank the lord for that. I made it. Halfway at least. Out of breath but relieved, he grabs his bottle of water from his kit bag and swallows half of it down in one. Following his team mates to the roll call point as he drinks, he looks for Phil but can't see him.

"Fall in!" The corporal hollers.

An overwhelming sense of fear and dread wash over Tom as he realises it's the wrong corporal.

Shit!

Backing away from the group, desperately hoping he hasn't been seen, Tom rushes into the nearest bush, stooping down until the group start their run back to the beginning.

Yanking his map out of his pocket, he studies it with greater concentration this time. Horrified when he realises he's five miles adrift of the checkpoint and that there is no other way except to retrace his steps. Clawing his way out from under the bush, it suddenly dawns on him. When he makes it back, he will have to do it all again. His shoulders sag. *What a bloody idiot that'll teach me to pay attention and learn to map read properly!* His mind is in overdrive, and exhaustion threatens to take over. *This is too much.* He mutters to himself.

Retracing his steps back to the crossroads to take what would have been the left turning, he continues to berate himself silently. Cursing his plight, his grandfather, his parents, even Reg in the pub, he blames them all for his current situation. Conserving his energy for the second round of the exercise, he walks rather than jogs. Taking a sip of his water, his head feels light, but he also realises that he may not get another sip before doing the circuit again.

An hour and a half later, he rounds the corner to the halfway checkpoint.

"About time, Gold, what kept you?" demanded Corporal Daily, currently manning the halfway checkpoint.

No point lying, Tom responds, "wrong way at Coopers Cross, Corporal."

"Right you are then, back to the beginning and round again. And don't bother stopping in between."

Knowing he isn't joking, Tom takes a deep breath and continues on his route, unsure whether to laugh or cry at his stupidity but certain he won't let it happen again.

***

Three hours later, mentally and physically exhausted, Tom reaches the end of the exercise. Corporal Daily waits to greet him.

"Gold, finally. You interrupted my dinner waiting for you, and you're going to pay. Drop and give me fifty.

"Corporal?"

"Drop and give me fifty. Now."

He attempts to take his kit off his back.

"Leave it. Drop and give me fifty. I won't ask quite so nicely next time." His nose almost touching Tom's, he shouts in his face. His spittle sprays Tom's face, making him reel in disgust.

Tom, his brain haggled from exhaustion and dehydration, drops to his knees, the corporal close behind him ready with his foot to push him to the floor. The penny drops when he cottons on that he now has to do fifty press-ups. Tom assumes the position, attempting to ignore the additional weight from the force of the corporal's foot.

Pulling himself up afterwards, his arms and legs shake uncontrollably as he gags and retches for all he's worth.

"Shower, then mess hall, Gold."

Tom drags himself away without responding to the orders, his feet burning with blisters, his head pounding, and his tongue sticking to the roof of his parched mouth. He staggers to the showers and stands under the water for what feels like an eternity. Emotions threaten to bubble over as he reaches for his towel, his eyes closed against the sting of the water. Feeling blindly, he can't put his hands on it; opening his eyes, he looks to the space where he left his name tagged towel. *Where the hell—am I losing it or what?* He mumbles to himself, wondering if the exhaustion from the day has haggled his brain more than he realises.

Stepping away from the open bank of showers, he looks all around, dumbfounded—no sign of it.

"Lost something, Gold."

At the high-pitched sound, he turns round and comes face to face with one of the uglier members of the other

33

team. He remembers him vaguely from his faux pax this morning.

He was last too, wonder if they made him do it again? Standing stock-still, his huge arms folded across his chest, a scowl on his face.

Confused, Tom answers, "yeah, my towels gone."

"Ah, would this be it then?" Questions the offensive youth as he dangles Tom's towel in front of him.

Making a grab for it, Tom stumbles on a tile protruding from the floor and falls.

"Ha, ha! Jerk. Here, have fun with this." He shouts as he smears whatever is on the towel into Tom's hair.

Dazed and shocked, Tom rolls onto his back, grabs the towel to dry himself when he catches a potent whiff of something rather offensive. Unable to compute in his brain what's happening, the smell makes him wretch. He grapples to his feet and pushes the button on the shower again.

"Bastard! You'll pay for this!" Tom screams out loud.

"That I doubt," retaliates the squeaky voice as it rounds the corner and leaves the shower room.

Great, I thought he'd gone.

Making sure his tormentor has finally left, Tom finishes showering, the tears free-flowing as he stands once again under the tricking water.

With the stench still rife in his nostrils, he dresses quickly. His body is still glistening with the water, his clothes are hard to put on. Once dressed, he heads to the mess hall, throwing his towel in the rubbish on the way past.

He will pay for this!

***

Entering the mess hall, Tom spots Phil and meanders over to him, "hey, I looked for you at lunchtime. Where were you?" Phil asks.

"Mate, you don't want to know."

"Woah, what's that smell?" Phil cries, looking around him.

"What smell, mate?" Tom responds, looking sheepish.

"Shit mate, it smells like shit."

Unsure whether or not to say anything, Tom looks down and gobbles a mouth full of food. *Can I trust him?*

"It's you, isn't it?"

Nodding, his mouth full of food, Tom looks away from Phil, tears still stinging the corner of his eyes.

"I never expected it to be this hard, and I didn't want to join up either. Right now, I hate everyone for putting me here." Tom complains, his anger against his family rising with a force he can't quite understand.

"Nah, mate, you hate yourself for what you've become. Get used to it. It will get worse."

"How is that possible? This has been the worst six weeks of my life so far. And you keep saying that, how do you know it will get worse?"

"My uncle, remember."

"Ah. If you knew it would be hell, why did you join up?"

"No choice, mate. This or prison."

"Oh." Was all Tom could think to say.

"Come on; you need an ally, we both do. You can protect me from my uncle, and I can make sure you don't get covered in shit again."

Tom's head snaps round, facing Phil but not quite looking him in the eye. Embarrassed, he says, "how do I stop it happening again?"

"You don't. Happened to my uncle when he first did his basic training. Don't let it get to you." Phil says, seeing the look on Tom's face. "It's just a boyhood prank, I'm surprised it took this long. Get through the training, and things will be different. We will go on to learn a trade if we finish basic training. So, come on, tell me what happened today?"

Hardly knowing where to start, Tom pours his heart out, barely stopping for breath in his running commentary of his day's adventures.

Listening intently until he's finished, "Oh, is that all? Wow, you got off light with all of it, mate. I've heard worse stories, believe me."

Looking over Tom's shoulder at the youth who has just entered the mess hall, Phil points, "that him there is it? Your tormentor?"

Tom's eyes follow Phil's finger as it points to the far corner of the room. "Yeah, that's him."

"Makes sense. That's Shaun King."

"How do you know him? There's a hundred of us here. Do you know everyone?

"Mmm, pretty much, yeah. I make a point of knowing who's around me. I have a past, Tom.

So do I but not as bad as yours by the sounds of it.

"Ah, say no more then."

"You'll have to stand up to Shaun, by the way, don't let him push you around, and whatever you do sort it out between you, don't ever involve a higher-ranking officer. You will be ostracised if you do."

"Thanks for the warning. I appreciate it."

"Right, time to hit the sack, Tom. Get some rest; you're going to need it." At that, Tom finds himself staring at Phil's back.

Jesus. I'll never get through basic training at this rate.
Tom mutters out loud, shaking his head in disbelief.

The Following Day
Tuesday 19th August

Lying in bed later that evening, sleep eludes Tom. It's been a few weeks since he last had a dose of biting snakes and his cravings are getting stronger. His limbs shake despite the oppressive heat of the room, and the rock-like bed does nothing for his aching bones. His sweaty body sticks to the faded white sheets like glue.

No, no, stop, I can't breathe. His arms flail around like a demented octopus as one of the tentacles scratches at his hair, as short as it is, trying to pull it out. Retching as the pain rushes through his body, his head bounces around and bangs on and off the bed. The stench from his hair still strong in his nostrils. Still retching and tossing and turning, he notices the octopus has a face. An ugly, angry, sour face. Realising it's his tormentor from the showers, Tom tries to back away. Where do you think you're going? The face says as it contorts into a ghost-like vision, eyes ablaze like burning embers on a bonfire.

Moving closer to Tom, their noses virtually touching, one of the tentacles reaches around him, grabs his kit and lifts it over his head.

"Gold, what have we here?" Rifling through Tom's kit bag, he pulls out the locket his grandfather had given him for luck.

Diving off the bed, Tom grabs for the locket, just managing to yank it out of the tentacle. Anger burns inside him; he squares up to the monster before him. Leave... My... Stuff... Alone. Asshole. As Tom tries to reach for the contorted face, it disappears, only to reappear behind him, taunting him. Come get me then, it shouts.

Tom spins around, still clutching the locket in his right hand, holding it in the air as if it were some kind of talisman.

"Ha, you think that will protect you? Think again, Gold, I've got your number."

Tucking the locket down his shorts, the creature rears up again, entangling Tom in its tentacles, squeezing as if attempting to squeeze the life out of him.

"Stop, stop, I can't breathe."

"Tom, Tom, wake up, man, what the hell, what's going on?" Shaking him, Phil notices he's sweating profusely. *I know it's hot in here, but this is crazy. I wonder if he has a fever?*

"Should I call the medic? You're burning up, man."

"What, where am I?" Tom asks as he half opens his eyes to see Phil sitting on the edge of his bed. "Oh, It's you, Phil."

"Yeah, who did you think it was?"

"Oh, no one, it's OK."

"You have a bad dream, Tom?"

"Er, yeah, something like that."

"Watch yourself, mate; you were flailing around like someone demented. They'll think nothing of sectioning you if you keep that up."

"Cheers, mate, that makes me feel so much better. I don't usually have bad dreams, but that was… weird."

"Well, try and get some rest, sleep with one eye open, eh? Keep the bad monsters away." Phil laughs as he makes his way back to his own bed and into a peaceful slumber.

Tom shakes himself until he's half awake and rummages around in his shorts. Panic sets in. No locket.

What the hell? Looking around for Shaun, wondering whether he did get the better of him, he notices Shaun is fast asleep. That's the loud snore he can now hear in the dead of night.

Leaning over to his kit bag, he feels around for the tiny flap inside the bag. *There you are, you little beauty, right where I left you. What on earth was that all about then?* Tom shakes his head in disbelief.

More awake now than he has been all day, the pitch black of the room emanates an eerie feel quite alien to Tom's senses. Staring at the ceiling, his mind in turmoil, slowly going over the day and how bad it has been. Every bone and muscle in his body ache like never before.

How can even my eyelids be aching? He asks himself. Tossing and turning again for what feels like hours but is only a couple of minutes, he gives in and lies flat on his back, staring into the abyss. The glint of light from the toilet block gives off just enough light for him to see the cracks in the ceiling. *Oh, well, I suppose I could count them. Not quite sheep, but they'll do.*

Having only just managed to doze back off into another fitful sleep, the sound of the 6 am roll call frightens the life out of Tom as he sits bolt upright in bed. His head is pounding, and his whole body still aches from the previous day. *I haven't felt this rough since I had the flu a couple of years ago.*

Shaking himself out of his reverie, he notices everyone else is up and racing towards the shower block.

"Tom, man, come on." Phil grabs his arm and drags him out of bed on his way past. "Get to the showers, double-quick, or you'll regret it." Phil bellows as he races off with the others. Glancing around, Tom realises he's going to be last if he's not careful and suspects that wouldn't be good.

Pulling his wash bag from the makeshift table at the side of his bed, he follows the others to the showers. Quickly washing, drying and dressing, he wonders why the rush.

"Hey, Phil," he shouts as he spots his mate wandering over to the mess hall, looking as fresh as a daisy. "Why the rush with the showers," he asks.

"Come with me, and I'll show you."

Following Phil back around the shower block, Tom stops short as he sees the last trainee in line. The freezing cold temperature of the water felt from their hiding place behind the tree at the edge of the fenced field.

"Wow, that water must be freezing now. I can feel it from here."

"It is, think about it, a hundred people. Twenty showers, minimal hot water."

"Why?"

"Get us used to life in the fast lane, mate, not much hot water where we're going. If we get through training."

"You reckon?"

"You really do have a lot to learn, don't you, Tom?"

"Guess so." Pushing himself further back against the tree to ensure no one can see him, Tom stands up straight and settles in to watch the drama unfold before him.

"Last one in is a sissy." Tom hears one of the new recruits' shout, at six feet five with a build like the side of a house and only 16 years old, no one was planning to argue with him. The last few stragglers dash to get there.

"Ah, look at him, the little squirt! Think you're hard, do you, walking, last in?"

"No, I just don't mind a cold shower. What's the problem?"

"Ooh, brave. We like to reward bravery, don't we, boys?" The giant looks around him at his two mates, twins by the looks of them, leaning against the wall with their arms crossed, awaiting orders.

"Being as your so brave and we like to reward bravery, you get an extra minute in the shower, isn't that nice?"

"Whatever," came the response. A shrug of the shoulders follows.

"Get yourself in there then, don't be shy."

Tom couldn't see the trainee's face from where he was standing, but he will never forget the piercing scream that resounds around the camp. Pushing himself off the tree, he makes his way towards the showers, but Phil's hand on his shoulder stops him in his tracks.

"Not so fast, mate. You do not want to get involved."

"What are they doing to him?"

"You really want to see?"

Tom nods, uncertainty and curiosity aroused in equal measure.

"OK, follow me, stay close and make sure no one sees you."

Sidling further along with the trees at the edge of the fenced field, they crouch behind a bush. From their vantage point, they have a perfect view of the action.

"What's he holding him under with?" queries Tom, turning to look at his new friend.

"Probably an old broom or a rusty post from an old metal fence. Who knows?"

"But, why?"

"Because he's a bully. He's not doing himself or his career any favours. He will get caught. He won't get grassed on. It doesn't work like that, but mark my words, he will get caught."

"Keep watching," Phil says as Tom turns back round to face the action.

For what seems like hours, Tom stares, mesmerised at the lashings this young man receives from his peers.

"It's a broom handle, Phil, look."

"Yep, he's lucky today then. He'll get ten of those."

"I just don't get it."

"They are attempting to show the group who's boss."

"What. No one is, except the soldiers training us. What makes them do these things?"

"Who knows why anyone does the things they do?"

Very true, Tom muses to himself.

Another piercing scream breaks Tom's concentration as he sits up to see the trainee being pushed back under the water yet again. Straining to see, he's sure the lashings have drawn blood.

"How come I didn't know about this before?" Tom asks, genuinely dumbfounded at the behaviour of some of his peers.

"You're never normally late rising, so you wouldn't have seen it happen."

I wonder if Gramps knew this when he encouraged me to join up? Tom ponders to himself, slightly nervous about the remainder of basic training.

"The last person to the showers every morning can expect this treatment, Tom until they get caught. Don't ever be last."

"Thanks, Phil, I'll remember that. I owe you one. That was nearly me this morning."

"I know. Look, he's coming out now." Phil points to the young lad staggering across the footpath, barely able to hold himself upright. Tom turns back to look towards him and stares in disbelief, nudging Phil in the ribs.

"Look who it is, Phil." Tom stares, aghast.

"Why if it isn't your mate, Shaun," Phil says.

"What a turn up for the books? I didn't recognise his voice, bit different now, isn't he?"

"Probably goes a long way to explain why he's the way he is, Tom. Didn't you notice the scars on the side of his face? They weren't from shaving."

"No, I was too scared yesterday and too gobsmacked today. The way he was with me was evil... pure evil."

"It was him who was last yesterday morning too. I think he secretly likes it, don't you? Why else would you be last two days running?"

"He'll probably be last tomorrow then," Tom mutters under his breath. His mind is working overtime. *Looks like someone else is having my revenge for me.*

"Don't even think about it, Tom. Revenge is never a dish best served cold. Or any other way, for that matter." Before Tom can ask how the hell he knows what he's thinking, Phil pulls at his sleeve, "come on, let's go; we don't want to be late for breakfast."

Scurrying out from behind the bushes, they both jog to the mess hall in companionable silence.

***

"Hey, Phil, fancy hitting the town on Saturday evening, assuming we pass the drill test?"

"Yeah, why not? Naff all better to do other than have a wank, is there?"

Laughing, Tom responds, "I was planning to find someone to do that for me while I was out."

"What type of girl are you looking for then, Tom?" Phil asks as they empty their breakfast trays on their way out of the mess hall and make their way to the rendezvous point for today's exercise.

"Not fussy, mate, as long as it has a pulse and a pair of tits, I don't really care. You?"

"Oh, I'm a bit more selective than that. They have to have a nice arse too." Phil guffaws.

Both laugh and enjoy the banter. "Seriously though, Phil, what is your type?"

"Small petite brunette, the gentile type who can hold a conversation."

"Really? I had you pegged for a tall leggy blond, mate."

"No way, my mother was like that. *Mine is too.* No, thank you. My girlfriend is the exact opposite."

"Wow, I didn't realise you had a girlfriend. What made you sign up and leave her behind?"

"No choice, mate. As I said, I wasn't about to go to prison. If I don't pass the training, I might get away with a lighter sentence or community service, and I fancy those even less than this, to be honest."

Tom didn't like to ask what he'd done for fear he may not like the answer, but he was saved the indecision by the bellow from the corporal.

"Right, you horrible individuals, let's be having you."

Falling into line, feeling ready to take on the world, Tom feels better today than he has for a long time, surprisingly.

"Your day today will be split. The morning will be spent on the shooting range, the afternoon out on an exercise."

Shooting range. Woo hoo. Tom thinks to himself, he'd enjoyed the weapons handling lesson they'd had a couple of weeks ago, this was his chance to see what he was made of.

"Your exercise this afternoon will push you to your limits and beyond. You need to be alert at all times as you will have targets on you. You will split into two teams

46

again, and you will be shooting at each other. Luckily for you, for today, they will be blanks. Get hit, and your punishment will be worse than death. Tomorrow the roles will be reversed, and the day will be repeated. Grab your maps and kit bags, and let's go."

At the shooting range, the corporal yells the orders, "work in pairs, and choose very wisely."

Tom and Phil immediately gravitate towards each other, neither of them quite trusting anyone else to do such an exercise with.

It turns out Phil is quite handy with a gun and does exceptionally well at target practice. Disappointingly, Tom is not so good. Hopefully, working as a team, they will counter each other's skills.

"My uncle gave me some good advice, Tom; his words to me were: you need eyes up your arse and arses in your eyes."

"What the hell does that mean?" confusion is apparent on Tom's face.

"Simply put, never, ever, let your guard down, no matter how rough you feel and keep your enemy close."

Now he tells me.

Following the rest of the team after lunch to their positions marked on their individual pair's maps in companionable silence. Both are wondering what punishment could possibly be worse than death.

Surprisingly light on their feet, given their body weights, they operate from a stealth-like perspective, using the trees, buildings and thankfully overgrown field as camouflage to navigate the ten-mile course over rough terrain whilst avoiding the shots.

"That was loud," Tom ducks as they hear three bangs in quick succession. "Someone brought it already then?"

"Sounds like it. Glad it wasn't us."

Crawling along the edge of the field through the trees, low down on their bellies looking around them every few seconds for tell-tale signs of the enemy. The crack of a branch to the right of them signifies the enemy's approach. Staying stock still, holding their breaths so as not to be discovered. The crunching of fallen twigs under foot warns them of the proximity of the other troop members. They dare not move a muscle for fear of exposure—both of their legs and arms shaking with the pressure to remain still.

Luckily, they are partly hidden behind a row of trees, their camouflage gear hiding any exposed parts well.

The footsteps slowly recede, and both young men breathe a sigh of relief.

"Close call there, Phil."

"Not half, come on, let's get to that tree there and check the map." Phil points as he starts to manoeuvre himself. Tom smiles to himself as he follows Phil's pointing finger. The tree Phil points at looks rather like someone doing a yoga pose. The twisted branches resemble oddly placed arms and legs. *Well, I've heard of women doing yoga, but never trees.* Tom smiles to himself as he follows Phil closely.

The base of the tree, charred with a hole, obviously having been set on fire previously, means they could easily fit themselves inside. Slowly, they make their way over, ever vigilant of potential enemy interaction.

Studying the map, they are shocked and also pleased to discover that they are only a quarter of a mile from the finish point. Phil double checks the map to make sure, given Tom's dubious track record of map reading.

"Yep, we're only a quarter of a mile away, Tom."

"I know. I just told you that."

"It looks like the best way is round the edge of the field but not the forest side, so we are going to have to move very slowly." Luckily the tree is close to the field, and the weeds are overgrown enough to ensure they aren't spotted.

Their attention is heightened even more for the last stretch; they take it at a snail's pace, much to Tom's frustration, who keeps trying to overtake.

"What did I tell you, Tom? Eyes and arse. Stay behind me or stay dead," Phil whispers to him.

Breaking out through the trees, they reach the finish line to raucous applause. Somewhat bemused to discover they are the only two out of fifty to have made it without getting shot. Unable to help themselves, they jump up and down and end up in a brotherly embrace. Elated at having finished. And surviving unscathed.

"Everyone, back to the training room for the debrief." The corporal shouts.

Marching in single file, all lost in their own thoughts, most of them filled with a sense of dread with what surely is to come.

"So, we have mostly dead people in the room then, congratulations. In a couple of hours, you've wiped out almost an entire platoon. I hope you're all very proud because this is where your life gets a whole lot worse." The Corporal shouts, despite the fact that you could hear a pin drop, and it seems no one in the room dares breathe.

The Sergeant, second in command of the team, Simon Pearson, who has studied the proceedings through binoculars from the watch tower in the field, stands up slowly next to the Corporal. His bald head almost bounces off the ceiling as he unwinds his body from the low plastic chair.

As he speaks, the entire room visibly straightens, knowing that this soldier would not take any prisoners despite his softly spoken voice.

With his hands behind his ramrod-straight back, he addresses his audience, slowly eying his prey, delighting in the fear etched on their faces.

"I've been watching you. All of you. Let me tell you, you have a lot to learn. You are only a few weeks into your basic training. Nerves are to be expected; it's all new to you, but if you think we have pushed you to your limits today, please leave. Now. Your place is not here."

A handful of the recruits rise from their chairs, heads bowed and make their way from the room. Tom and Phil, glued to their seats are surprised, but adamant they will see it through. After the scraping of chairs and the murmurs of goodbye have died down, Simon continues.

"The rest of you. Pay attention—the only two of you. Yes, the only two who didn't get shot or even injured on this exercise were the two who worked together. They sussed out their strengths and weaknesses and played to them. Checking the maps, marking out the area, developing signals for each other. They came close at one point but supporting each other, pulling each other out of danger, pushing each other to succeed was the single most important part of the exercise—teamwork. The rest of you, by god, you'll learn. You have to trust your partner and your team. I don't care whether you like them or not. You have to trust them. It may just save your life. Gold, Armstrong. Well done." Simon states, clocking them both, knowing they will go far if they keep their noses clean.

Tom can barely contain his excitement or his utter surprise at doing so well after such a poor day yesterday. *Long may it continue.* He smiles to himself.

"Get into groups of four. You are going to assess some of the notes from the trainers. Tomorrow, you will change roles, get out there and get practising."

Tom and Phil pair up with a couple of mouthy 16-year-old lads. Despite there only being an age difference of a year or so, both Tom and Phil are getting frustrated by their immaturity.

Was I like that? Tom muses to himself. *No wonder Gramps sent me here if I was.*

Tom is enjoying this part of the exercise, especially the feedback from the officers. Discussions get heated as they spot some glaringly obvious mistakes. Taking meticulous notes, Tom writes down everything. All four of them pay particular attention to the shooters in preparation for the exercise tomorrow and think they've picked up some valuable tips.

Once the session's feedback is over, the rest of the afternoon is spent on exercise, all four of them praying they will get through tomorrow.

"Calls for a celebration, Phil?" Tom asks as they leave the mess hall together later that evening.

"Yeah, definitely, mate, when is your drill test?"

"Tomorrow morning, yours?"

"Tomorrow afternoon."

"Town on Saturday then, assuming we pass."

"Of course, we'll pass, Tom, we're the A team."

They laugh as they walk together back to their billet.

Cassie
Saturday 23rd August

Having both passed their drills, they head into town for the first time since their arrival, Tom and Phil try to find a bar that isn't full of trainee soldiers.

Stumbling across an Irish bar, aptly named, *The Irish Bar*, hidden at the end of a dark and dingy alleyway, "this do, Tom?"

"Yeah, they have a singer on tonight, look," Tom points at the peeling poster haphazardly glued to the main grey wooden door.

"Cool," Phil drools as he opens the door to let them in, the picture on the poster seducing both men. "God, she's giving me a hard-on."

"Phil man, give over." Tom slaps him on the arm.

Walking into the bar, Tom looks around. The whole place has a grey air about it, with pale grey walls and ceiling. Walking through the second set of doors, both men's feet stick to the beer-stained, grey carpet. Amazingly the place is already full to bursting. They manage to secure a seat near the stage; Tom ambles off to fetch the drinks and eye up the totty, as usual. Eventually, he arrives back at the table; he shouts over the noise, "blimey, it's like a rugby scrum at the bar." Sitting opposite Phil, "spot anything you fancy yet?"

"Loads, mate, the place is full of it; it even smells horny."

Suddenly, the noise dies down, and a short, slightly built man appears out of nowhere with a microphone.

"Ladies and gentlemen, please welcome to the stage, the best Irish act in Peace Hampton, Cassie."

The compare leaves the stage as the lights dim, and the voice of an angel reverberates around the building. The whole club is in awe of the young singer, slightly older than the two of them, her long blond hair accentuates her tiny face. The end of her first song is met with ear-piercing applause.

"Wow."

"Yeah, wow," Tom echoes. *I think I'm in love.*

As the evening progresses, so does the flow of alcohol. Both Tom and Phil stagger out at closing time, hanging back in the hopes of catching a glimpse of the Irish beauty.

"What kept you?" the smooth Irish accent asks as the boys slide down the steps.

"Woah, hello, gorgeous," Phil smooches at her.

"You can call me, Cassie," she admonishes as she pushes his lecherous hand off her backside. "Enough already, soldier."

Feeling verbally slapped, Phil stops pawing and gawps at her. "How did you know?"

"This place is always full of them when training is on. Hence the lack of salubrious décor."

"Oh, we didn't recognise anyone from the troop," Phil states, somewhat unnecessarily.

"Too pissed, that's why."

Tom, too love-struck to involve himself in conversation, stands back, open-mouthed feeling suddenly remarkably sober.

Cassie turns to him, "who is this handsome fella?"

"Er, I'm Tom, that's Phil." Is all Tom could think to say.

"Lovely, so, you coming back to mine then?" She purrs, walking over to him, her long green dress swaying in the gentle breeze and her stilettoes giving her the same height as him.

Not used to women being so forward, he usually does all the asking, "erm, well…yes, I suppose."

Tongue-tied but excited, Tom turns to Phil, gives him to thumbs up. *I'm in here.* And winks at him.

Phil, mighty displeased, walks away. *I'll have my day with her—Mark my words.*

Grabbing Tom's hand, Cassie walks him to the end of the alleyway and the new build block of flats.

"Are we having a taxi?" Tom enquires.

"No need, I only live here," Cassie responds as she lets go of his hand to unlock the door. "The lift still works too. Come on, let's ride in it." Cassie winks at him.

Following her into the lift, the doors have barely closed before she grabs his face and kisses him like he's never been kissed before. *Wow.*

As the lift reaches her destination on the 2nd floor and judders to a stop, Tom feels like he's in heaven, and he doesn't want this moment to end. Dragging him out of the lift and into her small but serviceable flat, Cassie slams the door and pins Tom against it. Unbuttoning his shirt, she rips it off him.

We're doing it here? Against the door? Tom wonders to himself.

Starting on his trousers, she is surprised when he grabs her arms to stop her. "Not here. Not like this. Can we make ourselves comfortable first?" he asks.

Shocked, she retorts, "I thought all you trainee soldiers were up for casual sex."

"I usually am. That's what I expected, but…"

"But what? I only do casual, so don't get any ideas, Mr Tom," she commands as she releases herself from his grip and runs her fingers up and down his stomach and across his nipples. Tingling with delight, Tom can barely catch his breath.

No… no… not like this. What the hell is wrong with me.

Realising he isn't going to give in as easily as the others, she propels him towards the living room, indicating to him to make himself at home on the small hippie patterned sofa.

He does as she wishes while she fetches them a drink from the kitchen.

"What drink do you want, Tom?"

"Just water, please."

Sticking her head around the door in shock, water?"

"Yes, my throat is dry. I've had far too much to drink."

And I want to remember this night, not add it to my collection of times lost.

Looking around him at the red and yellow stripped wallpaper, a bit too psychedelic for Tom's liking, he jumps when she comes into the room and places his drink on the coffee table at his knees.

"I know, bit garish, isn't it?" Cassie comments, seeing his eyes search the room.

Taking a much-needed drink, he nods.

"The previous owner was only here a few weeks, but it was his decorating. I've never got round to changing it."

Before he can stop himself, the words are in the air, "I can help you if you'd like?"

"Would you? Would you really?"

"Of course. I'd like to."

Cassie, somewhat lost for words, unusually, sits down next to him, about to grab hold of his knee and start fondling him, thinks better of it given his earlier reaction.

"How long have you been singing?" Tom asks to break the silence.

"Since I was little, I've always sung. I'd like to do it in different environments, but this has been regular work for a couple of years now, hence this place. I also work behind the bar there too."

"Isn't it a bit much, being on your own, I mean?"

"I've never thought about it. I always knew I wanted to sing in pubs and clubs... and bigger stages... one day." She sighs.

Amazed at her strength of character, Tom keeps asking her questions. They talk well into the early hours. Finally realising the time, Tom jumps up off the sofa.

"Shit, I'll be locked out and on a ticket. I'll have to try and sneak back in. Somehow."

Jolted by his sudden movement, "Ah, that's easy."

Staring down at her, "Eh, how do you know?"

"I've shagg... dated enough would-be soldiers to know a thing or too. One of them being how to sneak back in."

Receiving the benefit of her knowledge, Tom bids her goodnight, making a date to see her in a couple of weeks, once she's purchased the items they need for decorating.

Shaun Gets Caught
Monday 25ᵗʰ August

With a spring in his step, whistling an Irish tune. Badly. Tom heads for the showers, praying he isn't last there.

"Yo, Tom, wait up." He hears Phil shout from behind. "So how was the… you know what?" He asks, nudging Tom in the ribs.

"What?" Tom asks innocently.

"The rumpy-pumpy with the blond Irish bombshell?"

Wary, given the face Phil had pulled when he copped off with her, Tom shrugs his shoulders.

"Come on, man, spill."

Knowing there is no point in lying, Tom explains that they just talked.

Ribbing him like mad, Phil sounds like a broken record, "I don't believe you, man, she was hot for it."

Bored with the probing, Tom turns the tables on him. "Did you find an unsuspecting woman on your way home, then?"

Strutting like a peacock, "As it so happens. I did."

Relieved, Tom congratulates him, slapping him on the back.

"Come on, Phil, we don't want to be last to the showers."

Breaking into a jog, they both shower quickly and are about to head to the mess hall when they hear Corporal Daily shouting, "not so fast!"

Both frozen rigid to the spot, assuming he's calling them, they turn to see Shaun eyeballing the corporal. Looking at each other, they wait and watch the scene unfold. The runt of the troop having had severe beatings from Shaun over the past few days can be seen cowering in the corner of the row of showers. Afraid that the rest of the troop will think he's grassed. He stays there, not daring to move.

Within minutes, Corporal Daily is marching Shaun off to the administration office at the front of the compound.

"No bullying or abuse will be tolerated on my watch. Your military career is over," they hear him say. "Do you understand?"

Shaun hangs his head.

Staring after him until he's out of sight, Phil turns on his heels towards the mess hall. "Told you he would get caught."

"I can't say I'm not pleased, but how did he get caught? Do you think he was shopped?"

"Nah, they aren't stupid, you know, they see everything. His card was marked from day one. He had that look in his eyes."

"What look?" Tom asks, confused.

"That, don't mess with me. I'm a nutter look."

"That's not nice."

"Didn't you clock it? He needs help, man, not the Army. Serious help. I just hope he gets it. But I very much doubt it."

Before the breakfast is finished, Shaun is a long-forgotten memory. His dismissal is instant.

Decorating Duty
Sunday 7th September

Taking the overalls Cassie waves in front of him; Tom pulls them on, ready to take on the decorating challenge. Cassie has already stripped the walls and almost striped herself, judging by her attire. Skimpy boob tube and mini skirt are not his idea of decorating clothes, but who is he to argue?

Tom, now sober, finally appreciates the chemistry between them.

"Aren't you putting any overalls on?" Tom queries, smiling.

"Whatever for, that's just one more layer you'll have to peel off later." She winks.

Laughing, Tom takes the bucket and paste to the kitchen to mix, leaving Cassie cutting the lengths of wallpaper.

A couple of hours later and somewhat sticker than when they started, the living room is papered. A simple but pretty pale green four-leaf clover design now adorns her walls. Tom stands back to admire it. Nodding his head.

"Better?" He looks down at her standing next to him.

"Better." She nods.

In a playful mood, Cassie picks the brush up, turns to face him and flicks the small amount of remaining paste at the front of Tom's overalls.

"Hey, Miss Cassie, what was that for?"

Laughing as he scrapes it off with his hand and flicks it back at her. It lands on her barely covered breast.

"Ooh, Mr Tom, that's very naughty. I think you need to scrape that off me." She coos as she takes a step closer to him. Taking his hand, she places it on her breast. "How are you going to get this glue off?"

Without too much thought, Tom pulls the boob tube over her head and throws it on the settee, only then realising she isn't wearing a bra.

How very sexy. Becoming increasingly hard, he pulls her into him and kisses her gently, savouring the taste of her mouth. While kissing him, Cassie pulls at the overalls, the press studs popping as she pushes them off his shoulder. Stopping to let him slip out of them, they head to the bedroom. She pulls his t-shirt over his head and throws it on the floor. Her hands roam up and down his torso. His hand strokes her up and down her back. She arches against his erection. "What have we here, big boy?" she pouts. Reaching down, she stokes him through his jeans.

Tom takes her right breast in his mouth, sucking and licking her as she purrs with desire against him. Reaching down, he puts his hand up her skirt, pulls her skimpy knickers to the side and slides his finger inside her. A contented groan escapes her lips as they part to kiss him again.

Pushing her gently onto the bed, he quickly removes the remainder of their clothes, fuelled by a desperate need to be inside her.

Straddling her, he kisses her breasts, making his way down to her belly towards her pubic area. Gently he licks the inside of her thighs. Teasing her clitoris with his tongue, she moans loudly and arches her back. *Take me, for Christ's sake.* She riles beneath him, willing him to enter her.

Licking her fingers, she grabs his now solid penis and slowly pulls back his foreskin, teasing the tip with the end of her thumb. Tiny amounts of precum make it easier to tease him. Slowly sliding his foreskin backwards and

forwards, she tries to guide him between her legs.
Enjoying the pleasure of her playing with him too much, he resists. For a short time. Arching his back, the pleasure threatening to take over too soon. He moves swiftly and places his legs on top of hers. He gently slides himself inside her and slowly, pinning her down so she can't move; he penetrates her a few times before positioning himself so she can wrap her legs around him. Finding a natural rhythm, they kiss passionately so as not to cry out as the orgasmic groans threaten to escape from their lips—both in the perfect position. Tom thrusts a few more times before they both reach a mind-blowing climax.

Thank goodness that's over. She sighs to herself.

Lying on top of her. Spent. Tom feels the happiest he has for a long time.

She's the one.

Betrayal
Friday 12ᵗʰ September

Training continues in the same vein, with the corporals and Physical Training Instructors pushing the trainees to their limits. Tom, having found solace in Cassie and his ever welcome sneaked drinking binges, often comes back to barracks ten sheets to the wind.

"Man, this is soooo boring," Tom complains to Phil as they run yet another circuit of the field followed by a session in the gym. Looking good and feeling even better, Tom still craves more excitement.

"This is what it will be like, mate unless we get called up for active duty," Phil answers, feeling the same himself but not quite as wild as Tom can be. Not wishing to be thrown out.

"I thought it would be more… exciting than this, though. You know girls, booze, action in the field."

Hysterical Phil tuts at him, "you haven't passed your training yet, mate. And you have one girl. Isn't that enough? Come on; I'll race you back to base; that should give you a bit of excitement."

Adrenalin pumps through them as they do their last circuit, finishing neck and neck before they hit the gym. "You going out with Cassie tonight, Tom?"

"Nah, mate, she's working in another bar, apparently. I said I'd go and see her, but she says I wouldn't like it."

"Mmm, oh well, quiet night in then?"

"Yeah, wouldn't do me any harm, I suppose."

Having finished their training for the day, they both head to the showers, then the mess hall. After eating, they head back to their bunks.

"Here, Tom, some light reading for you, being as you're having a quiet night in." Phil laughs as he throws his latest edition of Playboy magazine on Tom's bed.

"Oh, ha ha, very funny. I have several books to read that my grandfather sent."

"Ooh, check you out."

"Right, I'm off. Enjoy your… reading."

"Thanks, man. See you later."

Not even ten pages into his first book, the original *Hitchhiker's Guide to the Galaxy*, Tom is getting itchy feet.

Stuff the night in. Taking a pair of jeans and a t-shirt from the drawers next to his bed, he quickly changes and heads out for a solo night on the town.

Not short of offers for his attention, Tom, for once, doesn't take the bait. Preferring to see where his relationship with Cassie will take him. For reasons unbeknown to him, Tom's legs carry him to *The Irish Bar*. Butterflies in his tummy surprise him. *Why do I have butterflies? I come here often enough.*

Strolling past the bouncers who nod courteously to him, Tom makes his way to the bar. Lost in the crowd, he scans the room for a familiar face, assuming this is also where Phil has ended up.

Feeling a nudge at his elbow Tom looks around at a familiar face. One of the younger lads he worked with a few weeks ago if memory serves him well.

"Hi, Tom."

"Hi," for the life of him, Tom can't remember this lads name.

"You looking for your girl?"

"How do you know I have a girl?"

"Seen you together, like."

Nodding. *Nothing escapes anyone's attention round here, it seems.*

"Nah, not really. She's working somewhere else tonight."

"Ha, that's what you think."

"What do you mean?"

"She was in here earlier, with your mate, Shaun."

"What, Shaun's not my mate, and he was dismissed weeks ago." *Does he know about my incident with Shaun? God, I hope not.*

"Aye, I know." The Scottish accent becomes even more pronounced as he continues talking.

"He won't leave. Says he's meant to be here. He's OK, you know, just a bit… lost."

"You trying to rile me up?"

Tom squares up to him, but the lad puts his hands up in surrender. "No way, I have to live there too for a few more weeks, don't want no shite kicking off. You treated me right that day. I'm just returning the favour."

As Tom is about to shake his hand and thank him, he catches a glimpse of Shaun standing by the main entrance, his back to him, but he'd recognise that ripped jacket anywhere. Def Leopard fans being few and far between amongst the troop.

Pushing his way towards to door but holding back slightly when he's level with Shaun, he watches. A few minutes later, Cassie comes to him from behind the bar. Embracing each other, they kiss passionately; Cassie laughs with Shaun as he drapes his arm around her and leads her out into the night.

Quickly finishing his drink, Tom follows slowly behind, not quite believing what he's seeing.

Bile rises in his stomach as he realises how stupid he's been. The hurt tearing him up. Not wanting them to see him, his anger burns within him at every step. Fighting to keep a lid on it, he hangs back in the alleyway, watching as Cassie lets them up to her flat. Seething, Tom punches the door of the flats before he slowly walks away.

Now I know what the butterflies were for. What the hell have I ever done to him?

Tom in Trouble
Saturday 13th September

Another boring week. Gym, march, check stores, jog, eat, sleep. With too much time on his hands, Tom's anger is bubbling inside him.

How could she? And with him of all people. My arch-enemy.

"Tom?"

Phil breaks his reverie.

"Yeah."

In the middle of changing out of his combat gear and into his tight-fitting jeans and Calvin Klein t-shirt, Tom stares up at Phil.

"You going to town tonight?"

"Yep," Tom would have thought it was obvious but refrains from saying so.

Having heard Shaun is still in town, Tom is determined to find him and have it out with him. Man to man.

"Cool, a few of the others are going to *The Irish Bar.* You could kill two birds with one stone. Get hammered... and laid." Phil laughs.

"What?" Tom's brain takes a while to catch on. "Oh, you mean Cassie?"

Even the thought of her name causes the butterflies to summersault in his stomach.

"You are still seeing her?"

"Allegedly."

"Tom, you've lost me. What do you mean?"

Not wishing to cause himself further embarrassment, but if he doesn't tell someone soon, he may just explode. Explaining what he'd seen just yesterday that was festering in him. Phil listens. The shock on his face making it apparent that he didn't already know.

"But he was dismissed. Why is he still in town?"

"Death wish, screw loose. Who knows, but I'm going to find it and have it out with him."

"Woah," Phil puts his hand up to Tom as if motioning him to stop. "Not so fast, man. He's not worth it."

"He is. I need the satisfaction that he hasn't won. He's one-nil up on me at the moment."

"But he will win if you start a fight. Be the bigger man. Walk away."

"You in cahoots with him?" Tom rounds on him, his nose almost touching that of his best friend. His only friend.

Taking a step back, Phil has never seen Tom this angry before. "Of course not. How could you even think that?"

"I'm a laughing stock, Phil. After what he did. And now he steals my girl. I'm not having it."

"Mate, no one knows. Only me. Let it go."

"And those two rowdy lads we worked with, they know."

"How?"

"No idea, but they do."

"Leave it, Tom."

Tom harrumphs and walks away. The last person he wants to fight with is Phil.

Those two rowdy lads are hovering near Phil. "You two going to town?" the plumper of the two asks.

"Yeah," Phil answers, "you coming?"

"There's a few of us going, but you seem to have found the best bars, so we thought we'd tag along."

"Sure, I'll grab Tom and meet you at the gate in 10."

Their eyes light up like all their Christmases have come at once.

Phil is on tenterhooks as they enter *The Irish Bar* an hour later, he watches Tom looking around. Clearly on the prowl for his vengeance on Shaun. Unable to see either Shaun or Cassie, Phil heads to the bar to fetch their drinks. Having just been paid, he's making the most of his free time this week and his money. Next week it will be back to books and wanks, until his next pay packet if he gets through training.

Handing Tom his pint, "they ain't here."

"Really." Tom snipes at him.

"Come on. The others are waving at us; they must have found a decent table." Steering Tom in their direction, Phil prays neither of them will come in and spoil the night.

As the evening wears on, the lads relax more, enjoying the entertainment. Fortunately, it's a male singer tonight, so they aren't climbing over each other to get on the stage for a piece of the act. Closing time rolls around too quickly. Tom has to admit he's enjoying the evening, his thoughts not distracted by Cassie. For once. Proud of himself, he hasn't had as much to drink as usual. Just enough to make him wobble.

"Right lads, I'm starving," Tom announces. "Let's get a Chinese." Staggering out into the street, they head for *Dragon Eye*, the only Chinese takeaway for miles around, situated on the corner of the alleyway opposite Cassie's block of flats. They won't win any awards for hygiene, but the food is delicious.

Most of the group disperse as they leave the bar. Six of them grab their orders and wobble over to the bench opposite the takeaway. Still in high spirits after such a good evening, they are singing their heads off between mouthfuls of food. Tom stops mid *Sweet Caroline* as he notices a green dress out of the corner of his eye. Cassie's green dress, and she's in it. With her arm around Shaun. Adrenalin courses through him, and within seconds he's thrown the remainder of his meal at Shaun from across the street. On his feet, faster than lightning, he races over to him. Tom headbutts him in the gut as Shaun, hearing the commotion, turns to face him.

Shaun, winded, gasps for air, Cassie screams. Two of the lads run off, not wanting to get involved. The others remain frozen to the spot, gobsmacked at the weird turn of events, not used to seeing Tom behaving this way.

"Tom! No!" Phil shouts, dropping his food tray on the floor, running after him. "It's not worth it!"

"Tom, now stronger and savvier than he was a few weeks ago when the previous incident occurred, has Shaun pinned to the floor, delivering blows to his torso and stomach. The anger and humiliation of the encounter, the pain of seeing him with Cassie, plus 17 years of bottled-up emotions pour out of Tom onto Shaun.

Hearing the sirens in the distance, one of the neighbours must have called the police, the three of them pull him off. Phil curses him under his breath, grateful they only have a few more days here.

"Tom, come on!" Phil shouts as the sirens get closer, pulling him by his jacket; Tom keeps trying to get back at Shaun.

Racing down the street, they all run back towards base, not stopping until they reach there.

Back at the barracks, Phil asks, "better now?"
"No, not really."
"Why the hell did you do it then?"
"I saw red. I told you he wouldn't win."
"He will have if one of them grasses you up."

72

Lying face down on his bed. Tom stares across the room, not seeing anything there.

What have I done?

Praying he won't get found out. He vows to keep his nose clean at least until they finish training.

***

Early next morning, as the troop warm-up for their first exercise, Sergeant Pearson call's out, "Gold."

"Yes, Sergeant."

"My office. Now."

Shit, shit, shit.

Standing to attention in front of Sergeant Pearson's large mahogany desk, Tom swallows hard. His mouth is dry as he awaits his fate.

"It has come to my attention, Gold, that you like to disgrace the Army whilst on your nights out. Is that correct?" Sergeant Pearson takes his seat behind his desk and sits with his fingertips touching, elbows on the desk, back straight.

"No, Sergeant."

"No, really. That's not what I heard. A little dicky bird tells me you had a fight with a former trainee last night. Is this or is this not, correct?"

Tom has no choice but to say, "yes, Sergeant."

"Now we're getting somewhere, lad. I have only one question. Why?"

Swallowing again, Tom is unable and unwilling to admit why. And he's sure the sergeant won't want to hear it anyway.

I messed up. I let my emotions get the better of me. I'm a loser. Should I go on?

"I don't know, Sergeant."

73

Rising from his chair, the Sergeant walks around the desk and stands behind Tom. In his ear, he bellows. "Because you're an idiot."

"Yes, I am Sergeant." Tom can't argue with that. He feels like one at this moment.

Finishing his walk around his desk, Simon sits back down. In a strangely calm and more gentle voice, confusing Tom, he continues.

"Gold, you had an excellent military career in front of you. Why would you throw that away for a fight? We know what King was doing, and we dealt with it. Why couldn't you leave it alone?"

"I'm not sure, Sergeant." Tom's heart is beating so fast he thinks it's going to jump out of his chest. *Had an excellent military career in front of you. Guess that's me out then.*

"You are so close to finishing training, Gold. Do you really want to face a court-martial now?"

"No, Sergeant."

"I thought not." Well known for not giving second chances, Simon is as shocked as Tom when he says, "you have the remainder of training to prove to me that you can control yourself and you are soldier material. Do you understand?"

"Yes. Thank you, Sergeant."

"Get out of my sight and keep your nose clean."

Tom almost weeps with gratitude for the second chance and vows not to screw up again.

Leaving the sergeants office, he re-joins the troop for circuit training, he catches up with Phil.

"Hey, Tom, you still here?"

"Yeah. How I don't know, but yes." Elated and still in shock, Tom jogs a little faster, and Phil makes pace with him.

"Do you know how lucky you are?"

"Yes, I do. I'm determined to keep my nose clean, at least till after training."

Phil laughs at his friend. *Unbelievable.*

Just a Bit of Fun
Thursday 18th September

The last day of training is tomorrow, and Tom can't think straight with worrying whether he will pass. He sneaks off base and into town, and before he knows it, he's in a strange lady's arms.

"Come here, let me do that for you."

Tom pulls Ruth onto his lap, deftly flicking the clasp of her bra with one hand, watching it fall from her breasts. Eyeing them greedily, he manoeuvres her around to face him, legs straddled around his waist, her long dark hair flowing down her back, reminding him of Rapunzel. Leaning into him, her hair tickles his face as she nibbles his right ear lobe noisily.

Running her fingers down his spine sends shivers of pleasure to his extremities,

If only she wasn't so blasted noisy.

Tom moves her face away and begins to push her head down towards his throbbing penis.

What the hell? I'm paying for it. I may as well get my money's worth.

Lying back against the fluffed-up pillows in her large bedsit, his arms behind his head, savouring the sensations of her mouth clasping his member, a huge smile on his face as he thrusts in time to her movements.

No, not yet, not yet.

She knows instinctively what will have the desired effect and ensure he reaches orgasm but, he isn't ready yet.

I'm paying for half an hour, and I'm having it on my terms, he murmurs under his breath.

Without any thought or concern for Ruth or her feelings, he flips her over onto her back; in such a practised move, it's obvious this isn't the first time.

Staring at her pert breasts again, Tom positions himself between her legs, his erection screaming to enter her.

Opening her legs wider to accommodate him, Ruth lies back to accept the inevitable.

Placing a condom on his wildly throbbing penis, he gently pushes himself inside her. Getting comfortable before he thrusts for all he's worth. It's all over in under a minute. Again.

What's wrong with me? I should be able to go for hours. He admonishes himself.

Flopping onto his side, he reaches for the bottle of Hooch he brought with him, *disgusting stuff, but it does the job.* Already feeling the heady effects of his orgasm and too much booze, he stumbles off the bed in a rush to leave. Fumbling with the laces on his boots.

Ruth dresses herself and watches him out of the corner of her eye, thinking to herself, *this must be his first time. He's so nervous.*

Leaving his money on the side, he flings the door open and disappears into the night.

Immediately he's out of there, and he starts to sprint to the barracks. He has ten minutes to make it before curfew, but he's at least 20 minutes away.

Sprinting along the streets, his mind racing almost as fast as his feet. Disgusted with himself.

Final Training Day
Friday 19th September

"Yo, Tom, that was a close call last night, mate," Phil shouts from his bed.

"Hey, keep the noise down, man, my head!"

Phil laughs, "Corp won't like that. You look like shit mate; thought you'd knocked all this on the head.

"Yeah, I had, but… you know, one last time, before we leave, whether we pass or not. Couldn't resist."

"You know he's going to make you suffer. He saw you come in too."

"Bollocks, he didn't, did he?"

"Yup."

Tom sits on the bed with his head in his hands. Mentally preparing for the beasting, he would take for his stupidity yesterday. Praying it won't affect his result.

Barely able to hold his head up from the shocking hangover, Tom attempts to look normal so as not to arouse the suspicions of the corporal.

"This is your last day of training before passing out next week." The corporal announces, stating the somewhat obvious. "How many of you to pass out remains to be seen, and looking at some of you this morning, it could be a whole different type of passing out happening here. You know what you need to do. Let's do it!"

Tom's head is throbbing as each sound from the corporal reverberates through him like a poker piercing the back of his eyes. *I didn't have that much to drink. Did I?*

"Come on, boy! Are you a man or a mouse? This isn't playschool. Get moving."

Deep breathing, he struggles to catch his breath, Tom tries to speak, but fatigue and the awful hangover are threatening to take over.

I can't do this anymore. I can do this. I have to do this. All kinds of thoughts go through his head.

"Move it, boy! Move it!"

The burn in Tom's chest, his head feeling as if it's about to explode, the Corporal screaming in his ear is almost too much for him. Stopping to catch his breath, the Corporal is unrelenting in his shouting. Tom drags himself off again, through the mud, under the rope forming part of the assault course. On his forearms and belly, he pushes himself through the mud.

I can do it. I have to do it.

The Corporal, sadist by nature, Eric by name, or evil Eric as the lads like to call him, is a tall, stocky man who towers over Tom. "Faster boy! Are you trying to fail this course?"

Dying to respond but unable to get the words out, Tom pushes even harder, the bile in his stomach threatening to extricate itself at any second. Closing his eyes to try and reduce the nausea makes his head spin. *How much longer?* He wonders. *Surely, it's nearly over.*

By some miracle, Tom makes it through the assault course.

Stopping to catch his breath, Phil pulls up alongside him. "You look like shit, mate. Lost your breakfast yet?"

"Nah, man, never had any, nothing to come up."

Phil laughs as he walks away. "That's what you think."

Despite the past ten weeks of punishing training, nothing could have prepared Tom for this final day of challenges.

The Corporal is shouting out further instructions, Tom barely registering what he's saying, watches Phil, fit and ready to take on the world, a smug look glued to his face. Tom still feels like shit.

"Attention!" shouts the Corporal.

"Yes, Corporal." Is the communal response from the troop.

Giving his orders for the next part of the task, a two-mile jog followed by *The Hill*. They all begin to run.

And they're off. Tom sniggers to himself. *We look like the 2.30 at Cheltenham.*

Pacing himself so as not to embarrass himself, Tom starts slowly, the others all racing ahead. The Corporal is on his tail, again.

"Gold, this is your last chance!" he shouts. "Fail this, and you're out, boy!"

Tom, unable to do anything other than nod, keeps his eyes on the ground and carries on at the same pace.

"What's wrong with you, Gold?" Corporal Daily yells. "Did you not hear your instructions for *The Hill?*"

Shaking his head. Tom feels the colour drain from him, partly from his stomach gurgling and complaining at the lack of food and too much alcohol, and partly because he has a sudden flashback to the first day of training and his experience with *The Hill*.

Pushing himself harder, Tom can't believe what he's hearing.

"Not good enough, Gold! You're not trying hard enough. You've not giving it everything you have. A Failure! That's what you are!"

Hearing these words, words he's heard all his life increases Tom's determination to get to the top of *The Hill*. And fast.

I just hope I can make it without vomiting.

Calming his breathing to enable him to gather momentum, he feels his chest tightening even more.

Everything feels like it's about to explode. All he can hear is that word reverberating around his head. Failure. Failure. Failure.

Now he has something to prove. Every bone in his body is crying out for him to stop, to rest. His feet are bleeding through his endless layers of socks, the straps of the rucksack he's carrying chafe his shoulders. They too are bleeding. His head feels like it doesn't belong to him, like he's going to pass out, and the gurgling in his stomach finally reaches its crescendo, and without stopping, he finds himself vomiting violently.

The smell is enough to make him vomit again, this time collapsing heavily onto his knees at the side of the road. Certain he's about to pass out. Heaving for all he's worth.

"Get up, Gold, get moving."

Tom is sure he can hear the Corporal, but he can't understand what he's saying.

"Gold! Get up."

I didn't drink that much. Alcopops obviously don't agree with me.

Attempting to reach into his rucksack for his water bottle earns him another torrent of shouts.

"Get moving, Gold. Now!"

Dragging himself along the road, his legs weak beneath him, head spinning now from dehydration.

How much further? He wonders. *I'm never going to make it. I can't do this.*

Gazing ahead, apart from seeing stars, he can also make out the outline of what must be the last one of the rest of his troop. His head still splitting, but thankfully, his stomach is now calmer. He wills his legs to keep working.

I have to catch up with him. I have to catch up with him. He repeats to himself over and over. *If I can overtake him, at least, I'll have a fair chance of passing.*

Blocking out the shouts, which have now become just noise to Tom, he keeps hearing 'failure, failure.' This and this alone are what drives his legs to power up the 12-degree gradient.

Catching up with the fellow trainee he spotted earlier, Tom is shocked to learn that it's Phil, the strongest and toughest member of the group.

Not looking so smug now, are you Phil? Tom muses to himself as he pushes even harder, no idea where the strength and energy are coming from, overtaking him.

The thought that he will no longer be last gives him the impetus to push even further through the pain.

Able to see the brow of *The Hill*, his heart almost skips a beat as he realises he's almost there.

Now, who's a failure, eh? He smirks to himself.

The sudden realisation hits him that if he leaves Phil behind, his mate may not make it through basic training.

Not my problem, he tells himself. He didn't think of me when he raced ahead off the starting blocks with that smug face on.

Staring straight ahead, he can smell the finish line. Striving to give it that extra push to see him to the end, the nagging feeling that he can't leave his comrade behind just won't let up.

Pulling himself back slightly, waiting for Phil to catch up, he can sense rather than hear the words Evil Eric is screaming into Phil's right ear. Willing Phil to push himself harder and catch up with him, Tom slows his pace a little more, the adrenalin pumping through his veins. *Come on, Phil, come on.*

Tom hears the rattle of Phil's chest and him desperately sucking in air, bearing upon his left-hand side. Then he hears the shout of the Corporal.

"Gold, what the hell are you doing?"

Tom, panting for breath himself, is unable or maybe unwilling to answer. He catches Phil's eye and motions to him with a slight, almost imperceptible nod, letting him know that he can do this and they're in it together.

Falling in step with each other, Tom pushes himself even harder and hopes Phil will do the same. It works. They both forge forwards—the end in sight.

They spot the rest of the team just slightly up ahead, and both give one last push to complete this part of the day's challenge. Exhausted, they fall on top of the rest of the troop in a heap in the middle of the road.

Barely having enough time to take a long and well-earned swig of water, most of them choking, their mouths are so dry.

Called to attention within seconds of finishing, they are given their instructions for the rest of the day. More gruelling tasks lie ahead—all of them are praying that they will make it through.

The Results
Monday 22nd September

"Hey, man," Phil says as he taps Tom on the shoulder. Tom looks up at him from the rickety chair in the mess hall.

"Hey yourself."

"Tom."

"Yeah."

Embarrassed, Phil averts his eyes from Tom's gaze. They hadn't seen each other since Friday.

"I just wanted to say thanks, er, and good luck. Today's the day, eh?"

"Yeah, sure is."

Phil sits down opposite Tom. "Not many would have done what you did. I owe ya."

"You don't owe me anything. Any mate would have done the same."

Thinking to himself that he wasn't sure he would have, Phil changes the subject.

"You nervous about the results?"

"I guess," Tom answers, shrugging his shoulders nonchalantly although he feels anything but nonchalant.

"I have to pass. I have to," Tom murmurs, almost to himself. "I can't go home. That will just give them another excuse to label me a failure."

"What do you mean, Tom?"

"Oh, I didn't realise you were still there. My parents have always been so wrapped up in their own little world, they often forgot about me. I think they really wanted a girl... then I popped out. A disappointment from day one."

"No way. I never knew. I've heard you on the phone. It is them you call, isn't it?

"Mmm, sometimes, I like to speak to my grandfather. He gets me, but he's busy with his business."

"Oh, man, I'm sorry. I thought you were all OK. Nowt we can do till we know, though."

Phil, nosy as he is, pushes Tom with more questions about his past. "So, what's with your parents, then?"

"Dunno. One dodgy geezer and an alcoholic."

"That's rough, man. No wonder you're the way you are."

"Hey, what the hell does that mean?" Tom shouts back, his fists tensing, ready for a fight.

"Woah, sorry, mate, I didn't mean anything by it. It's just... you know... drinking, missing curfew. Sneaking about."

"Hey, that's my business, and I'll thank you to keep your nose out of it." Now nose to nose with Phil, Tom pushes his chair back and slams it on the floor before storming out of the mess hall.

Fuming with Phil and angry with the world and with a little time to spare and not much else to do, Tom walks towards the little park area in the centre of the training facility. Unsure why he's there, and more to the point, why the park is, he ambles along, kicking the tiny stones around the trees. Thinking of Cassie and Shaun and praying he hasn't messed up his chances. What the hell he is going to do if he doesn't pass?

The wind howls around the gaps between the old metal buildings. The rain stings his eyes as he makes his way towards the shop.

"Good afternoon. What can I get for you?" The pretty brunette asks Tom as he pushes the door of the barracks shop open, the tell-tale bell dinging to let the staff know he's there.

Ooh, that's a pretty fine specimen, young, dark and fit. Perfect for a bit of end of training fun. Tom thinks to himself, his knee jerk reaction to his current emotional state. Catching sly glances at her as he wanders around the store. He picks up a couple of bottles of hooch, a large bar of chocolate and a packet of extra strong mints, sticks his chest out and swaggers towards the counter.

"Just these, please," he says, leaning on his elbows on the counter, eyeing up the figure of the young girl serving him.

"That will be £2.54, please." Handing over the coins, Tom asks, "What are you doing tonight?"

Shocked at his forwardness, she stumbles on her words but recovers herself just in time, "you might have asked what my name was first," is her jaded response. On her guard now, knowing exactly what this trainee is after. *Just like all the others*, she tuts to herself.

Cringing at his own stupidity, Tom has the grace to look slightly ashamed, "I'm sorry, of course, I should, I just got carried away with your beauty."

Oh. My. God. Give me a bucket. Debbie wants to scream, but remaining civil, she answers, "my name is Debbie, and I'm washing my hair tonight." Handing Tom his few pennies change, Debbie stands with her hands on her hips, staring at him, waiting for him to leave.

"What about after you've washed your hair?" smirking to himself, as he coyly looks up at her once he's put his change in his pocket. He loves a challenge and is now determined to get this beauty into bed, or on the floor, or in the woods, anywhere really as long as he can empty himself.

"Drying it. Now, if you'll excuse me, I need to carry on working."

With that, Debbie turns her back on him and begins to stock up the cigarettes on the shelves behind the counter.

Shrugging his shoulders, *oh well, you can't win them all,* Tom heads out into the street. He's amazed to see that the weather has turned, the wind has dropped, and the glorious sunshine dazzles his eyes. Bumping into Phil,

"Sorry, man. That sun's bright."

"Yeah, listen, I'm sorry about earlier, Tom. I didn't mean to pry. Let me grab a coke, and I'll walk back with you."

"Coke, don't you want something stronger?"

"Nah, I want a clear head for when they give us the results later."

"Fairysnuff, I suppose," Tom shrugs, leaning up against the lamppost to wait for his mate. His earlier outburst is now forgotten.

"What will you do if you don't pass?" Tom questions as he falls into step with Phil.

"Dunno, not really thought about it. Just move on, I guess. Go home and get a job. Hope they keep me out of jail. What about you?"

"God knows. My parents wanted me to get an education, go to university, do an engineering degree… you know the usual? I was supposed to be training with my grandfather. Learn his engineering business, but I screwed up."

"Wow, some pressure there, man. That why you joined this regiment?"

"Yeah, made sense to do the engineering part."

Tired of Phil's constant probing, Tom asks about his family.

"My parents are like, do whatever makes you happy. How did you end up here then, why not just on the job training with the family?"

"Had no choice. I got sick of the arguing; exams went pear-shaped, so I never made the grade. Did endless shitty jobs, tried to work for my father and my grandfather, but that just made it worse. Uni was out. Gramps threatened me with the Army. It was this or the streets. Can't believe it was only ten weeks ago."

"What about you?"

"Oh, you know, the usual. Just hope we make the grade. I'm off for a run before they make the announcements."

"Catch ya later," Phil says as he races off, leaving Tom standing and staring after him. He can't help but think Phil is being a bit cagey, asking too many questions but not giving an inch.

Mmm, maybe it's me, but something isn't quite right here.

Tom, feels apprehensive as he heads back to the billet.

Within minutes of his return, he is called to Sergeant Pearson's office. Dreading the fate which awaits him, Tom smartens himself up, pops a mint in his mouth to quell the smell of alcohol and heads off.

"Enter," Sergeant Pearson calls in response to the forceful knock on his door.

Taking a very deep breath, Tom, presenting with more confidence than he feels, does as instructed and shuts the door quietly behind him.

"Ah, Gold. Good."

Standing to attention, Tom awaits his fate. *Just put me out of my misery, and I can go and find a new home.*

Sitting in his usual pose, elbows on the desk, fingertips touching, the sergeant looks at Tom. "You remind me so much of me when I first joined the Army, Gold. Rebellious, insubordinate, piss head."

Tom hangs his head, not daring to speak.

"You have what it takes if you put your mind to it."
Sergeant Pearson watches Tom closely. Knowing it's
pointless lecturing him.

Tom remains stock still, praying the sergeant puts him
out of his misery. And soon.

"I suppose you'll be wanting your results then, Gold?"

"Yes, please, Sergeant."

"You'll be pleased, and I would imagine, somewhat
surprised to learn that you passed. By the skin of your
teeth, after your warning, you still came back drunk. You
will learn, and you may even rise through the ranks, but
you're on very thin ice. Remember that."

"Thank you, Sergeant." Barely able to contain his
shock or excitement, Tom makes to leave.

"Before you go, it is also my pleasure to inform you
that you have been awarded best at drill."

"What..." Forgetting himself for a moment, "Oh, sorry,
Sergeant." Unusually, Sergeant Pearson only laughs
putting Tom, a little more at ease.

"You'll be wanting to practice your moves ready for
the parade on Monday, I assume?"

"Yes, Sergeant."

"Off you go then. And, Gold. Keep your nose clean
and stay out of trouble you could make corporal in a few
years."

"Thank you, Sergeant."

Saluting his senior officer as he leaves, Tom can't stop
the huge grin spreading across his face.

***

"Gramps, yes, it's me, Tom."

"Tom, you finished your training then?"

"Yes, today, I've just been given the results."

90

Tempted to say, see you tomorrow, but he doubts it from the sounds of his grandson's voice. "You passed?"

"Yes, Gramps, I passed. Can you believe it?"

No. Maurice is tempted to answer.

Yes, Son, of course, I can. I knew you'd do it. *Prayed you'd do it.*

"Will you be home before you're stationed?"

"Yes, Gramps. I will."

"Will you be coming to the parade, Gramps?"

"I doubt it, Son. Work is busy."

Why am I not surprised?

Feeling disheartened, Tom wants to change his response to the previous question. Trying not to let it get to him, he hangs up and heads off to practice, ready for the parade.

Passing Out Parade
Monday 22nd September

Standing to attention, looking smart in his full dress uniform, alongside his troop, Tom is wondering how many he will see again. Each name is called individually to collect any awards they have earned.

"Philip Armstrong." Tom hears,

"Sir, yes Sir."

Tom smiles to himself; he'll certainly need strong arms for this job.

"Congratulations, you are awarded best recruit."

Phil looks round and catches Tom's eye, both equally shocked and overjoyed at passing their training.

Tom, barely able to contain his excitement, almost misses his name when it's called.

"Thomas Jackson Gold."

"Sir, yes, Sir."

"Congratulations, you have been awarded best drill."

Stepping forward to collect his award makes Tom want to dance with joy. Still in shock, he catches Phil's eye again. Both are grinning like Cheshire cats.

This is it. Tom tells himself. *Your new life has just begun.*

After the commiserations and congratulations and some shocks, given some of the troop who got through and some who didn't, Tom can't help thinking himself very lucky. Some of these people were tougher, stronger, better disciplined. Born to be soldiers. He was just an angry young man looking for an outlet for his frustrations and a place to hide from his dysfunctional family.

"This calls for a celebration Mr Armstrong." Tom laughs as he slaps his companion on the shoulder.

"Yeah, it sure does."

Heading into town later, everyone who has passed causes mayhem in the bars. Most of them passed out up alleyways, and all will live to regret it when they face the Sergeant in the morning for their instructions on what to do next.

Tom and Phil break away from the crowd and make their way to the town's only nightclub. Tom has one thing in mind. Well, maybe two. Getting pissed and getting laid. Phil secretly hopes Debbie from the shop is in the club. She told him she would be when he left the store earlier.

Drink in hand, Tom moves away from the bar and leans on the railings, surveying the land for suitable bait.

Spotting Debbie, he starts to amble over to her, but Phil is quicker on the uptake.

Bollocks! Oh, what the hell? Let's have a bit of fun.

"Hey, you two," Tom shouts over Blondie's, *Call Me*.

Oh, great, Debbie groans, hoping her face doesn't betray her dislike of him.

Phil shakes hands with him, "I wondered where you'd got to."

"I'm here now."

Miming that he can't hear him, they troop off the dance floor towards the toilets where the music isn't quite so loud.

"I was saying," Tom began, "I was talking to Debbie earlier, wasn't I?" Attempting to place his arm on her shoulder, she shrugs him off and moves closer to Phil. "I see you washed your hair then."

"Yeah, I washed my hair," Debbie retorts, somewhat put out that she has to listen to this chump. She'd much rather be snogging his friend. "Friend of yours, Phil?"

"Yeah, this is Tom. It's only because of him that I passed my training."

"I don't believe that. I've seen you around, and you're always working out."

Pleased that she's noticed him, Phil turns a dark shade of crimson and takes a swig of his drink to hide his embarrassment.

"Oh, I guess I am. I do run a lot anyway. Have to keep trim, don't I?" He laughs until he clocks the look on Tom's face. *Oh, great, may as well give in now if he's interested in her.*

Sinking slightly away from them, ready to make a quick exit, Phil is surprised when Debbie grabs his arm. "Where are you going?"

"Oh, nowhere. I just thought you too might want to be alone."

Horrified, Debbie glances back to Tom, a look of disgust on her face. "Are you kidding? Alone. With him? No chance." Putting her best flirting face on, she turns back to Phil, "but I wouldn't mind being alone with you though."

Gulping to himself, pleased, shocked and a little unsure of himself, Phil's smile beams across the room.

"I know when I'm not wanted," yells Tom, expecting them to respond, but when he turns round, he's faced with their lips locked together, and they're completely oblivious of his existence.

July 1990

Preparing For Battle
July

Tom works hard in the years following basic training. Passing all the courses he undertakes with flying colours. Although bored a lot of the time, he finds enough to occupy his time. Horses. Women. Drink.

For the first time in a very long time, Tom's troop of Royal Engineers is called to a briefing. Lieutenant Bills stands in front of them and calls the room to attention.

"As you are aware, there is trouble in the Middle East. The US Army has already deployed soldiers there. Some of you may be next."

Waiting for the gasps and murmurs to die down, the Lieutenant takes a breath, as much in shock as the rest of the troop.

"You will now go into pre-deployment training. The initial threat and the training you have all been undertaking needs to be amended, and as such, we are now upgrading your training regime. Your new schedules are in the envelopes you were handed as you entered the briefing." Blunt and to the point. "We strongly recommend that you ensure your personal administration is up to date too."

Tom and Phil sit at the back of the room, staring at each other. "The fucking dessert, man. And what does she mean, personal administration?"

"No idea. Phil, this is exciting." *And bloody nerve-wracking. What if I'm not up to the job?* Tom bites his lip in contemplation. Looking around the room, it appears most of the soldiers have that same look.

Unsure whether he has heard correctly as his mind is racing, Tom whispers to Phil. "Did the Lieutenant just say CS gas?"

"Yep."

Jesus.

The days seem to merge into one; between extra PT sessions, equipment and stock checks and briefings, additional and new exercises are added.

The dilapidated metal wilding, not used, it appears since the first world war, is cold and damp. The Sappers, as they are now referred to, are forced in one by one as CS gas is leaked through holes drilled into the side. Respirators need to be checked. According to Captain James, the soldiers have to feel the effect of the gas in order to make sure.

Portraying it like a game, Corporal Masters, a giant of a man, standing at 6ft 4 tall, calls out his instructions, "get inside, with your mask on. Take your mask off and do two press-ups. Stay in there as long as you possibly can."

Tom, first up, follows the Corporal's instructions. Unsure how long he can stand it, it feels like only seconds before he is banging the door, begging to be let out. When the door eventually opens, he falls out, his eyes and nose burning and streaming badly. Feeling his throat close up, he's unable to see. Struggling to stand to let the wind blow away the gas, his throat gets tighter and tighter. He can't breathe. *Is this the effects of the gas or a panic attack?* Tom wonders. He crawls away from the offensive building, determined not to let this beat him. On all fours, Tom is panting like a dog, forcing himself to regulate his breathing. Within half an hour, the effects wear off, and he's able to continue with training. Phil doesn't fare so well and ends up grovelling for a chitty. The vomiting induced by the gas, not letting him off lightly.

A few days later, every Sapper proposed for deployment is called to the mess hall. The furniture is rearranged. The chairs all lined up in long rows.

"What on earth is going on, Phil?"

"How should I know?"

Tom and Phil are in the middle of the queue, staring straight ahead. Tom wonders why all his colleagues appear to have their hands in their pockets. Their elbows are sticking out. Moving closer to the front of the line, he can see the needles lined up. Signs on the tables, anthrax, botulinum. *What the hell.*

"Arm out, Gold."

Not a fan of needles, Tom puts his arm out, receiving two or was it three jabs, he can't tell. Looking away so he can't see what's happening. *This is scary shit.*

February 1991

War Zone
Sunday 24th February

There's shrapnel everywhere. "What have we let ourselves in for?" Shouts Tom over the roar of the Combat Engineer Tractor's engines. The large formation of tanks and vehicles travels slowly across the sand in the middle of the night, the camouflage rendering them virtually invisible to the naked eye.

"Not long now till we arrive; our safe area is a mile or so south of here." Corporal Masters assures Tom, now a fully-fledged Lance Corporal. Phil and another mousy looking Private in his 30s, Brian Smith are traveling in a Land Rover behind them.

"This is exciting, Sir," Tom's response falls on deaf ears. Staring through the night vision scope, Tom's brain can't or won't compute the carnage he sees. As the vehicles continue their journey, the vehicle fire to Tom's left lights up the sky, allowing him to see some of the carnage more clearly. Natives, lying by the roadside, covered in blood and cowering like frightened animals. Shaking his head, he tries to lose the image. The latest casualty, a woman barely past 20 years of age, her right arm contorted so badly it turns Tom's stomach over. Feeling powerless to help these people, Tom looks away, instead focusing on his job at hand as a Plant Operator Mechanic.

Arriving at their destination, they jump from the vehicles and enter the stinking filthy, half derelict building, which will be their home for the next few months—the sound of mortar bombs from enemy forces all too close for comfort.

"Stand by for debrief, lads, 04:30." The commanding office shouts.

Wow, that's only two hours away, Tom is shocked to note as he glances down at his watch, just to make sure.

A decade has passed since basic training, and they now have to face armed combat for the first time. Pleased he and Phil have deployed together. Tom, for all his bravado, is shitting himself.

"Right then, get your heads down for an hour, lads. See you at the debrief." These were the last words their commanding officer would utter.

Dragging themselves and their equipment to a mattress in the middle of a corridor, "what are we doing here, Phil?" Tom asks, somewhat shaken by the conditions he finds himself in. A bit different to the four-bed house on the hill back home.

"Fighting a war, mate, that's what we've trained all this time for."

"Mmm," was all Tom could think of in response as he questions again whether he's up to the task.

"Get your head down, Tom, not long now 'til debrief, and according to the rumours, it may be a while before we have another chance."

"OK, mate. Got ya."

Tom sleeps fitfully that night, his mind wandering, his heart gripped with fear, the like of which he's never known.

The sharp kick in Tom's side informs him that it's 04:30 and time to get up.

Already fully dressed after sleeping in his full kit, he clambers up and heads to the debrief.

Listening intently to the sergeant, Tom takes big gulps of air to try and steady his fraying nerves, concentrating on the sergeant's voice to try and hide his panic. For the first time since joining up, he's genuinely losing his nerve.

"Right then, company, you have your orders. Let's do it."

Following his orders, throughout the day, Tom and Phil on high alert for enemy fire, are busy digging shell scrapes. Working mostly in the sand, their heads below ground, the sound of enemy fire seems a long way off.

As the day begins to draw to a close, Tom pulls himself out of the shell scrape and grabs the camouflage netting, heading to their vehicle to hide it for the night. Praying it won't take him long to secure, Tom climbs up on top of the vehicle.

Ouch That Hurts
Monday 25th February

"I'm sorry, Gold, there's nothing I can do. That's just how it is. Rules are rules as they say."

"Can't you just give me a little while longer? I can rest, then get straight back out there."

"No, sorry, that's the way it is. The decision is final. It's too badly damaged to take the risk, not just for us, but for you as well. I know it's a lot to get your head around, but you're still young. You have years ahead of you to forge a career for yourself."

Shaking her head in dismay at the soldier, his dark hair almost shaved to oblivion and his once bright jade green eyes now as dull as dishwater, unsure what to do to help him as there is nothing.

Catching a glimpse of her greying hair and washed-out reflection in the soldier's shoes as she looks down, Jo Small picks up her stethoscope and notes from the bed, careful not to catch the wound as she does so. Turning to address the soldier, using his Christian name in an attempt to soften the blow, "Tom, I've seen so many like you pass through my care over the years. It's a dangerous job, and with it comes consequences. You'll get used to it. Give it time."

Tapping him gently on the shoulder as she leaves the shabby tent, a makeshift hospital in the middle of the desert, she cannot help but catch a glimpse of the scared look in the young soldier's eyes.

"Your life is only just beginning. Make the most of it, and don't waste it."

Lying stock still on the bed, if you could call it that, Tom battles to keep the tears at bay, but to no avail.

What the hell am I supposed to do now?

Panic and fear grip his heart, turning it cold as the sweat pours from his body and his brain attempts to compute the devastating blow which it has just been served.

"Hey, scrawny, what's up?"

Hearing the voice of his best friend of the past decade calling him by the nickname he has come to be known by, Tom wipes his eyes quickly on the back of his hand, attempting to drag himself upright in the bed.

"Don't get up on my account, ugly. You lie there and have a nice nap."

Laughing, they both catch one another's eyes. Phil knows instinctively that bad news is to be parted.

"I'm out, man, I'm out. This is the worst day of my life."

Phil perches himself on the edge of Tom's bed, utter shock tingling his fingers.

"You can't be. You only jumped from the vehicle, you've done worse than that before."

"I didn't even do that. From what I remember, I was trying to edge down the side to avoid injury. Ha, some good it did me. I may as well have jumped."

"How come you're out then?"

"They think it's how I landed which caused the problem. Must have landed awkwardly. Right mess it's made of my knee. At least, that's what I assume. I passed out with the pain as soon as I hit the deck."

"Buddy, that's shit. I can't get my head around it."

Trying not to show their emotions, they each look around the room as if trying to find inspiration in the air.

"Phil, what am I going to do? I don't know how to be a real person. I'm a soldier. That's all I've ever been any good at."

With no idea how to respond to his friend's desperate pleas, he taps his leg. "You'll be fine, man; you'll be fine."

The scream that escapes from Tom's lips at the gentle touch of his friend's hand shocks them both.

"Man, I'm sorry, that wasn't even a tap. Bloody hell, how much damage did you do?"

"A lot. I have to have an operation when I get home. They can't do it out here for obvious reasons."

Pulling the sheet back, Tom shows Phil his ever-swelling knee.

"Bloody hell," was all Phil could think of in response.

Reaching over to the empty ammunition box, which serves as a makeshift table, Tom grabs the pain killers. Fumbling with the bottle, he pours a few into his hand.

"Woah, Tom, not that many, here, let me."

Phil grabs the bottle and hands Tom two of the tablets.

"These look like they could take out a horse at ten paces. What the hell are they?"

"I've no idea, but I'm hoping they will."

Snatching the tablets and the water offered to him, Tom greedily swallows, the pain now more unbearable than ever.

Falling back across the bed and shutting his eyes, he is only vaguely aware of Phil bidding him goodbye.

The Journey Home
Tuesday 26th February

With great difficulty, Tom pulls himself onto the
Chinook; thankfully, all the training has strengthened his
arms. The pain in his knee doesn't feel as bad today. The
tablets must be working.

Sitting rigid in his chair, bracing himself for take-off,
he never did like that much, the sensations and the ringing
in his ears, then the popping sound and the shooting pain
from ear to ear. *Urgh*, he shivers. The sounds are being
exaggerated on this beast of an aircraft.

Feeling the bile rise in his throat, he struggles to
breathe as panic sets in. His chest rising and falling faster
than a hydraulic drill. His face, deathly grey, drips with
sweat—burning sensations in the tips of his fingers and
toes, but his body shivers with cold.

"Gold, Gold, what the hell you doing?" The sergeant,
who is being flown home on a family emergency, asks.

"Gold."

Tom feels like he is dropping in and out of
consciousness. *Must be the painkillers.* He wonders to
himself, his head swimming. The voice of the officer
sounds like he's underwater rather than 20,000 feet in the
air.

"Ouch, what was that for, mother?"

*"You're ten years old, and you're still pissing the bed.
What is wrong with you? Have you been at my Jack
Daniels?"*

"Ouch, stop that, Mom, it hurts."

"You want something to cry about, Son? Do you?"
Sylvie screams at him.

"No, Mom," Tom answers, sobbing for all he's worth as another lash of the belt lands on his knee, buckle first.

"Stop crying then, or I'll give you something to really cry about," Sylvie yells again. As another fierce blow lands on his knee. The pain throbbing, pulsating through his leg like a pounding fist.

"Please stop, Mom. I can't take any more." Tom sobs as he slowly side steps to the wall, sliding down it as his mother stands, staring at the marks on her son's legs, wondering where the hell they came from.

Tom flails his arms around as he sees Sylvie coming towards him for what he assumes is another beating.

"No. No. NO."

"Gold, Gold. Wake up, what are you saying?"

"What… Where am I?" Confused and feeling slightly delirious, his chest feels heavy, and his breathing is laboured. He looks around him, remembers where he is as he tries to piece together his thoughts.

"You look like shit, Gold." The Sergeant states.

Tom's attempts to respond are lost in a wave of nausea as his head spins, and he begins to gag.

"Take a breath, Son, take a breath, no chucking up on here."

Fighting his urge to throw up and desperately trying to get his breath, his panicking worsens. He tries to count sheep, sing, chant, anything to bring his breathing back to normal. His panic rises further as nothing seems to work. His heart feels like it's jumping from his body. *I think I'm going to die.*

Suddenly realising what's happening, his colleague springs from his seat opposite Tom and pulls his body forward, placing Tom's head between his legs.

"Breathe, Gold. Breathe."

114

Feeling slightly better as his breathing slowly starts to get back to normal, and his heart is no longer doing the long jump.

"If that happens again, Son, stick your head between your legs or breathe quickly into a brown paper bag."

"Why?"

"It works, that's why."

This would turn out to be the best piece of advice Tom would ever receive.

Feeling a little calmer now, Tom sits up straight, and as he does, his leg catches his kit bag. Squealing like a pig on a BBQ, he places his head back between his legs not only because his head starts swimming again but also to hide the tears.

Hearing the officer call him son has reminded him of his grandfather. *Jobless, possible cripple, useless, worthless and possibly homeless. What am I going to do now? I hope Gramps will take me in after all this time.*

Home Sweet Home
Wednesday 27th February

Hobbling up the long winding driveway of 1 Pebble Road, Birch Tree Town, dragging his kit bag behind him, Tom, bedraggled, filthy and in pain, is praying his grandfather will take pity on him. He's well and truly screwed if he doesn't.

Leaning heavily against the wall, he catches his breath before ringing his grandfather's bell, the sound loud enough to wake the whole town.

A few minutes later, an angry voice from behind the door shouts, "who the hell is that at this time of night?"

Barely able to say his name, Tom lifts the letter box and croaks, "it's me, Gramps, Tom."

Flinging the door open, stunned, Maurice immediately yells, "what the hell are you doing here, another job you couldn't keep down, eh?"

Too weak to argue, Tom slides down the wall and sits on the floor with his head in his hands.

"Even after a decade, he has no faith in me."

"What you saying, Son, get up. Get inside before anyone sees you in that state. Bloody drunk again, I suppose."

"No, Gramps, I'm not drunk. I wouldn't be here if I had any other choice."

"What do you mean?"

"I've had an accident, Gramps. My knee is shot to bits."

Rolling over, he drags himself through the door, using the wall to walk through the elaborately decorated porch into the homely kitchen, the Aga still burning despite the late hour.

117

Watching his grandson struggle as he follows him to the kitchen, he's shocked at the change in him. He looks strong, fit and healthy but the saddest he's ever known him. *He's either a really good actor, or he's in a hell of a lot of pain. I never wanted this for him. What have I done?*

Collapsing into his favourite chair in the kitchen, Tom stares up at his grandfather boiling the kettle and putting a tea bag in his cup and coffee in Toms. Everything seems to be moving in slow motion to Tom, his head is still spinning. He grabs the bottle of painkiller from his pocket, deftly takes the lid off and swallows two without even blinking.

"Coffee, Tom?"

"Please, Gramps."

"Coming up, so what the hell happened?"

"Can we talk about it later? I need some sleep."

"Sure, Son, I'll run you a bath first. You're not getting into bed in that state."

Shocked at his grandfather's sudden caring attitude, Tom is grateful for small mercies and a bit of peace and quiet.

"You want a hand in the bathroom?"

"Nah, I'll be fine, thanks, Gramps," Tom answers, wondering how the hell he's going to be able to get in and out of the bath.

Pouring some of the cheap bubble bath into the hot running water, Tom loses himself in the woody scent. Climbing gingerly into the bath, careful not to catch his knee, the soothing warmth of a long-awaited bath cocoons him in bliss. Tom tops the water up a couple of times, savouring the serenity, before scrubbing himself all over. Attempting to remove the memories of the past few days as well as the grime buried deep in his pores.

118

An hour or so later, Tom has lost track of time, he attempts to get out of the bath. Lifting himself isn't a problem. His arms are as strong as an ox, but he can't lift his leg over the side of the bath.

Choking back the embarrassment, he shouts, "Gramps, Gramps," *I hope he hasn't gone back to bed.* "Gramps. Gram..."

"I'm coming. I'm coming. Hold your horses; I'm not as young as I once was, you know." Maurice pants as he peers around the bathroom door.

"What's up, Son.?"

Distress churning his insides, Tom replies, "I can't get out the bath, Gramps."

Swallowing back the tears, he looks away as his grandfather strolls over to him.

"Do you think you'll be able to lift me?"

"I might not be as young as I once was, but I'm fitter than you, lad. Of course, I can lift you."

Positioning himself to grab Tom's arms, he anchors himself to the side of the bath and leans in, pulling Tom up as if he were a feather. Tom puts his arms around Maurice's neck as he manoeuvres his leg over the bath, finally sitting exhausted on the side.

Tom moves to cover himself up as his grandfather grabs his towel from its resting place on top of the toilet seat. Turning back towards him, Maurice can't help but notice the marks across the back of his legs and knees.

"Jesus, Son, the Army really have gone to town on you, haven't they?"

Perplexed, Tom shakes his head, "what do you mean, Gramps?"

Nodding his head towards Tom's knees and legs, "I know the Army is supposed to be hard and push your limits, but that seems a bit excessive."

119

"What does?"

Nodding again, Maurice points at the angry marks, noting how swollen his knee is, making the marks look even angrier.

Tom follows the line of his finger, "Oh, those, they're nothing."

Not the Army either.

"What did you say, Son? Not the Army? Where did you get them then?"

"Can we change the subject, please?" Tom asks, attempting to sidestep him but collapsing as his knee gives way.

Just managing to catch him, Maurice almost carries his grandson into his bedroom and sits him on the edge of the bed. Moving his kit back, which he'd brought up earlier, "get some rest, Son. I'll call the doctor in the morning. I can't believe the Army sent you home like this."

"No, it's fine. Honestly, I'll sleep it off and take some painkillers."

"I don't think so, Tom."

"Honestly, it's fine."

Reaching onto the floor to pick up the trousers he dropped there earlier, he finds the ever-faithful pill bottle hidden within, and as his grandfather leaves, Tom swallows three of the pink tablets, puts the bottle back in his pocket and lies back on the bed. Within seconds he's fast asleep.

"Come on, Son, where are you?" Sylvie asks, throwing her head back, laughing. Tom loves it when his mom does this, she looks lovely when she laughs, but he feels nervous. He can see her clearly from under his shelf in the bottom of the double wardrobe in his parent's bedroom. He loves to

play hide and seek. He plays it with his friends all the time, he's usually the one hiding, and it takes them ages to find him. This feels different today. His mother is talking funny, and she smells strange too.

Slurring her words, Sylvie asks again in a purring voice, "Oh, Tom, whurr arrr yooooo?" Bloody child.

Losing her patience, she shouts, "Get out here now, Tom."

Tom, still cowering under the shelf, holds his breath, but the sneeze decides now is the time to make itself known.

"Ah, there you are, you little shit," Sylvie shouts, grabbing him by the leg and dragging him from the wardrobe, bouncing him along as she pulls him to the top of the stairs. Taking the belt off her jeans, she drops his leg and lashes out, the belt narrowly missing his eye as he dives to the side to minimise the impact.

Scared and shaking, Tom shouts, "no, Mom, no," just as the belt lands its blow on the front of his right kneecap. Screaming in pain, he cowers again and edges away from her, but the belt is too fast, and its force catches the side of the same knee.

"Stop, Mom, stop," he yells, rolling himself over and grabbing the leg of the dresser. He used to fit under here to play hide and seek, but he's too big now, so he holds on and prays it will stop soon.

The slamming of the door startles Tom as he flails around on the bed.

"Hi, honey, I'm home. Tom, come and see Daddy too. Where are you both?"

In a hot sweat, Tom sits bolt upright.
"What on earth…"

Struggling to get back to sleep, Tom shakes himself awake, pushing the recuring memories away. *I'm taking too many painkillers.* He thinks to himself.

"Tom, Tom, are you up yet?"

"Yes, just getting up now, Gramps."

"Good, come and have a cuppa with me before I go to work."

Tom pulls his dressing gown on and slides down the stairs on his backside, not daring to try to walk down, the pain in his knee is excruciating.

Sitting in his favourite chair, Tom waits while his grandfather makes them both a drink.

As he hands Tom his coffee Maurice asks what happened.

"I fell off a vehicle, Gramps. Damaged my knee."

"I saw the damage last night. Why weren't you taken to their hospital?"

"I don't know, no one would tell me anything. Maybe I mis understood, but I'm sure they said I'm out and I was being medically discharged."

"That doesn't sound right to me, Son. I'll make some calls from the office today. See if I can find out what's going on."

"Thanks, Gramps."

"OK, Son, I called our doctor last night and he'll be here in a couple of hours."

Tom heads back to bed once his grandfather leaves, having taken more painkillers. Hearing a car pull up a short while later, Tom groans. Pushing himself up on his elbows, grateful that his torso has the strength of an ox, *I guess the Army did me more favours than I thought.* Swinging his legs over the edge of the bed, attempting to jump out, only to end up in a heap on the floor, waking

Charlie, the mongrel his grandfather brought a couple of years ago, the last time Tom was home on leave.

Whimpering, Charlie crawls over to his new master and licks his face, catching the salty tears as they fall.

"Oh, Charlie, what am I going to do? This isn't good; my knee is killing me."

Yelping in agreement, Charlie carries on licking.

"Stop now, Charlie," Tom commands as he drags himself to the bathroom to shower and dress. Finishing just as the knock on the front door lands.

"Mr Gold, Mr Gold, the doctor is here," Mrs Dainty, dainty by name but not by stature, Maurice's cleaner come housekeeper shouts, halfway up the stairs to try and make herself heard over Charlies barking.

"Shush, boy, I know it's the door. It's probably the bloody doctor."

"Ah, there you are, Mr Gold, Doctor's here."

"Thank you, Mrs Dainty."

She turns around and makes her way back down the stairs as Tom slowly slides down again, one painful stair at a time on his backside.

"Morning, Doctor Armitage," Tom stands and shakes his hand.

"Morning, Tom. Bad knee, I'm told."

"Yeah, you could say that," Tom laughs, his heart pounding, wondering what the doctor will say.

"I'm taking painkillers, but it ain't half sore doc."

"Mmm, that much is apparent. I don't see many grown men coming down the stairs on their backsides, even in my job." He responds, trying to make Tom feel a little calmer. He felt the tension in the lad from his handshake.

"Right, let's get you onto the settee, and I can have a closer look at that knee."

123

Towering over the short, rotund man, Tom follows him into the living room and falls into his favourite chair. Having had the forethought to put shorts on, he sits back to be examined.

"Tom, why didn't you go straight to the hospital yesterday when you got home?" He looks up at him over the rim of his rounded spectacles, his dark brown eyes dazzling from the light above him.

"I don't know. The taxi brought me here. I thought it would be OK with a few days' rest."

"Tom, you can't possibly believe that. It's twice the size it should be. This needs urgent treatment. I'm going to call Mr Howard, the orthopaedic surgeon from Malthaven, when I get back to the practice."

"But doesn't he only do private clinics now?"

"Yes, I've spoken with your grandfather, and he's told me to do whatever it takes. I hope you're grateful young man. That's all I can do. This can't be left any longer."

"But…"

"No buts, if you don't get this sorted, you won't be able to walk for much longer. Doesn't the way you came down the stairs tell you something?"

Bewildered, Tom hangs his head, knowing that what he's being told is the truth. Resigned to the inevitable, all Tom can say, is "OK, I'm in your hands then."

"I'll call Mr Howard, and I suggest you take whatever appointment he offers and get this sorted."

"OK, thanks for coming, doc."

"No problem, don't get up, Tom. I'll see myself out, and I'll call you later."

Slumped in his chair watching his knee swelling, Charlie pads up to him and rubs his nose on his hand, eager for a fuss. Allowing Charlie to jump on the chair next to him, Tom pulls him close.

124

"Oh, Charlie, what am I going to do? I know I'll have to have surgery, but what if it goes wrong or doesn't work?"

Burying his head in the mongrel's soft brown fur, Tom continues to mumble. All his fears and concerns lost on the dog.

"Mr Gold, would you like your breakfast in here this morning?" Mrs Dainty asks as she hurries into the living room, having seen the doctor off.

"Gramps will go mad. I'll come through."

"What Gramps doesn't know can't hurt him, can it? He won't be back for hours, and I won't tell him if you don't."

"You're an angel, Mrs D. That would be great, thank you."

Leaning his head back on the chair, sighing, *I'm so glad Mrs D is here. What would I do without her? I have a feeling I'm going to need her very soon.*

As Mrs Dainty brings Tom his breakfast in and places the tray gently on his lap, Tom hears a noise, "is that the radio I can hear, Mrs D?"

"Yes, Mr Gold, would you like me to turn it off?"

"No, no, turn it up, please." Mrs Dainty heads back to the kitchen and turns the radio up as loud as it will go, dashing back to the living room to make sure he can hear it.

"Breaking news," Tom hears, "A cease-fire has been called. Our troops will be heading home soon."

"Did you hear, Mrs D? The boys are coming home."

"I heard, Mr Gold, that's brilliant news. You must be pleased for your comrades."

"Oh, I am. That's about made my day." Tom heaves a sigh of relief as he finishes his breakfast. Within minutes he dozes off again.

Slumped in the chair, having taken several more painkillers with breakfast, Tom doesn't hear the phone ring.

"Hello, Mrs Dainty, how's the invalid?" Doctor Armitage asks.

"Oh, you know, stubborn, in denial, taking too many painkillers, the usual, I guess."

"Yes, I thought so. That's a worry with the painkillers too. I've managed to get him an appointment. Can you fetch him to the phone, please?"

"I'll go and wake him, just a minute."

"Mr Gold, the doctors on the phone. Mr Gold." Mrs Dainty shakes him gently awake.

"Mmm, I must have dozed off. What is it, Mrs D?"

"Docs on the phone. He has some news. Can you make it to the hall?"

Groaning, "can you take a message please, Mrs D?"

"Yes, of course." Dashing off again, Mrs Dainty picks up the receiver. "Are you still there, doc?"

"I'm still here."

"He asked me to take a message."

"Very well, please tell him I've booked him an appointment with Mr Howard tomorrow morning at 10 am at his practice in Malthaven. Please ensure he attends, Mrs Dainty. His situation will only get worse if he doesn't."

"Right you are. I'll let him know."

"Tell Maurice too, would you. I have a feeling he won't go unless he's pushed."

"Will do, Doctor. I'll tell them tonight."

After saying their goodbyes, Mrs Dainty walks back to the living room to check on Tom, just in time to see him put the bottle of pills back in the pocket of his shorts. She shakes her head, concern for him growing. This isn't the first time she's seen him sneaking the tablets away. Unsure what to do or who to tell, she walks away, muttering to herself. She's pretty much brought him up after finding him cowering in the wardrobe if the truth be told. Torn between her concern for his welfare and keeping her job, she keeps quiet.

At dinner that evening, Mrs Dainty informs them both of the doctor's message, knowing full well that he was right and Tom won't go if he can find a way out of it.

"Right then, Son, I'll drop you off on my way to work in the morning."

"That will be way too early, Gramps."

"That's alright. You can use the time to think about what you're going to do with your life now. I called your barracks, by the way."

Tom had forgotten, his mind elsewhere.

Looking up at his grandfather, Tom waits for him to continue.

"What they said didn't make much sense to be honest. They said they lost you when they landed the Chinook and have been looking for you ever since. Why they didn't think to call here or your parent's I don't know."

"I thought they'd put me in the taxi, Gramps. I'm sure there was someone else in there with me. Apart from the driver."

"I don't know, Son. They were expecting you at one of their military hospitals in the Midlands first thing this morning. Me calling them may go in your favour, Son."

"What do you mean, in my favour?"

"They have you classified as AWOL as they couldn't find you."

"Oh, god," Tom groans as he rests his head on the table. "I'm finished then."

"Not quite, Son. They did tell me to send you to their hospital but I declined, telling them the same as I told Doctor Armitage. I'll sort it."

"It doesn't work like that, Gramps. I'd better go. Did they tell you where the hospital is?"

Tom attempts to stand but his grandfather stalls him, his hand rests gently on Tom's arm. Like I said, Tom. I'll sort it.

Rising from his chair, Maurice leaves Tom. Feeling guilty. If he hadn't forced him into the Army, this would never have happened.

At least I may be able to help him get out.

As Tom watches his grandfather leave the house by the back door for his usual evening stroll, his heart begins racing again, his chest tightening. *No, not again.* A mixture of apprehension for the surely imminent surgery and frustration about his future. If he even has one. He puts his head between his legs to try and regulate his breathing. Grateful to the Sergeant for the advice. After a few minutes, but what feels like hours, his heart rate slows. Gathering his thoughts together, he leaves the table and makes his way to the living room to watch the news and unsure of his future in the Army, he begins to look for a job. *How the hell can I get a job when I can barely walk?*

Flicking through the Teletext and the papers, all the same, restaurant staff, bar worker, café operatives, quite a few to choose from but none which he wants to do. *Maybe I could go and work for Gramps again when my knee is better if he'll have me back?*

The Op
Thursday 28th February

"Right then, young man, which knee is it? Mr Howard asks as he looks down at Tom, his hospital gown perched high up on his thighs.

Horrified, Tom looks up at this ruggedly handsome surgeon, *the one that's the size of an elephant's foot, maybe.* He thinks to himself, sarcastically, not daring to voice his thoughts.

Laughing, Mr Howard says, "I guess it's the one which looks like an elephant's foot then?"

How the hell...

"You nearly had me there, doc."

"Thought so, Tom, you have to laugh. Life is too short."

"Hopefully not that short that I don't make it through surgery." Tom queries tentatively. Aiming at a bit of light humour himself but failing miserably.

"Course you'll make it, I have a magic scalpel, and I haven't lost a patient yet. That would be very careless of me. I can see you're nervous, Tom, but you have no need to be. I'm going to scribble on the leg now with a marker. Just to be sure we get the correct knee."

"I wouldn't think there could be much of a mistake, doc, but you enjoy your scribbling."

Tom lies back on the bed. The tip of the marker tickles his leg, making him giggle.

"That's better, young man, relax a little; it will make it easier to give you the anaesthetic," he is making small talk to ease the patient's nerves, "you weren't expecting this today, were you?"

"Erm, not really no. I thought I would have a few days to get prepared for an op."

"Normally, you would have had a few weeks, but Doctor Armitage was right. This can't be left any longer. Right young man, this nice lady will put you to sleep, and I'll see you on the other side."

Tom tries to look around to see her at the mention of young lady. *Who wouldn't, right?* She was too quick for him. No sooner had the surgeon said, young lady, Tom felt the prick of the needle and drifted off into the clouds.

"Take my hand, Tom; I want to show you something." Tom can't place the voice, and he can only see what he thinks is a woman in shadow. Taking her hand, she leads him high above the clouds into the deep calming purple of the universe, nothing but stars and the moon for company.

"Sit here and relax," the voice tells him. Looking around, Tom sees a seat on top of the cloud he walks over to and gently lowers himself into it.

Cocooning him in its warm, fluffy embrace, Tom visibly relaxes and feels a peace he hasn't experienced before.

"Who are you, Tom? What do you want?"

Tom lies back on the cloud and stares at the stars, counting them like sheep and making patterns in his mind. Ooh, look, a hammer and nail, a factory—a woman in shadow.

This is strange, Tom thinks. None of this makes any sense.

"Who are you, Tom? What do you want?"

The voice asks again.

"What do you dream of? A life of guilt and remorse or a life of success and wonder?"

Staring again at the stars as they all morph into the shape of a heart.

Visions of how life could play out in front of his eyes, nerve-wracking fear, irresistible temptation, success, love, passion. He reaches out but can't quite grasp any of it.

"Time to decide, Tom, just make sure you choose well."

Looking around to try and find this strange woman's voice, he notices a cottage at the edge of his sightline. Adjusting his focus, he sees what he thinks is a woman standing outside, waving at him. He can't quite make her out, but he can see the cottage clearly, a figure of eight door knocker, white washed walls, wrought iron gates and a butterfly perched on the fence post.

"Take me to the cottage," he hears himself say.

"Not unless you choose the correct path."

"How do I get to there then?"

"Take the path which makes you feel good. The one that makes you feel calm, comfortable, safe and helps you help others. Choose wisely, and you will visit the cottage soon."

Still staring at the cottage, the sense of peace and calm is still surrounding Tom as he gazes around him, looking again for patterns in the stars, counting them in his head, he curls up on the cloud. Never let this feeling end, he thinks.

"Mr Gold, Mr Gold, it's OK, you're coming round from the anaesthetic. Try to keep still for me, please, Mr Gold."

Tom slowly opens his eyes to see a gorgeous blond nurse checking his vital signs.

"Ooh, you can do that all day, gorgeous."

"What was that, Mr Gold? You aren't making any sense. Try not to talk for a while. You were doing some wriggling about in there. Nice dream under the anaesthetic, was it?"

131

"Mmm," Tom mutters, desperately trying to recollect the weird dream.

The Following Day
Friday 1st March

"Morning, Tom."

Wearily Tom responds, "morning, Mr Howard."

"Right young man, you are very lucky. That was a nasty injury and quite infected too. The fluid protecting the knee caused the excess swelling, was well, to be frank, a bloody mess. What the hell did you do?"

"I fell off an Army vehicle."

"Oh, and did this much damage?" Looking thoughtfully at his patient, "surely there's more to it than that?"

"No, I don't remember much about it, but I remember thinking don't jump, you'll injure yourself. The next thing I know, I'm on a plane home." Tom answers despondently.

"Well, I don't know what you did but, the cartilage and the ligaments were badly damaged, and the fluid, just plain nasty. All fixed now though. You may be left with a slight limp, but we won't know that until it's healed. Rest it for a few days at home, then start walking. Very short distances to begin with. The nurse will sort your antibiotics and pain killers before you go, and read this leaflet, thoroughly. Everything you need to know is in here. I'll see you in two weeks for your check-up."

"Is that it, doc. I'm going home today?"

"Yes, and don't jump off anything for a few weeks either, or fall for that matter."

Ha, bloody ha.

"OK, thanks, doc."

Left reeling, Tom sits up and drops his legs over the side of the bed, placing his foot on the floor. The pain shoots through him like a red-hot poker.

"Jesus, that hurts."

"Mr Gold, you shouldn't try to get up on your own." The gorgeous nurse he vaguely remembers from yesterday, her hand on his arm, helps him steady himself."

"Thank you, gorgeous." Staring at her name badge or rather staring at her breasts, he notices her name badge, "Gina, that's a nice name. I'm going home today, so I have to stand up."

"Home? Are you sure?"

"That's what the doc says. I'll miss you, gorgeous," he says again, glancing at her coyly.

Used to such comments, many people aren't used to tall blonds with a model like figure nursing them; she ignores him. "Let me go and find out for you. I'm sure that can't be right."

***

"What do you mean, Mr Howard? He can barely stand; how can he be discharged?"

"Nurse, he has a housekeeper?"

"What's that got to do with it? He's in our care."

"Soft on him, are you, Gina. Don't be fooled by those eyes. He's trouble."

Blushing, Gina asks what he means.

"Never mind, but he leaves today."

"Why, I don't understand?"

"Let me make it simple for you. His grandfather is paying for his treatment, and between you and me, he won't pay for any more. Do what you have to do, and no more was his grandfather's wish, and that's exactly what I've done. So, he leaves today. I'm not running a charity. Please sort his prescription and call his family to collect him."

Hands on her hips, Gina stands and stares. Disbelief washes over her as Mr Howard walks away.

Money really does talk, then. I'm in the wrong bloody job.

"Mr Gold, I have your prescription here, and I've called your grandfather for you as well."

"Thank you, Gina, that's so kind. When are you coming round to see me?"

Heeding what Mr Howard has just told her, Gina treads carefully. "You don't waste much time, do you? But I'm married."

"That's OK. I need a nurse, not a wife."

Mmm, I bet.

Checking his vital signs again and more to shut him up than anything else, she thrusts the thermometer in his mouth.

"You're good to go. If you'd like to wait in reception, I'll pop and fetch your prescription from the pharmacy for you."

"Thank you."

Phew, anything to escape this god's gift to women. Why am I bending over backwards to help him, and why the hell did I say I was married? Wonder whether I'll see him again.

Stop it. She berates herself.

Before she realises it, she's back at Tom's bedside, helping him pack his things, handing him the crutches he'll use for his recovery.

"What do I do with these once I've finished with them?" Tom asks.

"If you could bring them back here, that would be great, or I could collect them from you?"

What am I saying?!

135

Grinning to himself. *He shoots, he scores. Married my arse.* He almost wants to pump the air with his fist, but he refrains, just in time.

"That's very kind; I'll let you decide." Tom winks at her as he bends down to put his shoes on.

Blushing again, she walks away to treat the next patient. "Bye, Mr Gold."

"Goodbye, Gina and please, call me Tom."

Watching him out of the corner of her eye, despite the huge bandage and slightly ashen complexion, he has a lot going for him. Nice ass, nice face, gorgeous eyes. That twinkle. She is almost floating, thinking about that twinkle. When the voice of Mr Howard rings in her ears. *He's trouble.* Yes, I imagine he is.

Turning back towards her new patient, Gina misses the vacant look in Tom's eyes when he glances back towards her as he leaves the ward.

***

"Hi, Gramps."

"What took you so long? The nurse said you were ready to leave."

Nice to see you, too.

"I was. It just took a little while to get here with these," Tom replies, waving one of his crutches in the air. Feeling the anger rising within him, Tom hobbles past his grandfather and onto the car park.

"Come on then, Son, I need to get back to work."

Always bloody, work, work, work. No wonder he looks haggard.

"Your father called."

"Mmm."

"Asked how you were, how Army life was going, lance corporal and all that. Why haven't you told him you're back?"

Maybe because I don't want them to know, and I don't want the 'I knew you couldn't do it speech'.

Tom shrugs his shoulders. "Didn't think about it."

"That's your bloody trouble. You never do. Think about it. Call him when you get home."

"OK, OK."

The drive home in awkward silence disturbs Tom, having always been close to his grandfather, despite everything. Something feels… off. He can't quite put his finger on it.

"Gramps."

"Mmm."

"Can I come back to work for you once my knee is better?"

Pulling onto the drive, Maurice looks over at Tom as he opens the door to get out.

"I'd like that, Son. You should have some useful skills you can bring to the place. But you need to be sure it's what you want, and we need to wait until we hear back from your regiment too."

Staring in shock at his grandfather's words, *there it is again, that question. What do you want? To be back in the Army, that's what I want.* Tom opens the door and pushes himself up, grabbing the door jamb to help steady himself as he struggles to get out.

Wobbling on his crutches, Tom turns to shut the door; Maurice has already turned away, his foot impatiently tapping the accelerator. Once the door is shut, he drives away without a second glance, leaving Tom staring at the cloud of dust kicked up by the tyres. Seemingly unconcerned whether or not Tom can manage.

137

Hearing the car door, Mrs Dainty is on the doorstep before you can say boo to a goose.

"Good morning, Mr Gold. How are you?"

At least that's one person who cares. Tom mutters under his breath.

"I've had better days, but I'm OK, thank you. What's for breakfast?"

"Breakfast, didn't you have that at the hospital?"

"Yeah, sloppy porridge and an apple, hardly enough for a growing lad like me, eh?" he laughs. *Is this what I've become? Flirting with the help. The middle-aged help at that!"*

Already used to his abysmal ways, Mrs Dainty ignores his comments and heads back inside. Following her through the back door to the kitchen, Tom falls into his favourite chair.

"Hey, boy, what a welcome." *At least Charlie loves me.*

Laughing as the dog slobbers over him like he's just found his favourite chew toy.

"Woah, slow down, that's enough now," Tom states as he ruffles his head and gently pushes him onto the floor.

"Toast with your breakfast, Mr Gold?"

"Please, Mrs D."

Stretching his leg out in front of him, the throbbing feels like someone is playing the drums on his kneecap. Reaching into his pocket, he pulls out the bottles of tablets, taking the antibiotics and one too many of the pain killers, popping the bottle back into his pocket before Mrs Dainty's beady eyes catch him.

"Here you are, Mr Gold, enjoy. I'll be in the living room cleaning if you need me."

Without waiting for a response, she leaves him to it.

Feeling slightly sick after wolfing down half of his breakfast, Tom feeds the rest to Charlie, who thinks all his birthdays have come at once.

I guess that explains the measly hospital breakfast. He ponders to himself. *But I'm so hungry. Why do I feel so ill? Maybe the anaesthetic. Oh well.*

"I'm going for a lie-down, Mrs D," he shouts over the vacuum on his way past the living room. Finally getting upstairs after much deliberation and struggle, eventually choosing to bounce up on his backside, he collapses onto the bed and falls into a dreamless sleep.

***

Waking to the sound of a key in the lock, Tom is disoriented and perplexed, *bit early for Gramps to be home. What time is it?* Glancing at his watch, he is amazed to see that it's 6 pm. *I've slept all day. How can that be?* Struggling off the bed and making his way to the bathroom to relieve himself, only just making it in time, his knee is still throbbing, and the crutches hinder him. He downs more tablets and hobbles his way downstairs to the kitchen.

"Doing what the doc told you, are you, Son?" Maurice asks, already seated at the table for dinner.

"Not really, Gramps. I've been asleep all day."

"Mmm, so, after dinner then, you're going to start doing what the doctor told you?"

"How do you know what the doctor told me?"

"I read the leaflet, Son." Maurice waves the leaflet under his nose, "did you?"

"Erm, no, I forgot about it."

Reading the leaflet, Tom is dismayed to find he should be walking a little every day. Determined to get fit again, he vows to do everything he can to fix his knee in the

139

quickest possible time. *Wonder if they'd ever let me back in the Army? If my knee is fixed enough.*

"Here you are, liver and onions, keep you both strong and healthy." Mrs Dainty announces as she places their food in front of them.

Gagging, Tom looks down at his plate in disgust, memories of different times float around his head, the mess hall, the awful cooking, the torture, the girls. He doesn't want to think about that now. Swallowing the bile in his throat, he takes a small mouthful.

"Mmm"

"You like it, Mr Gold?"

"Mmm, yes, I do, actually. It tastes different to what I expected. Not like the muck, they served in the Army, that's for sure.

"Thank you for the compliment." Mrs Dainty laughs. "Enjoy."

"Aren't you joining us tonight, Mrs D?" Maurice asks.

"Not tonight, thank you, can't stand liver. I'm off home. My son is back for a few days anyhow."

Looking across the table at each other, Tom and Maurice burst into fits of laughter, Mrs Dainty's comment breaking the treacherous atmosphere of the house since Tom's return.

Consultation
Friday 15th March

"So, how've you been, Tom? You don't look like you're walking any better. Are you doing your exercises?"

"Yes, Mr Howard, the pain is still bad, though. I've had the dressings changed, but it still doesn't feel right."

"It will take time, Tom, you did some serious damage, but you need to strengthen the muscles around it now. Hop on the couch, and let's have a look at it." Turning away, Mr Howard calls, "nurse, can you take the dressings off, please?"

"Yes, doctor." Tom stares astonished, hardly believing his luck. "Hi, Gina."

"Hello, Mr Gold," embarrassed, Gina turns her back to Tom and feeling the need to do something to stop her shaking, she rearranges the dressings in the cupboard behind her.

What is it about this guy that makes my knees weak? She muses to herself.

Lying on the couch with his hands behind his head, Tom watches her intently, grinning from ear to ear. *She fancies me.*

"Bandages, nurse." Mr Howard squawks as he finishes writing up Tom's notes so far. Carrying Tom's file with him, he waits while Gina removes the dressings. Shyly moving away, she hides behind the curtain, feeling flustered.

"Looks like this is healing nicely, Tom. The swelling has gone down considerably, lots of bruising, but that's normal. I'm not too worried, but I'll order a scan just to be sure. You need to keep up with the walking. Did you talk to the physio?"

"No, I didn't know I was supposed to."

"Well, you need to see them; otherwise, you could do even more damage—if your grandfather will pay, that is."

Not likely.

"Can't you just give me a list of exercises to do?"

"No, they need to assess you. I'll make you an appointment, and I'll speak to Maurice. You don't need any more dressings. I'll sort the scan. You just keep walking and exercising."

"Thanks, doc."

Shaking his hand, Tom grabs his crutches and leaves the consulting room, catching Gina's eye on the way out and winking at her.

Waiting outside for Gina to pass by on her break, Tom leans up against the wall and pops three of his painkillers.

A few minutes later, he clocks her blond bob bouncing down the corridor, pushing himself off the wall, he calls her name.

"Hey, Gina."

Startled, Gina stops and spins round, finding herself almost cheek to cheek with him.

Oh, heck, I thought he'd left. Please go.

Regaining her composure, she asks, "did you forget something, Mr Gold?"

"Yeah, you could say that," he grins, blocking her ways, so she has no means of escape. "I forgot to ask you what you're doing later."

Caught off guard, she mumbles, "oh…erm… nothing…why?"

Tucking her hair behind her ear as she tries to turn away from him, embarrassed but not wholly surprised, she prays to herself, *please don't ask me out.*

"Fancy a night on the town?"

Laughing, "what, with your knee? I don't think so."

Joining in the laughter, Tom responds, "mmm, maybe you're right there. How about a drink at *The Black Dog* in Birch Tree Town instead?"

No, no, no.

"OK, then, I know where that is. Meet you at 8?"

Mightily pleased with himself, *I've still got it then.* He turns away from her and shouts over his shoulder. "It's a date then. See you later, Gina."

What... Am... I... Doing...? Mr Howards words ring in her ears... *He's trouble.*

***

Tom hobbles off to the bus stop, unable to stop himself smiling at his latest conquest. *How long will it take me to get this one into bed? One date, no, maybe the second or third. I should run a book on it.* He laughs to himself. *I'd definitely do better on that than the horses, that's for sure.*

"Hey, Larry, take me home, mate." Tom chants at the bus driver as he throws himself into the first available seat.

"Will do, dude. That looks painful."

"Yeah, it is."

Leaving Larry to drive, Tom sits back, planning his date in his mind. *Couple of drinks, quick snog, fumble, maybe. Mmm, sounds like a plan.*

***

"You're looking pleased with yourself, Mr Gold. Go well at the hospital, did it?" Mrs Dainty asks.

"Scan and physio, if Gramps will pay."

"Oh, you'd better be on your best behaviour then. I don't rate your chances."

"I know, but on the plus side, I have a date tonight with the nurse I told you about."

"Oh, Lord, I'll pray for her then." Mrs Dainty laughs as she turns to boil the kettle for their afternoon tea.

"Gee, thanks, Mrs D. I'm not that bad."

"Oh, yes, you are. Where are you going anyway?"

"*The Black Dog.*"

"Your Dad's place, blimey."

"I know, hope he's not working, and I hope *she's* not in there either."

"If you mean your mother, no danger of her being there, she'll be in the *Frog and Snail* in Rose Bush Village, but why there?"

"Can't drive, can I? So that's the only place anywhere near walking distance." *Literally, The only place.*

"Well, you enjoy, Tom, here's your cuppa. Do you need anything else before I finish cleaning upstairs?"

"No, thanks, I'll drink this then go for a walk. Hopefully, that will keep everyone happy. Try and do some of it without the crutches."

"Good idea, Mr Gold, you don't want to become dependent on them like you have the painkillers." Mrs Dainty answers as she leaves. Tom stares after her from his favourite seat in the kitchen.

How the hell... what... shit..., burying his head in his hands. *How the hell does she know?*

"Where you off too, Son?" Maurice asks as Tom stumbles out of his chair, having finished his dinner.

"Pub."

"What with?"

"What do you mean, what with?"

"Money. You don't have any, and I ain't paying for all your treatment for you to piss it up the wall."

Ignoring his snide comments, Tom simply says, "I'm meeting a girl there."

"Thought as much, who is it this time? Are there actually any left round here you haven't sullied?"

Stunned by his comments, "Gramps, it's not like that."

"Really." He responds, staring at Tom and holding his gaze, knowing full well it's exactly like that.

"Sit down, Son and listen good. I'll pay for your treatment, there's no point having that money sitting there if I can't help family when they need it, but you will pay it back. Every penny. Understand?"

"Why didn't you just send me to the military hospital then, like they said too?"

Maurice ignores Tom's question.

"I said, do you understand, Son?"

Knowing that pressing the point wouldn't get him anywhere, Tom answers meekly, "Yes, Gramps, I understand."

"You can start at the factory tomorrow, and we'll see what happens. You'll be starting from scratch, in the office making the tea and filing, before you go back on the shop floor. You need to know how it all works for when you take over, so you'll have no time for the ladies." *You can thank me later, girls.*

"You'd best get your head in gear; you have a lot to do. I won't be here forever, and you need to be able to step up."

"Oh, and, Tom, the money for your treatment will be taken from your wages, and you'll pay board here too."

"I might be left with enough for a pint then, Gramps." Tom laughs, the laugh not quite reaching his eyes.

"Aye, about that, Son, did the Army not teach you anything?"

Pushing himself up from the chair, Tom says, "I never expected adjusting to civilian life to be so hard, especially having an almost ready-made job."

"One which you need to work at. I've already said you have some valuable skills from the Army but running a business is a whole different ball game. Are you sure you're ready?"

No, I'm not. Tom thinks to himself, still hoping he will be able to go back into the Army once his knee is fixed.

Pondering for a moment, Tom doesn't answer, "I have to be, don't I, don't have much choice? I'm going now, I'm going to be late."

"OK. Oh, by the way, the doc called your scan, and physio appointments are Monday morning.

Date with Gina
Friday 15ᵗʰ March – Evening

"Sorry, I'm late. Please don't leave." Tom pants as he bumps into Gina in the doorway of *The Black Dog*. I had to walk, and it took me longer than I thought," Tom states as the throbbing in his knee bangs in time to his heartbeat. He glances at the clock above the bar as he gently guides Gina back into the pub. 8.15 pm, *not as long as I thought then, that's good, it's getting better.* Out of the corner of his eye, Tom spots his father pulling a pint and chatting to Alf and Fred, who have been drinking there since the year dot. *Great, I thought he'd stopped working weekday evenings.*

Hustling Gina to an alcove seat in the corner, Tom drops his crutches on the floor. *I don't need those anymore,* he tells himself, ambling back to the bar to get the drinks.

"What do you fancy?"

"Diet coke, please, Tom, I'm driving."

"Right you are." *Goodie, lift home then.*

"Snakebite and a diet coke, please."

"Coming up, Son. What are you doing in here?"

"On a date, aren't I?" Tom states as if it's obvious.

"No, I mean, we didn't know you were back, your mom and I."

"Why would you. I wouldn't be in here if I could drive."

Paying for the drinks, Tom picks them up and limps over to Gina.

"This is a lovely pub, Tom. I've never been here before."

Sitting opposite her, stretching his legs across the seat, "ah, that's better." He exclaims as he slowly starts to relax and unwind, his knee throbbing a little less than before.

Grabbing his pint, Tom takes a long swig and stares at her over the top of his glass, "delicious." *Shite father, great landlord, though.*

Staring a little longer than is polite, Tom looks away, thinking what a gorgeous woman Gina is, especially now she isn't wearing her uniform, her blond bobbed hair, blue eyes and ample breasts are enough to distract him from his troubles.

"So, how long have you been drinking here, Tom?" Gina asks as she takes a sip of her coke.

"I haven't, not really. Being in the Army for a few years, I rarely came home."

"Really, why not?"

"No reason to. We don't really get on, and this is my father's pub." Not wishing to elaborate and open up old wounds, he carries on talking, "I didn't think he'd be here, to be honest. I prefer *The Red Lion* in Malthaven. Not being able to drive, though, I'm a bit limited at the moment."

"You should have said; *The Red Lion* is my favourite pub. Their scampi baskets are to die for."

Tom laughs, "I hope not. That wouldn't be good for business,"

They both laugh, feeling the ice has been broken a little more; Gina starts to relax too.

"How's the knee?" she asks.

"Getting there, still sore, but I'm doing my exercises, being the good boy that I am."

Spitting the drink out she had just taken.

"Woah, what's that all about?" he asks.

148

"Sorry, I couldn't help but laugh. That's different to what I heard."

"Mmm, that doesn't surprise me; that's why I hate living in a small village. Everyone thinks they know everything, and they know nothing." Tom retorts, the anger rising in him, *not that they raise a finger to help when it's needed, though.* Taking another drink before he says anything he will regret, he looks at her again.

Putting her glass down, Gina responds, "don't shoot the messenger, Tom, I'm just saying."

"I know, sorry, can we start this date again?"

"Date, who said this was a date?"

Sensing the frostiness in the air, Tom ignores the question, "so what do you enjoy doing, Gina?"

"Walking, I like walking my dog."

Finding common ground, Tom breathes a sigh of relief, "What sort? I have a mongrel, Charlie, well, he's my grandfather's really, had him about two years. Soft as soap he is."

"Labrador puppy, and he's a handful," Gina laughs. "Wouldn't be without him though."

Smiling, Tom has a thought, "maybe we could walk them together when my knee is better?"

"Yeah, that would be nice."

Good incentive to get my arse in gear and strengthen my knee.

"I'll let you call me when you're ready," Gina says as she writes her number on the beer mat, she's been nervously ripping since they sat down.

Handing it over, she finishes her drink, "I have to leave. I need to get back to Snoopy."

"Snoopy?"

"My Labrador, he needs a walk before bed. See you around, Tom," she says as she picks her bag up and leaves Tom staring after her. *Oh, bugger, no lift then?*

Not relishing the idea of walking, "Dad, any chance of a lift to Gramps's?" Tom asks, almost choking on the last of his beer at the thought of asking him for a favour.

"When I close at 11, yeah, sure."

"OK, I'll wait. Can I have another then, please?" Tom asks as he ambles up to the bar.

"Sure, Son. Here you go, on the house."

"Cheers, Dad."

Jack pulls his cream Saab 900 up on his father's drive, spinning the wheels on the gravel chips as he turns her around.

"Thanks for the lift."

"No problem, Son. When are you going to speak to your mother?"

"Sometime. Never." Tom answers as he pushes the passenger door open.

Placing his hand on Tom's arm, Jack stops him. "Why?"

"Are you kidding me, Dad? You know what she's like. I'm not sure which Jack she loves more, you or the bloody bottle."

"That's enough, Son."

"But it's true, Dad, it's about time you faced the fact or are you trying to tell me she's stopped?"

Jack looks down at his lap, not daring to speak.

"Thought not. Why have you put up with it for all these years?"

"She's very loving. In her own way."

"She's got a bloody funny way of showing it."

"I know, Son, I know."

150

"I don't think you do, Dad, but thanks for the lift. See you around."

Tom steps out of the car, slamming the door behind him, walking away not daring to glance back."

Quietly, Tom opens the back door, not wanting to disturb his grandfather. As silently as possible, he tiptoes into the kitchen. Getting used to walking without his crutches, good job as he realises, he's left them in his father's car.

That's it then, no looking back now.

Popping the lid of the bottle of pills in his pocket, he takes three and slinks out of the kitchen and up to his room. He undresses and crawls into bed, falling into a deep sleep.

"Tom, Tom, walk with me," she says as her long brown hair blows gently across her face.

Tom reaches up and takes her hand, amazed at her short stature; her presence feels larger than life. Dressed in a gorgeous white dress, gold leaves as straps, she beckons him to follow her as they make their way through a dense forest. Battling with the sharp edges of the branches, he lets go of her hand so he can use it to protect his face. The forest becoming denser with each step.

Tom looks around, he can't see her anywhere, but he feels sure she hasn't left.

"Where are you? Where am I going?" Panic sets in, his breathing becomes more and more shallow. Stopping, he leans against a tree, the bark rough against his back. Forcing himself to take deep breaths, he can't see his hand in front of his face.

"Where are you?" All Tom hears is the eerie echo of his voice as it bounces through the trees.

'Should I turn back or try and carry on?' Tom muses to himself.

"Come along," she calls, "you can't stay there."

"Ah, there you are, were you hiding from me?" Tom laughs.

"Of course not," she responds, a twinkle in her eye, "let's get through these woods."

Following her closely now so as not to lose her again, Tom picks up his pace, still fending off the vicious branches, desperate to get his breathing back to normal.

Finally, after being cut to shreds, a small chink of light appears through the trees up ahead. The forest begins to thin out a little. Tom jogs towards the light, his breathing feeling a little better now.

"Why are you running, Tom?" the lady asks, "Who are you running from?"

"Stop." She commands.

Tom stops dead in his tracks, uncertain why the sudden change in the tone of her voice send chills down his spine. Frozen to the spot, he can feel the sun, see the sun, he even feels like he can touch the sun, but his feet won't move.

"Why are you running?" she asks again.

"I... I... don't know. I just want to get out of this forest. It's oppressive. I can hardly breathe." His chest feels tight and heavy.

"OK, I'll show you a little of the sun," she answers, come over here and stand by me. Tom does as instructed. That's weird, it's as if he wasn't frozen to the spot. The sun dazzles his eyes. He can't see anything apart from the glare. I'm not sure which is worse, the forest or the glare of the sun.

"I can't see anything. Why can't I see anything?" Tom panics.

"You will. Soon, you will. Come now, let's go back."
She leads him through the woods.

"Isn't there another way?" Tom asks.

"There's always another way, but this is the way you have chosen." Feeling a bump in the bed jolts him upright as he tries to scramble back against the wall and away from the bump, fear gripping his heart like a vice, his breath panicked and loud. 'What the hell is that? I have to get out of here, I have to get out of here."

Letting out a piercing scream causes Charlie to bark incessantly.

Shaking himself awake, Tom notices it's already 5 am.

"Tom, get up; you've got thirty minutes, then I'm leaving," Maurice shouts.

"What! Gramps, it's Saturday," Tom calls back."

Meeting on the landing, Tom scratches his head, "why are we going in on a Saturday?"

"We have a lot of work to do, Son, and the sooner you start, the better. Now get dressed. I'll be downstairs."

Leaning against the door jamb, Tom tries to piece together his life and the dreams he keeps having.

Tom's First Day
Saturday 16th March

By lunchtime, Tom's head and knee are throbbing. He's been standing for hours, filing, and staring at tiny writing on A4 manilla folders.

From his vantage point overlooking the factory and being able to see through the windows into the other offices, he has the chance to eye up the office totty.

"Is everyone working today, Gramps?"

"Mostly yes, we're very busy, we're only here till lunchtime normally, so we'll leave once we've all eaten."

Grateful, Tom concentrates on staring out of the window.

A young office junior by the looks of her, still wearing her hair in pigtails. *Mmm, thanks, but, no thanks, bit too young.* Another older lady walks past the window. O*oh, she must be the office manager, proper school ma'am appearance. Reminds me of Roald Dahl's Miss Trunchbull.* Tom shudders at the memory of her description in the book. *Best stay away from her.* Turning his head away to concentrate on his filing again, he sees her out of the corner of his eye. Tall, dark-haired. Confident looking, about the same age. *Mmm, she'll do,* he mutters to himself.

Pushing himself away from the filing cabinets. "Where do you think you're going, Son?" Maurice asks from his desk in the corner, not even looking up from the papers on his desk.

"Lunch," Tom answers, "thought I'd introduce myself to the staff."

Blimey, he's quick for an old duck.

"Oh, no, you don't. I know exactly who you've just spotted, so don't even think about it."

Christ, he doesn't miss a bloody trick.

"Gramps, she's stunning."

"Yes, I'm well aware of that, I may be old, but I'm not blind. And she's my best office girl. Leave her alone." Maurice responds in a tone that brooks no argument.

"I'll introduce you to everyone now, over lunch. We all go from one until one forty-five to the canteen. Lunch is provided by the company.

"Wow, I didn't know that Gramps, that's weird." Tom states.

"Why is it weird?" Maurice asks.

"Well, I've never heard of any other companies in a hundred-mile radius that does that." Tom answers.

"Why do you think my staff are loyal to me then? I pay them well, feed them and listen to them."

Tom laughs, "that's a bit out there Gramps, you sure you're OK?"

Maurice laughs back. "Oh, Tom, you have a lot to learn. Take heed that you do, otherwise, you'll live to regret it."

Hospital Check-Up
Wednesday 20th March

"Hello, stranger."

"Hello, Mr Gold, how are you? What are you doing here?"

"Just a check-up. Mr Howard should be releasing me this afternoon."

Gina laughs, "Don't you mean discharging you."

Tom laughs with her, pleased that he's been received favourably following their date. "That's the word. Discharged. So, how have you been, Gina?"

"Since you stood me up, do you mean?"

When did I stand you up?

Stumbling on his words, "I'm... sorry about that, family emergency," was the only thing Tom could come think to say, having not remembered making a date with her in the first place.

"Oh, I'm sorry," Gina smiles sweetly at him. "I hope everything is OK now?" Staring into his eyes for a sign. She's certain he's lying.

"Oh, yes, all good now, thank you."

"Glad to hear it."

"Mr Gold, please, Mr Gold." A booming voice calls from behind them.

Bugger, that's bad timing. Tom curses to himself.

"What time do you finish, Gina?"

"You're the last patient, so not long."

"That's great. Will you wait for me?"

Looking up at him, she begins to shake her head.

"Please, Gina." Tom pleads with her.

"OK then, I'll meet you out front when I've finished."

"Great," Tom claps his hands together in delight.

"Mr Gold, this way, please." Mr Howard calls to him.

Following the consultant through to his rooms, "How's the knee, Tom?"

"It's actually not bad, thanks, Doc. Better than I thought, all things considered."

"That's good. You do seem to be walking with a slight limp though, hop on the couch and let's have a look.

"Ouch."

"Mmm, that still hurts, does it?"

"Only when you push it like that."

Ignoring his patient, Mr Howard continues his examination. "Have you been doing your exercises?"

"Yes, I make sure I do."

"Good. You must do them, Tom, every day, not just when you feel like it." Staring at him to make sure he's got the message, Mr Howard continues. "I have your scan results from Monday."

"What's the verdict then, Doc?"

"I'm happy with the results. There are a small number of adhesions, nothing major, though. Did you go for the physio?"

"Yes, doc, I've had a couple of sessions, and I'm doing their exercises. They say I don't need any more, though."

"Mmm, this limp is concerning me." Instructing Tom to walk up and down his consulting room. "You might just be overcompensating after the initial surgery as there certainly isn't anything from the scan to suggest otherwise. We'll keep an eye on it, though. Any questions?"

"Yes, what do you mean by adhesions?" Tom asks, concerned.

"Oh, that's just scar tissue, nothing to worry about."

That's easy for you to say.

"Anything else?"

"Erm, yes. Will I be able to go back into the Army, do you think?"

Alarmed at the question as the doctor was under the impression Tom had been discharged, he stumbles over his words.

"Oh, erm, I don't know. You still have that slight limp, so I'm not sure whether that would go against you."

Disheartened, Tom stares into space.

"Oh, OK, thank you, doc."

I must remember, when I get home, to ask Gramps if he's heard anything.

After being discharged by the surgeon, Tom leaves his room, concern etched across his face.

"There you are, Tom. What took you so long? I thought you'd stood me up. Again."

Ignoring the dig, Tom responds, "lecture from Mr H. Mimicking the surgeon's voice, "you must do your exercises, Tom, every day... you get the picture?"

Laughing, Gina responds, "Yes, he is a bit like a nagging wife, isn't he?"

"Ha, that's a good way to describe him. Where is your car, Gina?"

"Staff car park, round the back. Where's yours?"

"Halfway back home. The car parks were full for some reason."

"Do you want me to drop you back at your car?" She asks.

"Would you?" Tom looks up at her, his gratitude apparent on his face.

"Of course, come on."

Walking round to her car Tom asks, "Gina, will you go for a drink with me on Friday?"

Swallowing hard, knowing this would happen but still unsure of him, Gina pretends she hasn't heard.

159

"Please?"

"What was that, Tom? I was miles away."

Repeating his request as they arrive at her car, Tom looks over the top of it, directly into her eyes. Gina feels her legs wobble beneath her.

What is it about this bloody man? No. Say no.

"OK then."

Jumping into her car, Tom smiles to himself. *Perfect.*

Travelling toward his car, he asks her where she wants to go.

"Oh, I don't mind, really. A nice meal, or just a drink? What do you think, Tom?"

"I think a meal would be lovely. *The Red Lion* in Malthaven is your favourite, isn't it?"

Wow, he remembered.

"Perfect, shall I meet you there?" Gina asks.

Just in case he doesn't bother showing up.

"OK, if you like. 7.30 OK with you?"

"Yes, thank you. I'll see you on Friday." She responds as she pulls up behind Tom's Audi.

Before Tom can lean over to steal a kiss, she turns her head away and puts the car into gear.

"Until Friday then."

"Yes, Tom, until Friday."

Second Date with Gina
Friday 22nd March - 7.30 pm

For the first time in years, if not ever, Tom is early for his date, smartly dressed and holding a bunch of flowers.

"Gina, you look stunning." Tom is gobsmacked. The bright pink baby doll dress, pink tights and pink strappy sandals give Gina an ethereal look. "Pretty in pink."

"Thank you, Tom. You scrub up well too." She grins at him.

"Why, thank you, madam," holding his arm out for her. "Shall we go eat?"

Walking briskly to the lounge, the evening turning a little chilly. Tom holds the door open for her.

"Hi, Ben."

"Hey, Tom, usual table tonight, is it?"

"Please, if it's free."

Ben seats them with the menus and takes their drinks order.

"What do you fancy?" Gina asks him, studying the menu intently.

"You."

"To eat." She giggles. Shaking her head, she looks down at the menu, pretending to be still reading it.

He's incorrigible.

"Ready to order, Tom?" Ben, pushing his glasses up his nose, is poised with his order pad and pen.

"Gina, what would you like?"

Proper gentleman, isn't he?

"Scampi basket, please."

"Ah, your favourite. I'll have the steak, please, Ben."

"Coming right up." Ben retrieves their menus and leaves them to it.

161

"What have you been up to, Gina?"

"Oh, not much really. Don't laugh, but I've started line dancing classes."

Tom, ungentlemanly like, spits the mouthful of his drink back into his glass.

"I said, don't laugh." Gina berates him, laughing herself.

"I'm sorry," Tom responds, almost in hysterics. "I can't imagine you line dancing, that's all."

"Neither could I until I tried it. I absolutely love it. Apart from that and reading, all I ever do is work, so I thought it was about time I got out there and tried something new. What have you been doing?"

"Working mainly. I wouldn't know what else to do."

"You need a hobby then, Tom."

"No time."

"I'm honoured that you have time for a date then."

Tom looks over his glass at her and smiles. She smiles back.

"Hey, guys, one scampi basket and one steak," Ben says as he places their plates in front of them. The precious shared moment is gone forever.

"Can I get you anything else?"

"Mustard, please," Tom requests.

Ben ambles away to fetch some and returns with a pot.

"Cheers, Ben."

"Enjoy."

Tucking in, they eat in relative silence, the odd exclamation escaping their lips in response to the deliciousness of their meals.

"That was lovely, Tom. Thank you for bringing me here."

"My pleasure, where shall we go now?" Tom asks as he pays the bill.

"We could go for a walk along the river and have a nightcap somewhere. What do you think, Tom?"

"A nightcap at yours?"

"I'm not sure about that. Let's walk first."

Leaning over the balustrades on the top of the bridge, Tom and Gina play Pooh sticks. They race each other to the opposite side of the bridge to watch their sticks flow with the gentle current of the water.

"Mine won, mine won," Tom shouts as he jumps in the air like a child on his first trip to the sweet shop.

"Best of three then?" Gina laughs as she runs off to fetch more sticks.

Tom stands and watches her go, her blond hair fluttering gently in the breeze, her demeanour carefree and childlike.

"There you go, I'll race you," she says as she hands Tom a stick.

Throwing their sticks, they race across the bridge, Tom slowing as his knee begins to twinge.

"Are you OK?" Gina asks as he turns to face her, the pain flashes across his face. "We can stop if you like?"

"No, no, I'm fine. It's just a twinge." Tom stands by her side and drapes his arm across the top of her shoulders. Relaxing into the crook of his arm, they walk slowly back to the pub.

"Who won that one?" Tom wants to know.

"Me."

"One all, that means we have to have a rematch for the decider. Next Friday, do you?" he asks, pulling her around as they reach the cars. Looking down into her eyes, their mouths find each other, and they kiss passionately. The slamming of the back door of the pub brings them both back to the here and now.

"I'd best be off, Tom." Gina pulls away from him and climbs into her car. "Same time next week? For a drink?" she queries when she sees the look on Tom's face.

Visibly relaxing, Tom answers. "Yes, I'll pick you up. Wait a minute." Tom searches for a scrap of paper in the glove box to take down her address.

"OK, goodnight and thank you, Tom."

Gina shuts her door and drives away. Leaving Tom staring after her.

I'm slipping. Romantic walks, meals, playing children's games. What on earth...

"Hey, Tom," Ben shouts from the back door.

"Yeah, it's me. I'm just leaving."

Ben walks over to Tom's car, and Tom winds his window down.

"Where'd you meet her?"

"She's a nurse at the hospital."

"Good, good," Ben responds as he strokes his beard.

"What are you thinking, Ben?"

"Oh, nowt, just what I said, she seems like a nice girl, don't mess it up."

"She is, mate, she is."

Driving away from the pub, Tom goes over the evening in his mind.

I haven't had such a good night in a very long time. And without the sex.

Arriving home after his date, Tom is surprised to see the light in his grandfather's study is still on. Although it isn't late, Maurice is usually in bed by 10 pm.

"Gramps, what are you doing?" Tom asks as he glances around the study door.

"Oh, hi, Son. Just finalising some letters, that's all."

"OK, then. Everything OK?"

"Yes, fine."

Turning to leave, Tom suddenly remembers, "Gramps," he calls, turning back into the room.

"Mmm,"

"Did you hear any more from my commanding officer? I haven't had any letters or calls and I'm quite surprised. I wondered whether I should report back there. What do you think?"

Glancing up from his letters, Maurice stares past Tom. "I told you, Son. I've sorted it. Think no more of it and concentrate on the factory."

Shrugging his shoulders, certain something is amiss, Tom leaves his grandfather to his thoughts.

I don't have much longer left, Maurice thinks to himself. *I really hope I did the right thing.* Picking up the letters from the Army, which were addressed to Tom but Maurice himself had opened, he wonders through to the living room and throws them onto the fire still burning in the grate.

Too late now. What's done is done. No way back for you, Son.

Struggling with his conscience, *what else was I to do. I need him here to take over from me. He's no use to me thousands of miles away.*

Maurice Passes
Friday 7th June

Strange, Gramps isn't about to lock up. It's gone 7. Maybe he finally trusts me to do it properly. For once.

By the time Tom has checked and triple checked that everything is locked and secured, it's already after half-past. With a feeling of trepidation and a sense that something is drastically wrong, Tom heads home.

***

"Gramps, where are you?"

"Gramps, it's so dark in here. Why haven't you turned on the lights?"

Dropping his briefcase and newspaper on the kitchen table, Tom flicks the switch to his left. The warm glow illuminates the kitchen.

Turning around, Tom gasps. Staring at his grandfather's favourite chair. The body slumped in it. Peaceful. Serene. Nothing like his grandfather. Edging towards him, he holds his breath.

"Gramps." He whispers.

Grabbing his pale hand. It feels cold and clammy to the touch.

"Oh, God, no, please, no!" Tom wails.

Keeping hold of Maurice's hand, he slides down the wall, his tears threatening to drown him.

Tom has no idea how long he's been sitting on the cold ceramic tiles floor. He's spent. Exhausted. Getting up, he reaches for the telephone.

"Hello, Doctor Armitage, it's Tom. Tom Gold."

"Tom. It's gone midnight."

Ignoring his indignant groans, "Can you come, please? It's Gramps. He's dead."

"Dead. Are you sure?"

"Yes, doc. I'm sure."

Shocked into wakefulness. "I'm on my way."

Dressing quickly, the doctor is on Tom's doorstep within half an hour.

Tom sees the headlights as the car pulls up the drive, opening the front door,

"Come in, doc, he's in the kitchen. You know the way."

"Yes, yes, of course."

Tom sits on the bottom step, not wishing to see the body of his grandfather again.

Once the doctor has pronounced death and made the necessary arrangements, he joins Tom on the stairs.

"How long has he been there… like that, doc?" Crying again, "I should have left work earlier. I thought it was strange he wasn't there at 3 o'clock, chucking everyone out as he did every Friday.

"What time did you get home?"

"About 8ish, I think. I was checking some paperwork. I only clocked the time about seven. I knew something was wrong, doc. This is my fault."

Gently, he places his hand on Tom's arm, "there was nothing you could have done, Tom. As far as I can make out, he died peacefully in his sleep. Natural causes. Nobody's fault. It would have happened, even if you'd been here."

"Really, doc?"

"Really."

"Come on. As the undertakers are here now, I'll see them out. Then we'll have a stiff brandy, and you can go

168

and get some sleep. You'll need to find his will, by the way."

"I know where it is, doc. Do you want it now?"

"No, it's fine, as long as you have it."

Hearing another voice as the doctor leaves, Tom follows him to the front door on his way to pour the brandy.

"Mrs D, what are you doing here?"

"The doctor called me; said you'd need some help... you know... with... everything."

Stumbling towards her, he embraces her, and they both cry softly for a while. The doctor silently takes his leave.

Katie
Sunday 9th June

The brandy works.

It's 9 am on Sunday morning before Tom stirs again. Still dressed in his suit from Friday.

I need some air.

After using the bathroom, not bothering to wash or change, Tom walks through the kitchen,

"Hello, Mr Gold."

"Mrs D, what are you doing here? What day is it?"

"It's Sunday, and I've cooked you some breakfast."

"I'm not hungry, and I thought you were at your son's on a Sunday?"

"You need me more than he does. Here, eat your breakfast." She pulls out a chair, almost legging him into it.

"Thank you, but I'm really not hungry."

"You need to eat. You've got to keep your strength up. Try just a little."

He does and soon realises he is ravenous. Wiping the plate clean with his now soggy toast.

"Thank you, Mrs D. You were right. I needed that."

"You're welcome. Where are you off too, dressed like that?"

"For a walk."

Grabbing his cap to keep the sun out of his eyes and pulling his wellies on, Tom leaves the house by the kitchen door and heads around the corner to his favourite bench.

Feeling rather worse for wear, trying to assimilate all that's happened in the last couple of days. Unsure whether reading the will he found before falling into bed on

Saturday morning or the death of his grandfather was the biggest shock.

Closing his eyes, Tom drifts off into a daze.

"Walk with me, Tom."

That voice again, "who are you?" he asks, still unable to see the person behind the voice.

"Tom, walk with me."

Taking her hand, he feels he's done this before. She leads him high above the clouds into the deep calming purple of the universe, nothing but stars and the moon for company.

"Sit here and relax," the voice tells him. Looking around, Tom sees a seat on top of the cloud he walks over to and gently lowers himself into it.

Cocooning him in its warm, fluffy embrace, Tom visibly relaxes. "Will you take me to the cottage now?" He asks.

Stirring slightly, Tom feels sure he's heard someone speaking to him. But it's just a dream. *Nope, there's someone definitely speaking to me.*

Tom brings himself around from his doze, confused he finds himself face to face with a frumpy stranger in black trousers and a grey high-necked sweater. She stands in front of him, a concerned look on her face and such a gentle voice, one he feels he recognises, although he's sure he's never seen her before. *And those eyes. Am I asleep?* Tom wonders.

How do I answer that question? Am I OK?

No, actually, I feel like shit. My knee hurts, I have no idea what I'm doing with my life, and I just lost my grandfather. However, all that comes out of his mouth is some rubbish about work.

172

Still feeling groggy, Tom tries to have a conversation with the stranger, but each sentence makes him seem weirder than he actually looks. Charlie, his ever-faithful mongrel, has done a runner, and he seems to have scared the young lady. No sooner had their conversation started when she made her excuses to leave. *I really did scare her then.* Not wanting the conversation to end, Tom calls after her as she picks her bag up and walks down the hill.

"What's your name, miss?"

"Katie. What's yours?"

"I'm Tom, Tom Gold."

Tom stares after her. Dumbfounded.

Why do I have to be dressed like a tramp, I ask you... when I meet such a strikingly beautiful girl, whatever will she think of me?

Staring into the distance, not really seeing anything, Tom starts to shiver. *Who is that woman? I feel sure I've seen her before, but I can't quite place her. She's not my usual type, a little overweight... and short... for my liking, but there's something about her...*

The sun has disappeared behind the clouds, and Tom feels the chill of the air through his thin suit. *A storm threatening?* He ponders to himself. Shaking himself out of his reverie, he whistles for Charlie and returns to the house.

"Are you OK, Mr Gold? You look like you've seen a ghost."

"Mmm, yes, I'm fine. Thank you, Mrs Dainty, fine."

"You sure?"

"Yes. It's very strange, though. I've just met a young girl. She was near my favourite bench, you know, the one overlooking the fields."

173

Mrs Dainty nods, not wanting to break his concentration.

"I feel sure, I've seen her before, but I know I haven't."

Shaking his head, he turns back to look at his housekeeper. "Strange. I'll go and wash up ready for dinner," he states as he leaves the kitchen and heads to the bathroom.

Bumping into Katie
Sunday 16th June

Tom loves to watch the horses race down the fields.
The adrenalin kick he feels is indescribable, euphoric.
Every Sunday morning, he walks to the bookies in Rose
Bush Village. It forms part of his weekly walk to help
strengthen his knee, and it's only four miles away. As the
far end of his garden overlooks his favourite bench, he sees
her, Katie, when she turns the corner from the forest into
the open landscape. *What a beautiful sight,* he muses to
himself *and not just the landscape.*

Cross with himself for oversleeping; he wanted to be
there early. Hoping she would walk this way again today.
Cursing, he quickly washes. Praying she will still be there,
he races out of the door and dashes over.

Standing over her for a while, soaking up her energy
and simple beauty, s*he looks like she's daydreaming.*

Having raced to get there, Tom struggles to find the
right words to speak to her. Although he does manage to
persuade her to walk to the bookies with him. The
conversation feels strange to Tom, like he's talking with
his younger self. Some of the phrases she comes out with
take him back to his childhood. *What a strange turn up for
the books,* Tom mumbles to himself as he rushes back to
the house to fetch Charlie any excuse to gather his thoughts
after their conversation.

Dashing around the house, Tom gathers up a few things
for his walk with Katie. Grabbing an old ruck sack, he
stuffs it with biscuits and drinks. Waiting for the kettle to

175

boil, Tom ponders their conversation. His mind wonders back to the days of old before his mother started drinking.

"Do it again, Mommy, do it again." Laughing, Tom loves it when his mom grabs his hands and spins him around and around, really, really fast. "Faster, Mommy, faster."

"I can't go any faster, Tom; I'll make us both sick." Stopping them spinning, she hugs him and kisses his cheek, placing him back on the picnic blanket.

"Here, Son, play with your cars," Jack says as the five years old, still feeling dizzy, grimaces at his parents.

Jack pushing Tom's favourite matchbox car around him on the blanket does nothing to appease the child. Tom continues sulking.

"What's wrong with you, Son? You look like you've lost a pound and found a blade of grass," Jack asks.

"I want mommy to keep spinning me."

"She'll spin you later, Son, let her have a breather for a while, eh?" Jack coos, trying to reason with the spoilt child.

Shaking himself out of his reminiscence, Tom has never heard anyone use that expression other than his father. *Lost a pound and found a blade of grass. Why on earth would Katie use it now?*

Making a strong flask of tea, Tom hopes Katie will like it. He whistles for Charlie, pulling his lead off the hook on the back of the door. He locks up and walks slowly back to the bench to meet Katie. Feeling lighter of heart after his chat with Katie. *I'm really looking forward to this walk now. Maybe I'll get to know her a bit better too.*

Despite her strange appearance, Tom is impressed with her thinking. Astonished that he is discussing his addiction with a stranger, he likes her idea of reducing his bets, though. Let's face it, a thousand pounds to win on a horse that places 4th in the Grand National is, well, ridiculous. *Brown Windsor isn't a name I'm likely to forget in a hurry, either.*

Walking and talking, Tom and Katie fall into step with each other until Charlie starts barking like a maniac.

Tom looks up, "Stop it, Charlie, what's wrong with you?" *Oh no, this is going to be embarrassing.*

Out of the corner of his eye, he can see Katie walking away, grateful for small mercies, as Tom comes toe to toe with Gina.

"What the fuck do you think you're doing, Tom? Who's this floozy?"

"There's no need for that, Gina. I only met her last week."

"Oh, only last week, and already you're taking her out. The rumours were true then." Gina retorts, her hands on her hips, and her pouting almost makes Tom want to laugh, but he thinks better of it.

"If you'll calm down a bit, I'll explain."

Taking a step back, Gina stares at him, waiting for a response.

"I met her last Sunday. She asked me if I was OK. *Which is more than you ever do.* I was sitting on the bench, dozing. We spoke for two minutes, and she left. She was there again this morning, and I asked her if she wanted to walk with me. She's only recently moved here.

177

I know what it's like to be the outsider, remember. I was just being friendly. OK?"

Why am I even having this conversation? Doesn't she trust me?

"Why didn't you tell me you met her last week?" Gina asks, slightly calmer but not quite sure he's telling the truth.

"Because there's nothing to tell. Do I have to tell you about every conversation I have? Are you that insecure?"

The look in Gina's eyes tells Tom he's touched a raw nerve. *Here we go.*

Expecting a thousand lashes with her tongue, Tom is shocked when Gina turns on her heels and walks away without another word spoken.

"Oh, bye then, Gina. See you later." He shouts at her, retreating back.

Dashing to catch up with Katie, he and Charlie are both out of breath. Tom draws up beside her again.

Grateful he and Katie had arrived at George's, Tom leaves her with Charlie while he places his bet.

Watching Katie and Charlie from the window, Tom is dumbstruck. Neither he nor George can believe how Charlie is letting Katie fuss him.

Tom grabs his change and betting slips from the counter and heads towards the door, stopping again to watch Katie and Charlie playing. Standing ramrod straight, his hands locked behind his back, a habit he is finding hard to break.

"Was he ever like this with Maurice, George?" Tom shouts over his shoulder.

"Nope, never. There's something about her, Tom, animals know, you know."

"Mmm." Silently leaving the shop, he feels confused by his feelings. *Why do I just want to grab this woman and hug her? Forever?* Shaking his head, he walks over to her. Suddenly remembering the biscuits in his bag, he breaks them out as they continue their slow walk back towards Birch Tree. Tom hasn't enjoyed a lady's company this much, without the sex, for such a long time. He doesn't want this walk to end.

Tom makes a valiant attempt to ask her out and is mortified to learn that she already has a boyfriend, and from his encounter earlier, it's clear Katie assumes he has a girlfriend. Still not wishing to give up, he wants to get to know this girl better. Shouting after her as she takes her leave, unsure whether she'd heard him say next Sunday, same time, same place. *I guess only time will tell.*

Wow, I'm learning so much today. Why have I never seen her working in The Black Dog?

She must be really shy, Tom thinks, *she never took her sunglasses off, and it's been overcast and cloudy all day.*

Tom slowly wanders up his driveway, lost in a daydream.

Mmm, that's lovely, Katie, do that again. Katie is gently stroking Tom's face, kissing his eyelids and gently nibbling his ears. Sighing contentedly, Tom relaxes into the moment. Savouring the tingling down his body. A sensation he doesn't remember ever having experienced before.

The honking of a car horn in the distance brings him back down to earth. *Wow, what a lovely daydream.*

Plans Go Awry
Sunday 23rd June

Up early to get ready for his… date… *should I call it that?* Tom is whistling whilst cleaning the kitchen.

"Mr Gold, what are you doing?"

"Oh, hello, Mrs Dainty, what brings you here?"

"I work here. If you still want me to. I've been coming in a normal."

"Well, I don't really need a housekeeper or cleaner, now Gramps has gone, and it seems I'm home permanently." *Sadly.*

Not wanting to lose this job, she's been here so long she is part of the family. No, it is her family.

Racking her brains for a reason to stay and fighting back the tears," Oh, OK, that's a shame Mr Gold, I… I thought it might help, me staying you know, as you do work long hours. I could still help. What do you think?"

Crossing her fingers behind her back and whispering a silent prayer, she's relieved when he says, "yes, that's true. I have enough to do at the factory. It's not really my thing, though, Mrs D."

"What isn't?"

"Factory life. Or housework. But I'm so used to cleaning and polishing everything to the nth degree. I'm finding it hard to let old habits die. I've already cleaned in here twice this morning."

"It looks like a shiny new pin, Mr Gold."

Only half-joking, Tom mutters under his breath, *Maybe I should go and get a job as a cleaner. Lord only knows I'm making a cock-up of running a business.*

Before Mrs Dainty could ask him to repeat it, there is a loud banging on the front door.

"Who the hell would be calling on a Sunday morning. Can't be anyone we know; they would use the kitchen door." Mrs Dainty states on her way to answer it.

The banging comes again. "I'm coming. I'm not as young as I used to be." She shouts. Mercifully, the banging stops.

"Oh, do come in, dear," Mrs D mutters under her breath as Gina slams the door back, almost knocking her over. *Why on earth is he mixed up with her?* She thinks to herself. *No good will ever come of it.*

Storming into the kitchen, Gina is shouting Tom's name on her way through the house. Hearing her yells, Tom's good mood disappears instantly.

"What are you doing here?" he asks, continuing with his cleaning. For some reason, he's finding it very therapeutic at present.

"I want to know what you were doing out with her last Sunday," Gina demands. Her hands were on her hips again. Pouting.

Trying very hard to control his temper, Tom takes a deep breath and turns to face her.

"Gina. I really don't need this shit every time I have a conversation with another woman. And it's been a week, so why storm in now demanding answers?"

When all I want to do is go and meet said woman. End it with her, stupid. Just say those two tiny words. It's over.

Sobbing now, Gina answers, "Because… Because I thought you loved me, and I thought you would be in touch before now, and I thought you loved me… and…"

"Gina, you're rambling. Calm down." Crossing the kitchen, Tom takes her in his arms and holds her head to his chest, comforting and soothing her. A first for him.

Just tell her it's over.

"Come on, I'll make a cuppa, and we can sit in the front room and have a chat."

Letting her go so that he can boil the kettle, Tom curses as she leaves the room. *Now I'm not going to be able to meet Katie, and she's going to think I'm a loser too. Maybe the rumours are right.*

Carrying the scorching hot drinks through to the front room, Tom is reciting over and over in his head what he wants to say, but he fears her recriminations and the possibility that she may also go after Katie.

I wouldn't bloody mind, but it's perfectly innocent, and already I'm feeling guilty.

"Here you go," Tom says as he places the drinks on the low oak coffee table. "Gina, we need to talk."

Anger bubbling inside her, she turns on him, raising her right hand. The blow he intercepts shocks him.

"Bloody hell, what's wrong with you?"

Tom picks up his drink and quietly leaves the room for fear of what he may be capable of if this gets out of hand.

Quietly he climbs the stairs, heads to his bedroom and closes the door. Hoping Gina won't be there when he goes back down.

"Tom, Tom, where are you? I'm sorry. I didn't mean…" he hears Gina calling but disinclined to answer her, he turns on the radio, drowning out her cries.

How do I get myself into these situations? Surely, I should have learnt by now. And I've missed Katie, so I suppose I'll have another telling off if and when I see her again.

The Funeral
Monday 24th June

Straightening his tie, Tom looks at the vision in the mirror. His vacant eyes stare back. *Woah, you look rough.*

"Mr Gold, the cars are here," Mrs Dainty calls to him.

"Just coming."

Climbing into the back of the funeral car next to his mother and father, they sit in silence for the journey, all lost in their own anguish. Tom stares out of the window, mentally preparing for the eulogy.

"You OK, Son?" Jack's voice penetrates his thoughts.

"Yeah, I guess so."

"Got your notes, you know, for what you want to say?" A lump rises in Jack's throat, making it difficult for him to speak.

"Mmm."

Realising Tom doesn't want to talk, Jack goes back to his own thoughts, cursing himself for being such a bad son.

Once the congregation is seated, Tom makes his way to the front of the crematorium. The piece of paper in his hand trembles as his hand shakes. Standing ramrod straight, arms by his side, the piece of paper on the lectern in front of him.

Clearing his throat, he looks around the room, a larger turnout than he expected, the cynic in him assuming they were only there so they could go to the wake for the free booze.

"Gramps was everything to me. He helped me so much, and I repaid him by rebelling and bringing trouble to his front door. I was young, foolish and... lost. When he forced me to join the Army, I have to confess; I hated him. I felt rejected. Why didn't he want me around?"

Taking a breath, the lump in Tom's throat growing ever bigger, "It's too late now, but I'm sorry, Gramps. It's because of you that I've grown as a person. The Army taught me so much, and if you hadn't forced me to go, who knows where I would be now. For that, I will always be grateful. I miss you so much, Gramps, but I know you're at peace."

There isn't a dry eye in the house as Tom retakes his seat.

Feeling a strange sense of peace enveloping him, Tom knows his grandfather approves. *I love you Gramps.*

Within a few minutes, the funeral is over, and before long, the congregation are heading to *The Black Dog* for the wake. As has always been the tradition in this family, wakes are a huge party. This one is no exception. Playing Maurice's favourite tunes by Glen Miller before the party gets into full swing. *Gramps would be proud. They sent him off in style.*

Tom, Sylvie and Jack are all seated around the same table, much to Tom's annoyance.

"Son, that was a lovely eulogy," Sylvie places her hand on Tom's arm. He flinches as if he's been burnt.

Feeling it, Sylvie recoils slightly. *Am I that bad?* But doesn't move her hand.

"Can we try and put the past behind us, Tom? I don't want it to end with a eulogy at my funeral, and there still be bad blood, like there was with Maurice and me."

Tom was expecting this,

"I don't know, Mom, I'll think about it. A lot has happened. A lot I need to get my head around still."

"I know, Son, I know. Maybe we could have lunch sometime?"

"We'll see. I'm not promising anything."

Jack sits sipping his lager, watching his wife and son, hoping they can start building bridges.

Not wishing to push her luck, Sylvie removes her hand from Tom's arm and turns to Jack to discuss the funeral.

Tom takes his leave. For the first time in a long time, he doesn't want to get drunk. Heading away from the pub, he catches sight of a young girl walking towards Vera's tearoom. *Is that Katie?* Quickening his pace, he catches up with her.

Making small talk isn't Tom's thing, but the cat's got his tongue, and he can't think of much to say. Leaving her to her afternoon tea at Vera's, Tom leaves her to collect his car ready for his meeting.

Well, she spoke to me, that's a good sign. I hope… And why the hell did I tell her I had to dash off. What is wrong with 'may I join you?' Stupid man. The meeting isn't until later, and he could have done with a friendly ear.

Tom Meets Katie, Again
Sunday 30th June

Lost in thought following his grandfather's funeral, Tom, intending to take his usual route on his morning walk to the bookies, is cross when Charlie appears to have other ideas.

Tom calls Charlie several times, muttering at him under his breath as he walks around the corner, taking the lead out of his pocket. *No, we're walking my way today, Charlie.*

Calling him again but to no avail, Tom can see why now. Slowing his pace, he stands straight and almost to attention. Watching Katie and Charlie, sat on his favourite bench, wondering to himself, *what's going on there? I can see her talking to him.*

Mesmerised by them. She seems to be telling his dog her life story. *Shame I can't hear them, or that Charlie can't speak, I might learn how to communicate effectively with women if he could. Tell me all their secrets, eh Charlie?* Tom muses to himself.

Not wanting to be caught staring, Tom makes his way over to them.

Calling her name, he is surprised when she almost jumps out of her skin. *Wow, she really was having a heart to heart with my dog.*

Trying desperately to make a good impression on her, Tom attempts to flirt with Katie, but she seems so distressed, he feels she's missing the signals. Not wanting to leave, but with the conversation drying up and Tom being desperate to get to the bookies before it closes, his attempts to make arrangements fall on deaf ears as Katie takes her leave.

Attaching Charlie's lead, Tom continues his walk, running their conversation over in his mind. *She wants to walk my dog to get her out of the house. Why doesn't she seem interested in walking with me too?*

Tom Lets Katie Down, Again

Saturday 6th July

I'm going for a walk, Mrs D," Tom shouts from the back door. "I should be back for lunch."

Shocked, she calls back, "aren't you going to work this morning, Mr Gold?"

"Not today, Mrs Dainty. I've decided I need a break."

"I'm glad. All work and no play is no good to anyone. You need to look after yourself."

"I know, Mrs D."

Stuck for anything else to say, she responds, "I'll leave you some cold meat and pickles for lunch, shall I? You can eat whenever you like then."

"Thank you, that would be lovely. Your money is on the kitchen table. See you Monday."

"Thank you," she shouts after him.

Instead of taking his usual route towards the bookies, the only walk he really knows or ever does, he turns left and makes his way down the hill towards Birch Tree Town, unsure why he feels the need to walk this way. Having grabbed his Walkman on the way out, Tom listens to Bryan Adams, *Everything I Do*. Singing along, Tom's thoughts drift to Gina, 'Don't tell me it's not worth fightin' for; I can't help it, there's nothin' I want more.' *Is it worth fighting for?* Tom ponders to himself.

Rounding the corner, the smell of baking from Vera's almost knocks Tom out. His tummy starts rumbling uncontrollably, reminding him he hasn't had breakfast.

Again. Peering through the window to see if there are any spare seats as Saturdays are always busy, he spots Katie sitting in the corner. She appears to be staring into space. He watches her for a few moments, unsure whether to go in.

Come on. Be a man. It's better to tell her than to leave her waiting. Again.

Joining Katie, Tom places his order with Vera, contemplating when he last took time out to do something other than work, drink or gamble. He finds he quite enjoys his morning with Katie, despite the fact that he feels he's let her down again. He can't make their walk in the morning due to work commitments.

No wonder she couldn't wait to part company with me. I must seem like a complete loser to her. At least she agreed to walk Charlie for me while I'm away.

Lost in a daydream, Tom ponders again how to ask her out.

Tom is walking through the carpet of sweet peas and marigolds, not a care in the world.

In the distance, there is a beautiful old cottage. It is white with black beams and a thatched roof. Tom ambles towards it.

Pausing at the black wrought iron gate, he can see that the walls of the cottage have been white-washed and a huge mural of a colourful butterfly greets him. Tom pushes the catch on the gate, surprised when it glides open smoothly. Closing it behind him, he walks along the path to the heavy wooden oak door, mesmerised by the intricate pattern and the unique figure of eight door knocker.

Gently pushing the heavy door, Tom is surprised when it creaks open.

"Hello, is there anyone here?" He calls. "Hello?"

Slowly walking through the door. Tom notes the colourful sofa and a mismatched armchair are the centrepieces of the lounge. Moving in between rooms, 'Why do I feel like I belong here?' Tom feels calmer than he has done for a long time, just standing in the kitchen staring at the matching mugs and plates which line the dresser by the back door.

Startled by a sound outside, he jumps. Making his way back through the lounge, he notices a framed photo on the fireplace. Intrigued, he picks it up, almost dropping it. It's a photograph of him and... is that, Katie?

Puzzled, he carefully replaces it in the same spot before heading outside. Walking back down the path, Tom glances behind him, wondering what the sound was which startled him earlier. He can't see anything, but for some reason, he is reluctant to leave...

Tom is startled out of his reverie by a tapping on the window. Looking over towards the noise, he feels his shoulders slump. *Oh, no, here we go again. I suppose I'd better acknowledge her.*

Finishing his drink, he leaves his money on the table and shouts his goodbyes to Vera. Exiting the tea room and making his way back along the length of the window, he stops a few feet away from the knocker.

"Hi, Tom."

"Hello, Gina."

Tell her it's over.

Stumbling on her words, Gina turns around from staring into the tea room to face Tom.

"Tom, I... I'm... sorry... I didn't expect to see you here. I thought you'd be at work."

Not sure whether she's challenging him to retort or expecting him to explain himself, Tom stays silent.

193

"I wanted to see you… say sorry for my behaviour. I know I was out of line; can you forgive me?"

Flashing her big brown eyes at him.

Tell her it's over.

When he doesn't respond, she asks, "can we go for a walk, Tom, please?"

Almost resorting to begging, she grabs his hand, he flinches.

"Tom, what's wrong. Don't you want me anymore?"

No, no, no, I don't.

"Gina, I don't know what I want, but I know it isn't this."

Her hackles raised, Gina retorts, "what the hell do you mean by this?"

"Exactly what I said. You immediately start getting uppity and nasty if I try to talk to you, it's just easier not to bother, Gina."

"It's her, isn't it. That… floozy."

"What on earth are you talking about? This is exactly what I mean, Gina. I've been in a tea room for a drink and cake, and you start accusing me of all sorts. Stop it. Before you really do destroy us."

Turning his back on her, Tom heads away from the tearoom, towards the hill bound for home.

"That's right, Tom, you just walk away. You can't face me, can you, because of what you've done?" Gina shouts at his back.

Turning round again, somehow keeping his anger at bay. He calmly calls back. "That's just it. I haven't done anything. It's over, Gina. Over."

"What, you can't finish it!" she squeals. "I love you, Tom!" She grabs him by his coat, almost pulling him over.

Laughing, he responds, "you sure have a funny way of showing it."

Before she can do or say anything else, Tom pulls out of her grasp and continues his walk up the hill, leaving her staring after him.

Somehow, he doesn't think he's seen the last of her.

Triggered Memories
Friday, 26th July

Tom has been busy at work since his run-in with Gina, and he hasn't seen Katie either. Finishing at lunchtime and locking up the factory after the last of the workers have left, Tom can't get Katie out of his mind, pleased that Gina had called earlier to cancel their evening out 'to talk about things'.

Climbing in his car and putting his Calvin Klein shades on to shield his eyes from the balmy afternoon sun, he heads for home. Pulling up on the drive, not wanting to get out. *Just do it, dummy.* He says to himself. Putting the car back into gear, he turns it around and heads back down the driveway. Parking a little further down the road as there's never enough parking here in July. Tourists somehow manage to find their way to Malthaven and the surrounding areas and take over; he walks back down Shell Avenue. He knows which flat it is; he's seen her walking back from the tea rooms before.

Whistling to himself, he heads down the narrow path and loudly rat tat tats on the door.

Strange, maybe she's working.

He knocks again, louder this time.

About to knock again, he hears what he thinks is a timid call coming from Katie. Unable to make out what Katie is saying and worried about the piercing scream he assumes has come from her lips, Tom listens again at the door and calls for her to let him in.

Don't get involved. He says to himself.

Oh, my word, hearing another piercing scream as he's about to walk away. Tom tries the handle of the door. *I can't just leave her; I have to find out if she's OK.* His Army training tells him something isn't right.

Shouting through the letterbox, her responses make no sense. "Let me in, Katie." Pushing down on the door handle, Tom is both relieved and apprehensive when the door opens, although it seems to be slightly stuck. Managing to get it open far enough to poke his head in, he looks around. His eyes finally rest on the sight of Katie lying on the floor covered in blood and cowering like a frightened animal, gently calling her name and asking her to move over. A tear escapes from the corner of his eye as his thoughts take him back. Back somewhere, he never wanted to go again.

Tom is staring through the night vision scope. The blood. So much blood and carnage. "Stop! Stop the vehicle," he shouts over the hum of the engine. The heat of the desert mingled with his feelings of pure horror, cause the sweat to pour from him. Wiping the back of his hand across his face, he squeezes his eyes shut. The vision will go away if he closes them tightly enough.

Stop! We need to help these people. The vehicle rolls on, oblivious to the torment tearing Tom up inside.

Tom stands over the limp body of the young girl, her arm severed by the recent blast; her eyes flicker with recognition of the soldier trying to help her. "There's nothing I can do," Tom wails indeterminately as the young girl takes her last breath before his eyes.

The bang of the front door closing as Tom edges into Katie's flat brings him back to the present day. Shaking his head to remove the memories, Tom sets about cleaning Katie up. *What am I going to do with her? I can't leave her here.*

Leaving her to have a bath, after he's removed her clothes, Tom wanders around the flat. The remainder of it so neat and tidy; it's like two different properties.

Struggling to compute the difference, he dashes back to help her when he hears the splash in the bathroom. Pulling her out of the bath, Tom holds her in his arms, not wanting to let her go. Ever. Their eyes meet. The emotional charge between them is intoxicating. Normally taking any opportunity to kiss a woman, Tom turns away. *She needs my help, not my kisses.*

After helping her dress and packing a few clothes in a black bag, Tom helps Katie out to his car.

Still trying to fathom out what to do with her, when she asks where he's taking her, his immediate response is.

"Home."

Tom settles Katie in one of his spare bedrooms. *At least she's safe here.* Quietly leaving the room as she falls asleep, Tom goes to his own room and climbs into bed. The warmth of the night air feels oppressive, but the sheets feel as cold as ice on his skin. Turning his thoughts to Katie and the mess she was in when he found her, he finds it hard to sleep.

Wrapping the sheets around himself, he eventually falls into a troubled sleep.

The Combat Engineer Tractor is bouncing along the sand, one in a convoy travelling at night in a bid to evade detection. Tom stares out of the window. Sunrise barely breaks, but he can make out shapes in the sand. Vehicles still smouldering from today's air attack, clothes strewn among the piles of rubble which were once someone's homes.

199

What is that?

Tom's stomach lurches as the glint of light casts a shadow across a car. The wedding ring twinkles on the mutilated hand. Jesus. Tom dares not look round to see where the rest of the body is. This is beyond evil, he thinks to himself, shaking his head in dismay.

The hand crawls across the sand, only two of the figures remain intact. The blood. So much blood. Tom covers his face as the hand moves closer to him. Stop. Please. Stop!

Tossing and turning, a bump on the bed jolts Tom upright. His hands grip the sheets to him. Eyes squeezed shut; his knuckles are whiter than snow. Fear grips his heart like a vice. His breathing laboured. Get me out of here.

His piercing screams scare Charlie into barking. Loudly. Almost like he's in competition with his master.

Sweat drips profusely into Tom's eyes. He dare not open them for fear of what he may see. Charlie edges over to him and licks his face, worried about his master. The licks calm Tom down, and he opens his eyes. Untangling himself from the sheets, he climbs out of bed, still in a daze, the vision still prominent in his mind.

I need help.

***

"Hello, Monica speaking."

The soothing voice on the other end of the phone immediately calms Tom's nerves.

"Erm, hello, Monica, my name is Tom, Tom Gold. I've been told you do counselling."

"Well, yes, I do, but you need a referral from your doctor."

"Oh, I'm sorry, I didn't realise."

"Call your doctor on Monday morning and ask him for a referral to me."

Monica is met with silence on the end of the phone. Concern grows within her.

"Mr Gold. Tom? Are you still there?"

Not for much longer if I can't get help.

"I need to speak to someone. It's all going pear-shaped. It's always pear-shaped. I need help."

"Tom, you need to make an appointment Monday."

This doesn't feel good. Monica thinks to herself.

"Please, Monica, I'll pay you."

"It's not about the money, Tom. It's about boundaries."

"What do you mean?"

"It's Saturday. And I don't know where you got my number from but…."

Feeling deflated and unsure where else to turn, Tom sighs, interrupting her, he says, "OK, I'm sorry. I shouldn't have called… what can I do?"

"There are charities for out of hours calls, Mr Gold."

"Are you saying I'm a charity case?" Tom all but yells down the phone.

Her voice still calm and soothing, Monica is used to dealing with such outbursts. "Not at all, Tom, but they are all there to help."

Met with silence again, "are you still there, Tom?"

"Erm, yes, I'm still here."

Against her better judgement, something about the tone in his voice tells her she needs to help this man today.

"OK, Tom, I can tell by your voice you're not in a good place. Just this once. I will make an exception, but please don't call again out of hours. I have half an hour before I'm due to go out."

"I can't thank you enough, Monica." Tom cries down the phone. In between sobs, he tries to tell Monica about his nightmares, but he isn't making any sense. Once his tears have subsided, and he's a little calmer, Monica suggests he comes to see her on Monday afternoon and books him an appointment for 3 pm.

A Trip to A&E
Saturday, 27th July

Tom is staring at project plans spread over the large glass-topped table in his office. He usually gets his best work done on a Saturday when there are fewer outside interruptions. Not today though. He's been staring at the plans for over an hour, and still, they aren't making any sense. *I just don't see how I can make it work.* Swallowing hard, he thinks to himself, *maybe I should ask Dad.*

Glancing at the clock, he notes it's almost half-past two. He's missed lunch, and he wanted to be home early today to make sure Katie was OK. Packing up the plans and grabbing his briefcase, Tom heads for home. Excited to see Katie.

Wolfing down a cheese and pickle sandwich while he makes drinks for himself and Katie. He'd brought her favourite peppermint tea bags a while ago. Ever hopeful he would one day be able to woo her into visiting. Laughing to himself at the irony. *Now I have got her under my roof, and I haven't even kissed her.*

Smiling to himself and still shaking his head at his thoughts, Tom taps gently on Katie's door. Receiving no reply, he pushes the door open. Surprised to see she's fast asleep. *It's gone 3.30; surely, she should be up by now.*

Entering her room, he wakes her, threatening Charlie to keep off the bed. The dog is just as keen to see Katie as Tom is.

Katie rouses herself while Tom places her drink on the bedside table, waiting as she tries to get up. She makes a fuss which Tom takes as flirting until he looks down to see the blood-soaked sheets. Katie sobs uncontrollably into her hand. Recognising this may trigger thoughts he would rather not visit, he busies himself with helping her to get showered and dressed.

Not quite what he had planned for this afternoon, but Tom insists on taking Katie to A&E.

***

While Katie is being checked over by the nurse, Tom sits in the waiting room, his head in his hands, pondering the situation he finds himself in.

Why the hell did I go round there yesterday?

Out of the corner of his eye, he sees the curtain on Katie's cubicle being pulled back, and Katie slumped in a wheelchair. He immediately demands to know where she's being taken.

Learning that she needs a scan and having been given permission to go with her, Tom follows the gentle giant of a porter to the x-ray department.

Uncertain how or why it started, but while they're waiting, an argument ensues. Tom is incredulous that she is defending the animal who put her in here in the first place. The venom in his voice surprises him as his anger rises. He wants to grab her and shake her to her senses. Vaguely registering something about her thinking about him, which caused the fight between her and her so-called boyfriend makes Tom see red. *Ungrateful bitch. I should have left you there.*

Before he says something he will regret, and just as Katie's name is called, Tom takes his leave as he has a meeting to get to, telling her to call when she's ready to be collected.

With his meeting being cancelled, Tom sits at his desk, going over his conversation with Katie in his mind.
Thinking about me? Why would she be thinking about me?
His secretary is constantly fielding calls from Gina. Katie, wow, Katie. *She must have put up one hell of a fight, but what do I do now? And why hasn't she called to be collected?*
Checking the clock on the wall behind his desk, he notes that it's gone 9 pm. Emotionally exhausted, he grabs his coat and keys and heads for the door. Switching off the lights and closing the doors on the way. Hungry but too tired to even think about food, Tom heads home and straight to bed.

"There you are, Tom. I've been waiting for you. Let's go for a walk," the stranger leads him up a winding terracotta path in the middle of a large overgrown field. The path seems endless, twists and turns all over, but in the distance, all Tom can see is a beautiful whitewashed cottage; although only able to see the top, it seems to be calling to him, but the stranger is taking him away from it.
"Why aren't we going to the cottage?" Tom asks.
"We will, eventually, not yet though. We need to keep walking through this field."
Surrounded by wildflowers, he carries on walking; the field seems never-ending. Although he feels calm, he wishes he could get back to bed. He's tired now...

Groggy and feeling mighty tetchy, unsure whether it's lack of food, weird dreams, his row with Katie, or just life in general, Tom drags himself out of bed. He's been lying awake for a couple of hours, and as he checks the clock, he is dismayed to discover it's almost midday.

Getting dressed, he heads into the kitchen. *God bless you, Mrs D.* Tom smiles to himself. His grumpiness vanishes as he sees the selection of pastries and bread left for him on the kitchen table. *You are a diamond, Mrs D. What would I do without you?*

Famished, he boils the kettle and makes his favourite coffee, demolishing the food before him.

Grabbing *The Telegraph* from the sideboard, Tom settles down to read the financial pages. His concern grows when he looks at his investments. *I hope George brings me some luck this week. I'll be in trouble if not.*

In Too Deep
Saturday 3rd August

"How many times do I have to tell you, Sid," by far the thinnest member of staff Tom has ever seen, "the job has to be completed by the end of the week."

"I know, Mr Gold, but the supplier hasn't dropped the parts off yet. It won't be for at least another three days. It's still manageable. If we get the parts."

Dismissing Sid with a wave of his hand, Tom looks down at the paperwork on his desk, the red letters and final demands.

This job HAS to be finished. If it isn't, then I am.

Burying his head in his hands, his thoughts turn to Katie; *maybe I could have a chat with her. She can't really help, but it will make me feel better.*

Looking out over the factory floor, Tom notes that the workers have left. Shaking his head as he stares out over the workshop, he realises he is going to have to stop the overtime if something doesn't happen soon. In his daze, he almost misses the ringing of the phone on his desk. *Really. It's Saturday, for crying out loud.*

Thinking, hoping, praying it might be a customer, Tom walks back to his desk grabs the handset.

"Golds."

"Tom? It's me."

His shoulders sag as he curses under his breath, *why, oh why did I have to answer it?*

"Gina."

Trying, but failing, to stay civil, "I'm a bit busy, what do you want?" Comes out sharper than he intends.

Putting on her smoothest voice, ignoring his cutting tone, "I thought we could go for a drink this evening, sort things out?"

"There's nothing to sort out, Gina, I told you. It's over."

Almost begging him now. "Please, Tom, I don't want to leave it like this."

Sighing, "OK, OK. Meet me at *The Black Dog* at seven tonight, then."

They hang up, and Tom goes back to his desk, tidies up and prepares to leave. Thoughts of Gina and Katie put aside for the time being. He has bigger things to worry about. *I have to speak to Dad now. I can't do this business thing. He'll know what to do.*

Arriving early at the pub, for once hoping his father is there, Tom waits, also secretly wishing Katie is working too, although it doesn't look like it. Feeling disheartened, he grabs *The Sun* newspaper off the bar and studies the form for the week ahead.

"Hey, Son, Michael says you were looking for me," Jack says as he flops down on the seat next to his son.

"Oh, hi, Dad," Tom says as he folds the paper and looks up at his father. Fear and stress contorting his features.

"You look awful, Tom. What's going on?"

Taking a sip of his snakebite and swallowing hard. "I don't know where to start, Dad."

"Girl trouble again? Will you ever learn?"

"Well, yes and no. Girls, work and other— stuff." Mindful that he doesn't want his father to know how bad the gambling is but also realising he may have to tell him, Tom talks about Gina, Katie, work and the bills he's facing."

"Oh, Son, why didn't you come to me sooner?"

"We weren't exactly getting on before Gramps died, were we?"

"But surely, Dad didn't leave the business in a mess." Jack states.

"No, no, he didn't. That's all down to me. I'm a failure at everything, Dad. What should I do? Without it being dodgy." Tom quickly states, guessing what his father would have done back in the day.

Ignoring the digs, desperate to make this relationship work, Jack continues, "well, I've had a few businesses, so I'll have a look at the accounts and see where we can make savings. Have you won any work recently?"

"Not much. I can't sell, Dad. I'm an engineer. I want to be on the factory floor with the workers, but I don't want to screw this up. Gramps worked so hard for it, as he was forever telling me."

Jack laughs, "he was rather fond of reminding us how hard he'd worked for us, wasn't he? God rest him.

Katie's doing well here, so I can spare a few hours in the week. I'll come to the factory on Monday, and we'll see what needs doing. OK?"

"Great, thanks, Dad." Thinking this will go a long way to repairing the rift between them, Tom feels a weight being lifted from his shoulders.

"I have been thinking about selling, but what would I do then?"

Patting his son on the shoulder, Jack stands and walks back to the bar.

Tom stares after his dad and hears the latch on the door go. Looking up from his drink, he sees Gina walk in. Feeling his heart sink into his boots, he stands and beckons her over, "what would you like?"

"You." She responds, a twinkle in her eye.

When she's lovely, she's adorable. There just aren't many times when she's either.

Faking a half-smile, Tom responds, "to drink?"

"You're in a bad mood."

"I've got a lot on my mind. What do you want?"

"Half a lager, please."

Tom turns back to the bar and orders the drinks while Gina finds them a seat near the back of the pub. Heading over to her, Tom braces himself for an argument. Gina is a nice as pie, talking as if they'd never had a cross word. Alarm bells ring in Tom's haggled brain, but he quite enjoys the conversation. Discussing their days and laughing at some drunks, his father has to evacuate from the bar.

Feeling quite relaxed and at ease again, the snakebites having calmed him down a little, Tom is surprised by Gina's question.

"Are you coming back to mine, Tom?"

Knowing he should say no, Tom can't help saying yes. Feeling he needs a release, she is, after all, looking stunning in a little black dress and stilettoes. And she knows exactly how to turn him on.

Waking up the next morning, Tom is horrified to roll over and see Gina's legs wrapped around his, her head resting gently on his torso.

Oh my god. What have I done?

Trying to ease out of bed without waking her, she murmurs softly, "Tom, give me a cuddle."

He does as she asks, and she immediately starts to nibble his nipple. *What happened to it's over.*

The sensation is almost too much; he pulls her up and kisses her roughly, his erection as keen to get inside her as he is to get away from her. Quickly and without emotion,

Tom flips her onto her stomach, pulls her backside in the air and thrusts inside her. Blocking out everything except for his desire to finish the job so he can leave.

Over in only a few minutes, Tom leaves her lying on the bed and heads to the bathroom to relieve himself.

What am I doing?

"Tom," Gina calls in her best sultry voice, causing Tom to roll his eyes and mimic her.

"Tooommm."

Opening the bathroom door, he shouts to her, "just coming."

Giggling like a schoolgirl, "I think you've done that already, big boy." Leaning against the bedroom door jamb, wondering where he's going wrong, his thoughts disrupted by Gina's comment. "I'm glad we're back together."

"Sorry?"

"I'm glad we're back together. Are you coming back to bed?"

Shocked, he grabs his clothes off the bedroom floor, "No, I have things to do today, sorry."

Pouting, Gina retorts, "seeing her, I suppose."

Just like Jekyll and Hyde.

Having no energy for another argument and unsure how he's landed himself in this mess again, Tom turns his back and races down the stairs, shouting "goodbye, Gina," on his way out.

Meeting with Jack
Monday 5th August

"Thanks for doing this, Dad." Tom looks up at his father as they go through the options for the business.

Jack takes off his glasses and looks at his son. "I'm so proud of you, Tom."

"What? But I'm a failure, Dad." Tom answers, surprised by his dad's words.

"Tom, you've always given your all to everything you do. An accident in the Army is not failure. Adjusting to life on civvy street and asking for help is not failure." *That's what Monica says too.* "We all need help at times, and I'm glad you came to me, Son."

Tom looks away, feeling himself choked up by his father's praise. "I nearly didn't, to be honest. I thought the rift between us was irreparable."

"I know, Son, I thought so too, and I'm sorry I was never properly there for you. I don't know the half of what you went through, but I'm here now. Let's decide what we're going to do. OK?"

Nodding his head in agreement, Tom looks down at the notes they've been making all day.

"It's not as bad as it seems, Son. It's not great either, but I think we can turn it around."

Relief floods Tom's veins.

"I hope so, Dad. I really hope so."

Writing a plan of action was alien to Tom, being used to not having to make decisions, just doing what he's told when he's told. He was quite enjoying it, to be honest. *Maybe I've finally found something I'm good at.*

"I'll put some money into the business, Tom so that we don't have to lay anyone off."

213

"Are you sure? I know you never wanted anything to do with it, and because I've ballsed it up, you're having to bail me out. I'm sorry, Dad."

Holding his hand up as if to say stop right there. Jack takes Tom by the shoulder and forces him to face him. "I knew Dad would leave this to you. I have no need for the money, and I'm not an engineer."

"No, but you're a businessman. You don't need to be an engineer to manage it."

Shaking his head in frustration, Jack continues, "I wanted Dad to leave this to you. I'm just glad it worked out the way it did, and you'd come home before he passed away. I didn't expect you to stick at the Army."

"I loved it. Once I got used to the way of life, it was easy for me. Not having to think. Maybe a bit too easy in some ways. Except for the desert, but I wasn't there that long."

"Are you glad you're home then, Son?"

"Yes and no. I loved it. The camaraderie was second to none. You had each other's backs whether you liked each other or not, and we had great fun. But I'm glad I'm home too. I have to face up to this challenge now."

"Yes, you do, and you have to curb your gambling."

Tom is horrified. Stumbling on his words, "How…wh... how did you know?"

"I'm your father, and people talk around here. People are worried."

Cursing, "has Katie been talking to you?"

Taken aback, Jack answers, "No, does she know then?"

"She's been… sort of helping me, she gave me a little tip, and it's working. I'm gambling less money now."

"That's good, but it wasn't her. I think you've found a good friend there, Son."

"The best, Dad. Who was it then? Who do I need to keep an eye on?"

"Tom, it's more than one, and I've also seen you there."

"Oh. I've never seen you there."

"I wasn't in the bookies."

"Oh, where were you then?"

"Somewhere I shouldn't have been, but let's leave it at that, shall we?"

Not wishing to pry but now curious about what his father is referring to, he opens his mouth to question him further. Seeing the look on his face tells him it's not a good idea.

I suppose I'll find out eventually. Tom thinks to himself.

Having finished the plan for the business and agreeing that the money Jack puts in will be a loan. Tom finally takes responsibility for himself and his actions, realising this is his chance to prove to the world and to himself that he's got what it takes to succeed.

A Lunch Date
Saturday, 10th August

Tom is more nervous than ever as he heads for his parents' house. Jack is working at the pub, and it's just him and his mother, Sylvie, for lunch.

Walking rather than driving allows Tom some thinking space. He racks his brains to come up with something to say. Unclear how to put into words the burning hatred he has held for his mother for so many years. He knows the purpose of the meal is to heal the rift that's been between them since his childhood. Apparently, he ruined her dreams of becoming a famous dancer, and she's never forgiven him. Although not having been present at the conception, Tom is at a loss to understand why.

"Hello, Son. I'm so glad you could make it." Sylvie says as she opens the door when she sees him walking up the drive. "No car today?"

"No, I walked. Thought the fresh air would do me good."

Astonished, Sylvie bites back a sarcastic retort and beckons Tom to follow her to the kitchen.

"I'm doing your favourite, steak, new potatoes and veg. Oh, and not forgetting the strawberries and ice cream for dessert."

"Mmm, OK, thanks, Mom." Tom answers. He's surprised she can remember after all these years. Tom's mind wanders back to the days when she used to scare the crap out of him.

In an attempt to avoid the conversation dredging up past experiences he would rather forget, Tom turns the conversation to Katie. He's worried, and he hopes Sylvie will have the answers.

Over their main meal, Tom explains to Sylvie what's been happening over the past couple of weeks. He's shocked to learn that Sylvie hasn't seen her either.

"That's odd, Mom; I thought she would have been into the shop. She was in a bad way."

"I haven't seen her for a while, but from what you're saying, I suspect she's ashamed. She probably hasn't been out since."

"Why should she be ashamed? It's not her fault that John is an arsehole."

"Now, Son, don't get angry. Anyone would think he'd attacked you by the way you're acting.

"I know, Mom, I wish he had. At least I'd be a fairer opponent.

"You really like her, don't you, Son?"

"Yes, Mom, I do."

"Would you feel better if we went round after lunch to see her?"

"Yes, I think I would."

Clearing the plates away and bringing heaped dishes of strawberries and ice cream to the table, Sylvie attempts a reconciliation.

"I'm sorry, Son."

Tom looks up after scoping the last of the ice cream into his mouth. Swallowing slowly, preparing himself for what is to come, he asks, "what for?"

"Everything. I've been such a horrible mother." Tears roll down Sylvie's face, but Tom isn't going to make it easy for her.

"Yes, you have, but I don't have the energy for this now. I'm going to see Katie. Are you coming?"

Knowing it would be pointless saying anything else, Sylvie nods and grabs her handbag before following Tom to Katie's. Walking in silence, Sylvie realises it's going to be harder than she thought to repair the rift between them.

***

Tom knocks on Katie's door and taps the window several times to arouse her but to no avail. Taking a notebook and pen from his mother, he scribbles a note and posts it through her letterbox. Knocking again on the off chance that she'll hear.

With no response to his knock's forthcoming, Tom turns away from the door and heads back down the path. Just as he reaches the hedge, he feels sure he hears a door open and his name being called. He spins around, horrified at the sight of Katie standing on her doorstep. Barely recognisable as the girl he took to hospital a couple of weeks ago.

Rushing back to her, leaving his mother standing there staring, he grabs her into a bear hug.

Rubbing her arms up and down, he discovers the bottle of pills. Prizing them out of her fingers, he sits her down.

Oh, lord, what have I walked into. Again.

Looking into Katie's turquoise blue eyes, Tom begs her to tell him how many she's taken. It isn't until he threatens her with the hospital that he discovers she'd been drinking again after the fight and the pills were for a hangover. Cursing under his breath as it turns out his mother was right. She did feel ashamed, and she hadn't been out since the fight with John.

Trying hard to hide his emotions as a tear escapes from his eye. Apart from the fact that he hates seeing her like this, and once again, he feels helpless to know what to do, he also knows how she feels and is glad he's getting some help. He hopes she is too.

"What are you saying, Katie? I can't hear you." Tom asks as he puts his ear next to her lips.

"You're my knight in shining armour."

Is all he catches before she declares her love for Charlie whilst waving his note in front of his face.

Oh, how I wished you loved me too, Katie. He says to himself.

Opening Up
Sunday 18th August

Looking forward to his walk to the bookies this morning, Tom had arranged to meet Katie. Partly to make sure she was OK and partly because he wants to get to know her better.

Walking towards Rose Bush Village, Tom asks Katie why she always walks with her head down. Laughing with her as he embarrasses her. He loves it when she blushes; it gives her an innocent glow.

She opens up to him about her past and lack of confidence. Not helped by the bullying she was subjected to at school. Tom resonates with her about a lot of what she's experienced. Katie teases him and makes him chase her. They laugh and talk with no awkward silences. Tom surprises himself by putting even less money on his bets than he'd planned. For some reason, he wants to impress Katie. The money he saves he wants to use to buy them lunch at his favourite restaurant, *The Red Lion* in Malthaven. Thankfully she agrees to join him. Tom hasn't had this much fun since his last walk with Katie, and he doesn't want the day to end.

They walk home quickly, and once they've collected Tom's car, they head straight to the pub.

Once seated with the menus, Tom asks Katie what she wants and places their orders at the bar. It's busy today, and Ben is short-staffed, so no waiter service. This suits Tom; it gives him a few minutes at the bar to gather his thoughts. He knows Katie is going to ask him about his past, and he's nervous about opening up to her for fear of scaring her off.

Chatting away over their food, and as expected, Katie asks Tom about himself, eager to learn more.

Surprisingly he opens up to her, just a little. He tells her about his experiences in the Army. Not wishing to drag up his childhood given that Katie is often in his mother's shop. He finds it hard to talk to Monica sometimes, but it feels different with Katie somehow.

Reconciliation Attempt

Saturday 31st August

Tom's counselling is going well. Monica is pleased that he's had lunch with his mother. She hopes he is finally facing one of the issues mentioned in their sessions, his childhood and his issues with his mother. Deciding not to work on this glorious Saturday, he takes himself off to *The Cave,* his mother's bookshop, in the hope he can talk to Sylvie without an argument ensuing. Walking through the door, he feels sure he can hear Katie's voice.

Standing next to her, he makes small talk then spots the books she is looking at. Turning them around to have a closer look, he is horrified to see that they are all about hysterectomies.

I wonder if this has stemmed from the beating she had? Tom wonders to himself.

Not sure what to say to her, he is relieved when he hears Sylvie walking into the shop from the kitchen.

Giving his mother a withering look but keeping his mouth shut at her insults, *this is going to be harder than I thought. Is it worth it?* Tom asks himself, also wondering why Katie looks horror-stricken as she puts her hand up to her mouth.

Sylvie, introducing Tom to Katie, is left staring after her as Katie picks up her bag and dashes out into the street.

Tom and Sylvie stare at each other as they try to piece together what could possibly have made Katie dash off. After realising that Tom must be the 'friend' Katie often refers to, she threatens Tom to keep away. Gathering the books together, it takes Sylvie a while to realise Tom is still there and must have come in to see her. With mixed emotions, she asks what he came in for.

223

Deciding that now maybe wasn't the best time for a heart to heart, *would there ever be a good time?* He wonders. Tom shrugs his shoulders, "oh, nothing important, it can wait. Has Katie paid for these?" He asks, pointing to the books she's left on the counter in her haste to leave.

"No, Son, I'll keep them for her. She's in and out of here a fair bit."

"No, it's OK. I'll take them over to her now." Handing his mother the money, "That's mighty nice of you, Son."

"I am nice, Mom." *Just misunderstood.*

Before Sylvie can answer, Tom leaves the shop and heads straight to Katie's.

Leaving Katie with her books, Tom walks away, wishing he wasn't going on his blind date this evening.

A Blind Date
Saturday 31st August – Evening

Silently wishing Sid hadn't set him up for a blind date, Tom dresses in his best turn-up jeans and Calvin Klein t-shirt. The sun is still bright; he hopes they'll be able to sit outside *The Black Dog* on this glorious evening. Grateful he doesn't have to drive as his date is meeting him there, Tom walks down the hill to the pub. *On-time again, wonders will never cease, he laughs to himself.*

Sitting in the last outdoor seat after fetching his favourite tipple from the bar, Tom watches the world go by from behind his shades. Not really one for people watching, he can't help noticing the leggy dark-haired girl glancing around the tables. Gobsmacked when she walks up to him, "Hi, you must be Tom." She says as she holds out her hand for him to shake.

"Er, yes, I am. Are you Kay?"

"I am. Don't tell me; you were expecting someone… shorter."

Their laughter breaks the ice.

"Don't worry; I'm used to it."

"Sorry, used to what?" Tom asks. Confusion apparent on his face.

"I get it a lot. The shocked looks. Being this tall is both a blessing and a curse." She laughs.

Laughing with her, Tom asks, "can I get you a drink?"

"Cosmopolitan please."

Tom laughs again, "that might be a bit of a stretch in here but, I'll see what I can do."

Ordering the drinks from his father, Tom is amazed when he delivers what looks like the perfect Cosmopolitan.

225

"Is there no end to your talents, Dad? I didn't think you'd cope with a cosmo."

"Cope with anything here, Son. New girlfriend?" Jack nods in Kay's direction.

"Nooo, blind date."

"Oh, blimey, well, enjoy then."

"Thanks, Dad."

Delivering the drinks to the table, the sun still beats down on them, but a gentle breeze makes the heat almost bearable. Tom stops his thoughts from wandering back to the oppressive heat he once experienced in the desert.

Sitting down next to Kay to ensure the sun doesn't dazzle him, he asks, "How do you know Sid then?"

"He's my brother's friend. Apparently, I needed a date, and you were the perfect fit."

"Oh, that's nice of them. I don't normally go on blind dates."

"Me neither, Tom, but Sid made you sound… intriguing."

"Oh, intriguing, am I? That's good to know." He grins at her, enjoying the banter.

Conversation comes easily to them, and Tom is even more heartened when she states that she's only looking for a bit of no-strings fun. The chemistry between them is apparent so flippantly Tom comments. "What are we waiting for then? Let's get out of here."

Leading her away from the pub, they walk up the hill to Tom's house.

An Unscheduled Visit from Jack

Thursday 12th September

"Hey, Dad, what are you doing here?" Tom asks as he looks up from the paperwork strewn over his desk.

"I just thought I'd pop in and see how you're doing."

"I'm good, thank you," Tom answers, certain there's more to his visit than meets the eye. "Just going over some paperwork for a new contract. I'll probably need your help with it soon."

Distracted, Jack waves his hand at Tom. "Anytime, Son, you know that."

"Dad, why are you really here?"

"Oh, Tom, it's Katie. I'm worried about her."

Tom, now all ears at the mention of Katie's name, "why, what's wrong?"

"She had to have a hysterectomy, Tom, and she's got no one to look after her." Looking down at his hands, Jack is unsure whether to ask but, he doesn't know what else to do to help the poor girl. He's done all he can.

Tom, not surprised at the news, looks at Jack, "Spit it out, Dad."

"I was wondering whether she could stay with you. Just for a couple of weeks while she recovers."

"Me? Why me?"

"She was going to stay at the pub, and I could keep my eye on her while I'm there but, she'll need more help than I can give her. Besides, you have Mrs Dainty, and I thought… you know, with her being a woman and all, she could help out."

227

"Oh, I see what you mean. Well, I have the room, and I'm sure Mrs Dainty would love to have someone else around to spoil."

"Great, Son, so I can tell Katie you'll pick her up tomorrow?"

"What? What do you mean pick her up tomorrow?"

"Yes, didn't you know? She had the operation on Tuesday. She comes home tomorrow."

Before Tom has a chance to reject the idea, Jack flees, shouting his goodbye's as he closes Tom's office door behind him.

Katie Moves In
Friday, 13th September

Driving to work, after delivering Katie her breakfast, Tom is reliving their giggles. An hour it took him to conjure up toast and jam with an apple and a peppermint tea maybe he should leave the domestic side to Mrs D.

He feels good that he agreed to her moving in for a while. Her smile brightens up the place, the smell of her Jasmine shampoo, Tom finds intoxicating.

And, is it my imagination? Or was she flirting with me? What was it, she said, something about being a sight for sore eyes? Tom laughs. Of course, she made out she was talking about breakfast. Is it too much to hope that she was referring to me?

He wishes he could capture the almost childlike innocence of her cramming a slice of toast in her mouth to stop her embarrassing herself further.

Pulling up at the office, Tom drags himself out of the car, constant worry about the factory plays on his mind. *I need a big win on the horses or a minor miracle at work.*

As he collects his messages from his secretary on his way to his office, Tom still can't believe Katie is under his roof, living with him while she recovers and still, he can't find the words to ask her out.

An Embarrassing Incident
Saturday, 28th September

Tom, still in bed, hears the door close. Getting up, he looks out of the window just in time to watch Katie leave. His eyes follow her until she disappears into the woods.

Oh, bugger, I was hoping to walk with her today. May as well go to work instead, I suppose.

Finding himself incapable of concentrating in the office, Tom gathers some of his paperwork up, fully intending to do it at home. Daydreaming about Katie, surprised that he had agreed to let her stay with him while she recovers. He has his housekeeper, and Katie has no one. *It's the least I can do, and I'm enjoying having her with me.*

Pulling up on the drive, Tom is excited, hoping Katie is back and they can grab some lunch together before he tackles his paperwork.

Cursing under his breath, *Who's that at the door?*

"Hi, Kay, what are you doing here?" Tom asks as he opens his car door just as Kay, all 5' 8" of her, her long black hair tied back in a ponytail, is walking back to her car, having received no answer to her knock on his front door.

"Hey, Tom, I was at a loose end for a couple of hours, so I thought I'd pop by. Sorry, I should have called first. I assumed you'd be home on a Saturday morning."

"No, it's fine, come on in. I've just collected some paperwork from the office. Would you like a coffee?"

"I'd prefer tea, if you have it, please, Tom."

"One tea, coming right up. Make yourself at home in the living room. You remember where it is?"

"Thank you."

Making herself comfortable on Tom's oversized sofa, Kay kicks her shoes off and tucks her feet beneath her.

"Here you go," Tom enters shortly after she's settled herself and places the drinks on the coffee table.

"I should really leave you to your work, shouldn't I?"

"It can wait, don't worry." Suddenly feeling incredibly horny, Tom sits beside Kay and pulls her into his embrace, kissing quickly, and roughly, the overwhelming desire to just to shag takes both of them by surprise, only stopping to strip off, they climb back on the settee, getting straight down to business, Tom enters her, his backside bobbing up and down on the sofa. The groans escaping their lips sound like a whimpering dog. Hearing the door latch click, Tom can't believe it. Looking around, he momentarily meets Katie's eye.

"Oh, Jesus, she's back."

Hanging his head part in shame and part in disbelief, the sexual desire seeps away from them both, and they stop. Lying inert in each other's arms for a few moments.

"Is that your girlfriend?" Kay asks.

"No," *Mores the pity*. "She's staying here while she recovers from an operation."

Slightly disappointed but not at all fazed, Kay stands and swiftly dresses. "I'll leave now then; she didn't seem too happy from the gasp when she opened the door."

"Thanks, Kay. I really appreciate it."

"No worries, that's what no strings is. We both have things to do, so I'll see you around."

Allowing Kay to let herself out, Tom takes a minute to gather his thoughts. *I can't stay in here forever, may as well face the music.*

232

***

That went well, not. Tom thinks to himself after speaking to Katie. *Why do I always say the wrong thing and end up upsetting her? I can't believe she's even thinking of going abroad. She'll never cope. I'll talk her out of it. On the plus side, though, at least she didn't mention the embarrassing incident, and where did she get the idea I had a degree from?*

Feeling a little at a loose end, no woman to keep him company, Tom grabs the paperwork off the kitchen table where he left it earlier and heads to his study. Beginning with the accounts, he's surprised but pleased to see the business is starting to turn round. *At least something is going right for a change.*

Hearing the kitchen door click, Tom stops work and listens intently. Katie must have come back, but where is she? He wants to find her, to apologise. Leaving the study, he looks around the ground floor rooms. No sign of her. *She must be upstairs. Maybe she's overdone it and is having a lie-down.*

Leaning on the door jamb of her room, he watches her fussing Charlie. Katie looks up at him; their eyes meet. His apology falls on deaf ears as Katie turns away from him and continues to cram her meagre belongings into black bags.

Listening to her explaining her reasons for leaving, Tom is dying to interrupt, to tell her she couldn't be further from the truth. His life isn't as sorted and glorious as she assumes. He's just as lost as she is. He's never known what he wanted to do. Still doesn't. He loves having her here, and he doesn't want her to leave; despite the fact that she is right about the women he keeps bringing home, it's her he wants here. Not them. Before he has the chance to catch his breath following her verbal battering, Katie picks up her bags and flies past him, leaving him in the doorway staring after her.

I love you, Katie, please don't leave me.

Jack is Worried
Monday 18ᵗʰ November

"Hey, Tom, it's unusual to see you in here on a Monday evening." Larry shakes his hand and offers Tom a pint.

"Thanks, mate, snakebite please, it's been one of those days."

"Oh, want to talk about it?"

"No thanks, mate. Cheers for the pint, though." Tom takes a large swig, savouring every mouthful. Trying not to drink so much anymore he finds he's enjoying this one more than usual.

"What's happening with you then, Larry." Tom places his drink on the bar in front of him.

"Oh, you know, same old, same old. Oh, except Katie was on my bus today. Poor girl missed her stop. I had to drop her on the corner. She didn't look like she would have made it back from the next stop."

"What!" Jack asks from behind the bar. Overhearing their conversation.

"She didn't look none too good, I'll say that."

"What you waiting for, fellas? Get round there and make sure she's OK," Jack demands, worried.

Leaving his pint half-finished, Tom, already having had the same thought, dives out of the pub, Larry is close behind.

Getting into his car, Tom races over to Katie's.

"Hey, man, slow down, we're no good to her dead, you know."

"I know, sorry."

Slowing down to a more respectable speed, Tom curses Katie under his breath. *Why didn't you ask me if you needed a lift?*

***

Finally, Katie answers the door after Tom bangs loudly enough to wake the dead. No sooner has she opened it when Tom grabs her a big bear hug. *I've missed you, Katie.*

Explaining their conversation and Jack's concern to her, Katie lets them in once Tom lets her go. As he releases her, he realises how tired she looks, but this doesn't stop him telling her off for catching the bus.

Realising that Katie may be uncomfortable having a stranger in her flat, Tom offers to fetch her a Chinese.

Driving more sensibly now he knows Katie is OK. Tom drops Larry back off at the pub and heads to *The Blue Dragon* in Rose Bush Village. Remembering the last time he had a Chinese takeaway all those years ago threatens to spoil his mood. Ordering enough for two, Tom decides to keep Katie company, more for his benefit than hers. He feels he wants some uncomplicated chill out time with his friend.

***

Settled on Katie's settee with their food on their laps, Tom and Katie fall into comfortable conversation. Tom is concerned, Katie doesn't look well, and he's pleased that she's going back to see her surgeon. Not wanting her to have to catch the bus again, Tom tells her he will take her to her appointment.

236

Talk of holidays ensues, and while Katie is discussing her plans, Tom's mind wanders to his holidays abroad, in Spain, when he was knee-high to a grasshopper.

The intrusion of work and the many phone calls he's had to make today to keep a customer from cancelling, all down to a stupid mistake on the paperwork. His stupid mistake.

Realising Katie has gone quiet all of a sudden, he looks over to her he notices her eyelids droop. Trying but failing to slide off the settee without disturbing her, Tom refuses her offer of payment for the meal, agreeing to let her take him out when she's better; he disappears into the night.

A Surprise Visit
Saturday 23rd November

Tom's counselling sessions are going well, he should be finished with them soon. Work is picking up. He is beginning to get his gambling and drinking under control, so to test his resolve, he takes his morning newspaper from the paperboy, locks the door and heads to *The Black Dog*. Throwing away the racing pages as he enters the pub, he senses before he sees his friend from the Army propping up the bar.

"Phil, is that you?" Phil turns to face him,

"Yeah, man, it's me, in the flesh. Miss me, did you?"

They embrace in an embarrassed bear hug, clinging to each other, melting the past few months away in a heartbeat.

"What brings you here? Did they finally throw you out?"

"Nah, I'm on leave, had to come and see me old mate, for a pint. I knew you'd be in here."

Tom laughs, "how did you know that?"

"You must have mentioned it at some point in the past few years. An elephant never forgets." Phil laughs.

"You're hardly an elephant. Look at you, skin and muscles now. Look at me, gone to fat."

I'm sure I never mentioned The Black Dog. Suppose I must have, though.

"Snakebite, is it, Tom?"

"Please, mate."

Leaving Tom staring after him, wondering why he's turned up out of the blue, Phil turns back to the bar for the drinks.

Carrying them over to the seat Tom has secured in the corner, "here you go, mate, enjoy."

"Cheers, Phil," Tom says as he takes a much-needed sip from his glass."

Both feeling as if it was only yesterday when they last met, get into an easy conversation.

"So, what's happening with you, Phil? Still enjoying the Army?"

"Yeah, I've been promoted to Lance Corporal."

"Wow, that's great, mate, well deserved."

"Mmm, I suppose. It was after our few days in the Gulf, so much happened I can't even begin to tell you, but it messed with my head."

Muttering under his breath, Tom responds, "you're not kidding."

"Sorry, mate, what was that?"

Not wishing to admit that he was finding life on civvy street somewhat frustrating and that he'd had to get help himself, Tom shrugs his shoulders.

"Oh, nothing, so what brings you here."

Grabbing his glass and swirling his drink around, pondering how to break the news. He looks up. Tom stares at him expectantly.

"Well, Phil?"

"I come bearing news."

Looking Phil in the eye, unsure what to expect, he wasn't really close enough to anyone to warrant Phil delivering bad news in person.

"What is it, Phil? What's happened?"

"I don't know how to tell you this."

"Just say it, whatever it is, it can't be that bad, surely." Tom questions.

"OK, I won't beat about the bush. It's Cassie, man."

Staring at Phil, his glass to his lips, Tom drops his gaze.

"What about her?" He thought she was in the past. Having fallen for her. Hard. He never thought he'd hear her name again.

"Please don't tell me she's had a baby, and it's mine. I was careful. Well, most of the time, anyway."

Tom couldn't think of anything else it could be that would bring Phil here to see him.

Still meeting a wall of silence as Phil sips his drink, avoiding giving Tom the news.

"Just tell me, man," Tom almost shouts.

"She's my wife," Phil blurts out.

Choking on a sip of his drink, Tom stares at Phil, looking for signs that he's pulling his leg. This is the last thing Tom expected him to say.

After the initial shock has worn off, Tom thinking maybe she was seeing Phil as well as Shaun and himself, asks, "when did that happen?"

"Shortly after we got back in February."

Maybe not then.

"She called out of the blue. Tracked us down, well tracked you down, but you were back home by then, so I spoke to her. I had some leave due and went to visit her. Shaun had attacked her."

"What? She was still seeing him, after all this time?"

"Yes, he stayed there after they dismissed him, never left."

Shaking his head in disbelief, *why do women put up with it?* Katie enters his thoughts again, and he shudders when he remembers the night he found her.

Turning his attention back to Phil, "so what happened then?"

"I went to see her as I said. You wouldn't have recognised her." Tom didn't need to imagine.

241

"To cut a long story short, I stayed with her for a few days, helped her get the police involved and get some help. Then I went back to Germany. Couldn't get her out of my head, so we started writing, and we spoke as often as we could. The rest, as they say, is history."

"Wow," surprised that Tom feels no emotion having heard the news, he mustn't have loved her as much as he thought, he holds his hand out. Happy his friend has found love. "Congratulations, mate."

"Thanks, I thought you'd be upset."

"No, I'm just glad she's with someone who will look after her now. I did love her, you know."

"I know you did. She realised she loved you too, a little late perhaps, but that's why she asked me to give you this." Phil slides an envelope across the table with Tom's name on it in the most beautiful handwriting he's ever seen.

Tom looks at it like it might bite him.

"Aren't you going to open it?" Phil taps his finger on the envelope.

Tom picks up the envelope and immediately drops it back on the table. "Nah, man. Not here. I'll read it later."

Picking up his now empty glass, Tom heads to the bar, "another, Phil?"

"Yeah, please."

With a lot to catch up on, they talk until late into the evening. Phil makes his excuses, and they both leave the pub together. Tom slides the letter into his jacket pocket before they leave.

"Do you miss us?"

"Yeah, I do. They were amazing years, but I'm adjusting slowly."

"Takes some doing, does it?"

"Yeah, it's a totally different life, but I'm facing my demons."

They walk together in companionable silence. When they reach the base of the hill, they stop, Tom is heading up it, and Phil is walking to Malthaven, where he is staying for the evening. With Cassie.

"Do you want to see her, Tom?"

"See her?"

"Yes, she's in Malthaven."

Stunned, it doesn't take him long to answer, "no, I don't think so; maybe next time?"

"OK, I understand."

Surprised that they are both relatively sober given they have been drinking all day with no food, they part company with a handshake and a brotherly hug. Tom, his tummy rumbling, heads to *The Blue Dragon*, pondering the turn-up of events.

Monica
Monday 25th November

Feeling pleased his friend had visited over the weekend and brought good news, Tom decided not to go to the bookies on Sunday, luck isn't on his side at the moment, and he's lost too much money recently. Even contemplating taking money out of the business, the only thing stopping him is the repercussions from his father when his loan isn't paid on time. Instead, he heads round to Katie's with Charlie to see if she's had her scan date yet.

Oozing positivity for her and promising to take her for her scan, Tom is looking forward to his counselling session with Monica this afternoon to give her his news about the bookies.

***

Tom locks himself in his office and takes the letter out of his pocket where he'd placed it on Saturday, feeling it was burning a hole in his jacket. He stares at it, unsure whether he wants to know what's inside.

A knock on the door breaks his reverie as he quickly pushes the letter under his desk pad. Standing to unlock the door, his secretary informs him that there is a Monica on the phone, but she can't put the call through.

Strange, the phone lines are OK. Walking back to his desk, Tom realises he has knocked it out of its cradle. Replacing it, he signals for his secretary to put his call through.

"Hello, Monica, is something wrong?"

"Hi, Tom, no, not really. I just wondered whether you could come this afternoon instead of early evening if it's not too much trouble."

"Of course not."

"That's so helpful, thank you. Is 2.30, OK?"

Tom checks his diary, even though he knows he has no meetings scheduled today. "See you then."

"Bye, Tom and thanks again."

Even more interruptions at work keep Tom busy for the rest of the morning. As he packs his desk up for the afternoon, the corner of the letter glints in the light. *I really need to read this.* He muses to himself as he picks it up and puts it back in his pocket, once again feeling like it's burning a hole there.

***

Tom arrives at Monica's practice a little early and sits in quiet contemplation, wondering what they will talk about today—buzzing with his good news from Sunday.

Sitting on either side of a large impersonal oak desk, Tom and Monica face each other. Tom bows his head. Monica, short but big-boned with dark brown hair, speaks first.

"Talk to me, Tom?"

His fears, destructive thoughts and pent-up emotions come flooding out as he finally begins to open up more about his issues. His Army days and the horrific flashbacks, his knee operation, his grandfather's death and his childhood. Sunday's good news is all but forgotten.

Monica lets him vent. Keeping quiet as this is the most he's opened up since he started seeing her. She takes notes as Tom continues. The raw emotion tumbles out, and

Monica can feel his energy draining away, almost like he's giving up. *I thought he was stronger than this. Please don't give up, Tom,* she muses to herself *you have so much to give. You've come so far.*

Not being able to hold back any longer, he sobs uncontrollably. Exhausted after his tirade and not used to sharing his innermost secrets in this way. With anyone.

As he stops to take a breath and wipe his eyes, Monica asks, "how do you feel now, Tom?"

"Mmm, a little better, to be honest, getting it off my chest. I've held back so much for so long; it feels like a kind of release.

I'm not surprised. Wow.

"I feel guilty for the damage I've done to so many people over the years. Especially to women. I wanted to jump off Pebble Bridge a while ago, you know."

Shocked at his revelation but hiding it well, "what stopped you?"

"Apart from the water being too shallow and the bridge too low, I thought of Katie and the state she was in a few months ago. She comes to see you, doesn't she?"

"You know I can't discuss that with you, Tom. What made you think about her?"

"I just thought, I can't leave her. What would she do without me? You know she lived with me for a while after her op, don't you?"

Remaining silent, Monica waits for Tom to continue.

"Not that I'm much use to her really, I can't even summon up the courage to ask her out. Tell her how I feel."

"Why do you think that is, Tom?"

Silent for a few minutes, Tom takes a breath to gather his thoughts.

"Scared, I suppose."

247

"Of what?" Monica asks.

"Rejection, ridicule, being hurt like I was with Cassie."

"I thought you had no feelings for Cassie."

"Quite the reverse, I was falling in love with her, but I caught her with some else. And would you believe she's now married to my best friend from my Army days?"

"Oh, how do you know that?"

"He came to tell me on Saturday."

"How do you feel about that?"

"I'm genuinely pleased for him, but then I think of the failure I am with women and life in general, and I seem to spiral down again."

Sobbing still, Tom tries to catch his breath. He's never experienced this kind of emotional release before. The talking and the tears combined feel like they've helped him let go of some of the past.

"Tom," Monica gently calls his name when the tears stop flowing and his breathing return to normal.

"Tom, I want you to write letters to all these people. The ones you feel you hurt and who hurt you."

Staring at her with a look of apprehension on his face, she quietly reassures him, "I don't want you to send them. In fact, I strongly advise you don't. I just want you to write. I think it will be good as part of your healing process."

"Mmm," Tom mutters, unsure how it could possibly help. He changes the subject, "I've thought about going to the spiritualist church in Malthaven. I keep having weird dreams and visions I don't understand. I wonder if they could help me too."

"Anything you think will help, Tom, go for it. You can try it; you don't have to go again if you don't like it. You need to do what's right for you. And you need to grieve for your losses, not just your grandfather but all the changes in your life." Tom nods his understanding.

The session finally ends, and Tom leaves Monica's office. Feeling slightly lighter-hearted, he decides to take her advice and write the letters. *I have many to write, including one to my knee! It's your fault I'm here and not in the Army.*

Letters
Monday 25th November – Evening

Leaving Monica's later than expected, Tom arrives home to find Mrs Dainty has already left. The glorious smell of the chicken dinner warming in the oven alerts his stomach to the fact that he hadn't eaten since breakfast. Lucky that Mrs D is so generous with the portions, Tom makes the gravy that's sitting on the hob and sits down to eat.

Not bothering to take his jacket off, lost in his thoughts of this afternoon, he suddenly remembers the letter in his pocket.

Pushing his plate to one side once he's devoured his dinner, he takes the envelope out and places it on the table. Staring at it, willing it to disappear. "I need to write my letter to Cassie before I open you."

Grabbing some scraps of paper, envelopes and pens from his study, he comes back to the table and writes. Pouring his heart out, Tom writes everything he can think of in the letter. Old and recent feelings, guilt and regret, seep through his scribblings. Unable to read most of it, he addresses it to Cassie, places it in the envelope and pushes it aside.

Suddenly feeling very tired and somewhat emotional still, he makes himself a cup of Horlicks, grabs the detritus from the table and makes his way to bed.

Washed and with no one to disturb him, Tom climbs into bed, wrapping the blankets tightly around him. Despite the fairly mild temperatures for the time of year, he is chilled to the bone.

Propping himself up on the pillows, he slides his thumb under the corner of the envelope on Cassie's letter, stealing

251

himself. He takes a couple of deep breaths, uncertain whether he wants to read what's inside but knowing in his heart that he must. It may just answer a few burning questions.

Taking a sip of his Horlicks, he begins reading.

Dearest Tom,

Do you remember the first time we met? I do. I'll never forget it. Your eyes were the colour of my dress. I spotted you in the audience, and I knew I had to wait for you. Sitting up talking for hours was... special. You were the first man not to jump into bed with me on the first night. I was so used to being used I was shocked, and I didn't know how to handle it. I realise now I probably pushed you away, and I regret it more than you'll ever know.

The night I met Shaun, he swept me off my feet, said all the right things, did everything he could for me, but I guess you know how that worked out. I tried to contact you, but when I found out you were no longer in the Army, I was devastated for you. I spoke to Phil, and he told me what happened, how badly you had injured your knee. Only you, Tom, eh, only you. Yes, I'm laughing, but not at you, with you. One day, I hope you'll laugh again like you used to.

Anyway, I just wanted you to know I'm happy with Phil, and I'm glad we met. In your own little way, you made me realise I didn't have to put up with the shit. I have no explanation for my stupidity with Shaun, but I feel he was using me to get back at you. I learned that lesson, and thanks to Phil's help, he's now behind bars. Phil and I are moving to Germany with his unit.

I wish you well, Tom; you're a good man.

With love
         Cassie.

Silent tears toll down Tom's face as he lovingly places the letter back in the envelope. *I well and truly blew that one, didn't I?* He admonishes himself, vowing never to make the same mistake again. *I'm glad she's happy.*

Monica
Monday 2nd December

"I'm so sick of crying, Monica. I feel so ashamed." Tom blurts out, his head bowed.

"What makes you say that, Tom?"

Stumbling over his words, again, "I… I don't know. It's… just… I'm an ex-soldier. And a man. I should be able to face anything and deal with it without blubbing like a baby."

Monica's soothing voice penetrates his thoughts.

"It's normal to cry, Tom. Human. It doesn't matter who you are or what you've done. It's a good way to release pent up emotions and, you have so many. Bereavements, injuries, surgery, let alone everything else. If you think about all you've been through, even in the short time I've known you, it's enough to make anyone cry."

She watches his face, trying desperately to find the right words to help him.

"You're stronger than you think, Tom."

"Mmm," not quite convinced, he looks up at her, wringing his hands in his lap. "Will I ever feel human again? Feel like me again?"

"That's up to you. What do you really want, Tom?"

Startled, he looks up at her. *Where have I heard that sentence before?*

"Your business is doing better now. You've recovered from your knee operation. Physically you're fine. You're exercising more, that will help. You just need to catch up emotionally. Give yourself time, though. Go out and have fun. Do something new. Meet new people."

Church. Immediately springs to Tom's mind.

255

"Did you write your letters?"

"Sort of. I wrote the one to Cassie before I read hers. That made me cry too. After everything I did to her, she wished me well. She had a shit life too. I just made it a million times worse. I should have made it better. I wanted to. But I ran away like I always do. I was too chicken to tell her how I felt."

"You're not running away anymore, Tom. You're facing your demons, and that's good. How do you feel now?"

"Honestly?" he asks.

"Is there any point other than to be honest?"

Pondering for a few moments, unsure how to put his feelings into words.

"Mixed. Relieved, guilty, angry, sad, upset, emotional. So many feelings. So much hurt."

"That's good. Now, what about the positives?

"I never give it much thought. To be honest, I don't feel there are any."

"What about the fact that you have a roof over your head? That's positive, isn't it?"

"Mmm, true."

"You think of some more. You were doing so well a couple of weeks ago."

"The business is picking up," Tom responds, deep in thought.

"Ooh, and last week, I missed my trip to the bookies."

"That's good, Tom. Very good progress. Now, when you get home, I want you to continue writing your letters, but I also want you to start writing lists. Negatives and positives. Negatives to get rid of the hurts and positives from each day. Start with the small and obvious ones. Include people as well as things."

"Really?" Tom queries in a grump.

"Really. I want you to carry on adding to the lists each day until the positives outweigh the negatives.

Huh, unlikely. Tom mutters under his breath.

"Come now, Tom, you can do this."

"It's a lot to do."

"Good, it will keep your brain occupied." Changing the subject, sensing Tom wasn't quite on board with her suggestions but hopeful that he would be up to the task, she asks, "you mentioned church last week. Did you go?"

Shaking his head in dismay. "No, not yet. I couldn't quite get the confidence to face it."

"OK, that's fine. That's your challenge for this week then, go to church, even if it's only for a few minutes when there's no service on.

Staring into space, Tom doesn't respond.

"What have you got to lose, Tom?"

My street cred, myself. Or maybe it will be quite the reverse.

"Nothing, I suppose."

"Good. I don't want to see you for a few weeks as you have a lot to do there. We'll pick up again in the new year."

A little disgruntled but accepting her decision. Tom thanks Monica and takes his leave.

Having walked to his counselling session, Tom detours to Vera's, hoping he might see Katie. Looking around for and willing her to be in the tearoom, Tom's heart sinks into his boots when he discovers she isn't there.

Passing the time of day with small talk with Vera, Tom has a slice of his favourite cheesecake to take out. Paying for it, his hand on the door ready to leave, Tom doubles back and, for some inexplicable reason, orders a Chelsea bun for Mrs Dainty.

I hope she's still there when I get back.

Arriving home earlier than usual, he gives Mrs Dainty the fright of her life.

"Oh, my goodness, Mr Gold," she squeals as she drops the feather duster from the top of the ladders.

"Sorry, Mrs D, I didn't mean to frighten you. Whatever are you doing up the ladders, by the way?"

"Giving the top shelves of the sideboard a dust. It's been a while, but being a shortie, I have to use the ladders to do this bit."

Tittering to himself, he walks around the ladders and puts the cakes on the table. "Come down from there; let's have a cuppa."

Shocked that he's asked her, she slowly comes down from the ladders asking on her way, "whatever are you doing home so early?"

"I had an early afternoon appointment, and I decided not to go back to work."

"Good for you. You look shattered."

"I am, Mrs D."

Emotionally drained would be a better description.

Tom sets about filling the kettle, much to her horror, "Mr Gold, that's my job, here, let me," she says as she attempts to take the kettle out of his hands.

"It's OK. I'll do it; you sit down. I've brought us a cake. Chelsea bun for you. Your favourite."

Mrs Dainty stares at her boss, shaking her head. *Whatever in the world has come over him. The aliens have finally landed.*

"Oh, erm, thank you, Mr Gold, but why and how did you know they were my favourites?"

Ignoring the why, "I've seen you bring them here before. Your secret treat. Don't worry, I won't tell." Tom teases her. Blushing, she turns away as she takes over to make the tea.

"Make one for yourself too, let's sit and have a natter. I'm just going to get changed first." Tom shouts as he races through the house.

OK, the aliens really have landed. Maybe he's going to get rid of me.

Settling at the table, Tom and Mrs Dainty sit in companionable silence, both enjoying the rarity of doing nothing but savouring the moment. Mrs Dainty finally breaks the silence.

"Mr Gold."

"Yes, Mrs D."

"Can I ask you something?"

"Yes, of course, everything is OK, isn't it?"

"Yes, yes, everything's fine. It's just... I..."

"Yes,"

Nervously she blurts out, "I wanted to ask if you knew of any jobs." Unable to express his sense of dread at the thought she might leave, his mouth full of cheesecake, he stares at her. Noticing, she laughs, breaking the delicate atmosphere. "Oh, sorry, not for me, for my son."

Relief washes over him; he waits until she's finished. "It's just, he lost his job recently and to be truthful, he gets under my feet, and I'm worried he's getting into bad ways. I didn't like to ask... but..."

"It's fine, Mrs D. I'm glad you asked. I'd like to help if I can. I have a big meeting in a week or so. Something may come of that. What can he do?"

"Well, not much, he was working in a bar, but they finished him, not sure why." She fails to tell him that it was his father's bar. "He's not good with people, in all

honesty. I just want him to have a chance at a decent life."
Like you have.

"I can understand that. Ask him to come and see me at the factory next week. I'd like to help if I can." *It would be nice to give him a chance.*

Gushing and slightly embarrassing herself, Mrs Dainty thanks him profusely as she excuses herself from the table.

"I'd best prepare your dinner, Mr Gold."

Jack's Allotment
Saturday 7th December

"What you doing here, Son?" Jack asks as Tom gets closer to him. Straightening himself up, Jack drops the spade he's using to dig up his brussels sprouts and rubs his back, stretching to click his spine back in place.

Coming straight to the point, Tom replies. "I need your help again, Dad."

Taken aback, Jack looks at him, "My help?"

"Yeah, you've run businesses, and I can't do this on my own anymore."

"You've got a great team though, Tom. Your Gramps would be so proud of you."

"I know, Dad, but I have a huge prospect interested in working with us, and I don't think I can take it on. I can't make the sums work. I need a fresh pair of eyes. I'm seeing them on Tuesday."

Heartened that his son is turning to him for help again and grateful for the break from digging. Jack looks up and smiles, "it would be my pleasure, Son. Do you want to go over the stuff now?"

"Do you have the time? I've brought it with me. Or we could go back home and do it there in the warm?"

"Here is fine. It's warmer than you think in my little shed."

"OK, it will be nice to work somewhere different. Might even inspire me." Tom laughs.

"You never know, Son. You never know."

Pouring over the accounts, contracts and drawings with a nice cup of hot chocolate, it starts to go dark before they realise neither of them has eaten since lunch.

"I think that's enough for one day, don't you, Tom?"

Rubbing his eyes and dropping his pencil on the bench they've been working on, Tom agrees.

"Shall we go to the pub? Jack asks. "You can buy me an early dinner."

"You're on, Dad. Let's go."

Packing up all the paperwork and locking everything up, they head over to *The Red Lion* in Malthaven, Tom's favourite restaurant.

Over baskets of chicken and chips, Tom and Jack continue to rebuild their shattered relationship and, at the same time, outline the plans for the prospective client. The plan that would bring the company its biggest deal to date.

"Will you sit in the meeting with me on Tuesday, please, Dad?"

"Of course, Son, I'd love to."

Church After Dinner
Saturday 7ᵗʰ December

Dropping Jack back at his allotment to collect his car,
Tom notices it's only just gone six-thirty.

*Maybe today is a good day to try the church, see what
it's like.* The car seems to take itself there as if agreeing
with its master.

"Good evening, welcome to Malthaven Spiritualist
Church. Have you been before?" The kindly grey-haired
lady asks.

"No, I haven't. I'm not sure why I'm here to be honest,
or what to expect.

"That's fine. You're here for a reason. My colleague
will show you around if you like?" The welcoming smile
from the young lady, who seemed to appear from nowhere,
makes it hard for Tom to refuse.

*No. No. She's showing you around. Do not get any
ideas.* He screams to himself.

Explaining how everything works and who he needs to
pay his nominal fee to, she shows him into the main church
and invites him to take a seat. Already fairly busy, Tom
takes a seat at the back. Settling down, he wonders
whether he should have asked someone about his weird
dreams.

"Good evening, ladies and gentlemen," the grey-haired
lady shouts to be heard above the loud whispers of the
congregation. The effect of the stained-glass window
above her imitates a halo around her hair. Amused, Tom
giggles to himself.

Settling back in his chair, it's a while before he realises someone else is now speaking, and they appear to be speaking to him.

"You, Sir, at the back in the printed navy jumper."

Startled, Tom looks around him, then points to himself.

"Me? "Quietly escapes his lips.

"Yes, Sir, you. You've been having strange dreams. Fields and cottages are prevalent in some way?"

How the hell?

"Erm, yes, that's right."

"And, you've been having nightmares too." The speaker states, his long hair and beard make him look older than he sounds.

Tom nods.

"Please speak up, Sir. Spirit like to hear voices."

Obviously used to this medium's humour, the congregation giggle amongst themselves.

"Sorry, yes, that's correct, I've been…"

Holding his hand up, the speaker cries, "no, no, don't tell me anything, let me tell you."

Nodding again, Tom is speechless.

"I have a gentleman with me, sprightly in his old age, worked till he dropped, he's telling me."

"My grandfather."

"Good, yes, that sounds right. Don't tell me anything." The speak admonishes him again. "He's showing me a letter. It looks like it has some kind of insignia on it. Military. Army, Navy, perhaps. Can you take that?"

"Yes, Army," is all Tom can mutter.

"He says he's proud of you. What you've made of yourself and sorry that he forced you to make a decision you didn't want to make. He was trying to help. He realises maybe he shouldn't have done it. He should have

264

let you live your own life. It's not too late, he says. What do you really want? he's asking now."

The words stick in Tom's throat, too scared to utter them, he nods again.

"Please speak up, Sir. Does this make sense to you?"

"Absolutely," Tom answers, the strength in his voice returning in that instant.

"I've longed to hear him say 'I'm proud of you' for years."

"Thank you, Sir."

Crushed that he's let his feelings be voiced, Tom stares into space. *And those words, I heard those so many times, what am I missing?*

"Your spirit guides are with you, Sir; at present, he's one of them. Please follow your heart," he says. "Don't add to your regrets. Start to make good memories."

"Thank you," Tom answers.

"I'll leave you with that thought, Sir."

"Thank you, thank you very much."

The rest of the service passes Tom by in a blur. He doesn't hear anything else until the closing prayer an hour later. He's so absorbed in the messages. *What do I want? To be happy.* Tom thinks to himself as he bids the two ladies he met earlier goodnight.

On his way out, he sees a sign for the same medium. Private sittings. Retracing his steps, he asks the younger lady, "are there any spaces available, please?" as he points towards the advertisement.

"I'm sorry, Sir, that one is fully booked. He's our most popular medium."

"Oh, that's a shame. He just gave me a message. I wondered whether he could give me anything else."

"I heard the message, Sir. Take what you need from that first. He probably wouldn't have much more to tell you at the moment."

"Oh," slightly disheartened, Tom turns to leave.

"You always get what you need, Sir, maybe not what you want, but always what you need. That was yours. For now."

"Thank you, that's very helpful," Tom replies as he leaves the church.

What do I really want? Time to ponder. I must write that down when I get home. And do some of Monica's tasks too. Maybe the answer is in there somewhere.

Potential New Client
Tuesday 10th December

Tuesday morning rolls around far too quickly for Tom, still trying to get his head around his experience on Saturday. His stomach is in knots. Staring at his reflection in the mirror. *Looking better. Breathe, Tom. Breathe. It will be OK.*

Talking to himself, repeating his sales pitch and at the same time thinking, *what do I really want?* Apart from Katie, he struggles to think of anything. Lost in his thoughts, the ringing of the doorbell makes him jump.

"Good morning, Mr Gold."

"Good morning, Mrs Dainty. Is the wanderer in?"

"Yes, Sir, he's upstairs. Shall I fetch him for you?"

"No, it's OK, thank you, Mrs Dainty, I'll shout him."

Heading for the stairs, Jack shouts up, "ready, Son?"

"Coming, Dad." Returns the faint reply.

Feeling grateful that Jack is attending the meeting with him, he splashes his face with cold water and plasters a smile on his lips.

Be positive.

Grabbing his suit jacket from the top of the banister, Tom heads downstairs.

"You look tired, Son."

Really, I thought I looked good.

"I was up until 2 am pouring over the plans for today to make sure I have everything straight in my head."

"Good. And, have you?"

"Yes, I think so. I can't screw this up, but I'm so nervous. I'll never get an opportunity like this again."

"Of course, you will, Son, and you won't screw it up. Have faith in yourself."

Arriving at the office, Tom is heartened to see that his secretary already has everything laid out. The large glass-topped table in the middle of Tom's office is strewn with tea and coffee pots, cups, biscuits and posh mini cakes, which Tom can't remember the name of. Seeing them makes his stomach rumble, unable to face breakfast, he makes a beeline for them, only to be told off by his secretary, laughing as she leaves his office to greet their guests.

Fed and watered, small talk out of the way, the four men get down to business. Jack sits slightly back from the table to allow Tom to chair the meeting. Reminiscing of his times around dodgy boardroom desks, Jack's heart swells with pride as he listens to Tom standing tall delivering the project plans they had discussed only a few days before.

I've missed so much of this lad's life. What a crap father I am. Time to make it up to him. Willing Tom to do well, Jack prays he will win this business. *It will be the making of him.*

Lost in his own world, Jack shakes himself out of his reverie when he hears Tom say, "would you like us to leave the room so that you can discuss it together?"

Sitting down, more to stop his legs shaking than anything else, Tom awaits their response.

The older of the two gentlemen, everything about him is grey. His eyes, hair and suit, but somehow, it suits him, responds, "no, that won't be necessary. We have made our decision."

Tom and Jack sit bolt upright in their chairs and hold their breath.

Glancing at each other, the two men ask in unison, "when can you start?"

268

A whirlwind of emotions fizzles through Tom's body. Barely able to contain his excitement, he grabs both of the men's hands in turn to shake.

"We were thinking the first week in January," Jack responds, noting Tom appears to have been rendered speechless by the news.

"We want to give you the best service possible and, as outlined in the plans, there are things we need to put in place before the contract starts. Would that work for you?"

Glancing at each other, an almost imperceptible nod passes between the gentlemen. The younger of the two, also in a grey suit but with darker hair and brown eyes, responds in a gruff voice, "that works for us."

Tom finds his voice again and confirms, "I'll get the contracts drawn up and sent over this week." Tom asks as the gentlemen all make their way to the door. "Just out of interest, what made you choose us?"

"Your military background in the Royal Engineers." The older gent responds. "As you know, the end-user for this project is British Aerospace, and your background pleases our Managing Director. He knows discipline and precision are required for these jobs. You'd already won it before we got here."

Wow, the Army really did do me a favour.

Having seen the men move towards the door, Tom's secretary is waiting outside to show them out. Thanking her, Tom jumps up and down and grabs his father in a bear hug. "We did it, Dad. We did it."

"You did it, Son. I'm so proud of you."

Releasing his grip, Tom looks at his father, "do you know how long I've been wanting to hear you say that, Dad?"

"All your life, I should imagine. We have been such poor parents, Son. Can you ever forgive us?"

269

You don't know the half of it, Tom thinks but lets it slide, not wishing to ruin the elation he currently feels.

"I hope we can make up for lost time, Son."

"Me too, Dad."

Not wishing to lose the moment, Jack feels now is a good time to mention Christmas.

"Listen, Tom, Katie wants to do a get together on Christmas Day in the pub. Has she mentioned it?"

Tom's smile widens. *The day just keeps getting better.*

"No, I haven't seen her for a while."

"Fancy it then?"

"Do I ever? That would be lovely, thanks, Dad."

"Don't thank me, thank Katie. There'll only be a few of us, and it will do Katie good with everything she's been through. Get her out for a while."

Nodding, Tom is now suddenly very excited about Christmas.

It's all coming together very nicely. Tom muses to himself. *Now I just have to ask her out.*

"Talking of Katie, I'd best go, Dad, I promised her I'd pick her up from the hospital, and I don't want to let her down. Again."

"That's great, Son. I'll leave you to it then."

Tuesday 10th December – Evening

Finishing his dinner and leaving his plate on the table, Tom grabs the last of his coffee and retires to the study to re-read the draft contract he plans to hand to his secretary tomorrow morning for typing.

Sitting down at the large mahogany desk, Tom spots his letter to Cassie out of the corner of his eye. On top of it is a pure white feather. *How bizarre. How has that got in here?* Tom can't help wondering whether this is a message for him.

Picking the feather up, he places it gently in his wallet, unsure why but convinced that's what he must do. Putting his wallet away again, he grabs a new notepad from the desk and sets about writing the other letters as Monica had suggested. His mother, father, grandfather. All the women he has wronged. The hardest one, strangely enough, will be the one for Katie.

Staring at the blank page, Tom finishes his coffee, puts his cup down and grabs his pen. Fidgeting in his chair, he looks around to find a distraction, unsure whether he's ready to pour his heart out, even to a piece of paper. He hasn't told Monica half of it. Shaking his head. *Come on, you can do this. You'll feel better afterwards.*

Taking a deep breath, he begins with the letter to his mother. As Monica has told him, he needs to be positive as well as negative, but the only thing he can come up with is the fact that he hasn't spent much time with her. *I think this must be what they call a work in progress. I have a long way to go before I can forgive her.*

Tom pours his heart out onto the paper, the bullying, the drinking, his gambling which he firmly places at his mother's feet. The words are so fierce they almost burn the paper he writes on. Each sentence merges into the next.

271

The ink runs with his tears. Now he's started, he can't seem to stop, the pen runs away with him, page after page of hurt and anger free flow onto the paper. He sits there for hours, each letter rolling into another until he's finished them all. All bar the one to Katie. *Where do I even start? Katie is the future, that can wait a while.*

Putting his pen down, he leans back in his chair. *Wow, Monica is right, you know. I do feel better now.*

A little voice inside his head murmurs, *what about the positives?*

Quickly grabbing another new notebook he'd brought back from the office a few weeks ago, he starts to write down the positives in his life. Doesn't take long. It is a work in progress, after all.

Standing from his desk, Tom stretches and clicks his bones back into place as he straightens up. *Ooh, that's better.*

Rubbing his eyes, he picks his cup up and makes his way to the kitchen for his Horlicks fix, noting the time on the clock above the door as he goes. 2 *am, already. I need to get to bed.*

Ten minutes later, Tom climbs between the cold winter sheets, wraps himself in his blankets and falls into a dream-filled, restful sleep. The best he's had in years.

"Tom, Tom, come with me. I want to show you something."

Looking up, he sees a gorgeous girl, she's around his age, but she looks deathly pale. Her dress is a rainbow of colours, the patterns swirling one way they look like dancers, as she turns the pattern kaleidoscopes into aeroplanes, then into the deep blue ocean, fish, dolphins, turtles all swimming around him.

Grabbing her hand, he walks with her along a silver-white sandy beach, the sand tickles his toes as he steps along the shoreline. Arriving at a remote cabin nestling on a bed of rocks at the far end of the beach, the figure of eight door knocker intrigues him; 'I've seen that somewhere before.' Tom can hear music. Climbing onto the rocks to get a better view, he can see a party in full swing. Edging across the rocks, he reaches the bright white front door. Turning the rounded handle, he pushes; the door doesn't move. 'Maybe it's stuck,' he muses to himself. Turning the handle again and leaning his athletic weight into it. Still, it won't budge. Looking back at the girl, he asks, "why can't I get in?"

Staring into the room, he notices that most, if not all of the people in there are people he knows, family, old girlfriends, Army colleagues.

"What is this about?" He asks. When he receives no response, he looks around him; his companion is nowhere to be seen. He hears her voice gently in the stillness of the night. "What do you really want, Tom?"

'Those words, again,' Tom thinks to himself. "I want to be in there, having the time of my life," he murmurs, more to himself than to her. I've missed out on so much.

"Why have you brought me here?" he asks.

"To remind you to enjoy your life. Go after what you really want. Don't settle. You have so much to celebrate and be grateful for. You don't know how lucky you are. And will you please ask her out on a date!"

Tom moves away from the window and sits down on the rocks. Half staring at the party and half at the gentle push of the waves lapping up the rocks at his feet.

'Maybe I should go for a swim as I can't join the party.'

Stripping down to his underwear, he makes his way down the rocks to the sea. Gently lowering himself in, he's

273

surprised how warm it is. Paddling around, wishing he was by the sand, he could build a sandcastle. Just thinking about it makes him smile as he remembers one day, a very long time ago, before her drinking got worse, his mother helping him build a fortress of a sandcastle.

Splashing around in the water, calmness washes over him. "I'm enjoying this so much," he shouts to his companion. Even though he still can't see her.

"Good." She shouts back. "Do more of it."

Tom continues to splash around, enjoying the warming sensation of the water on his nearly naked body.

After what feels like hours but is only a few minutes, having drifted further out to sea than he likes, Tom swims back to the rocks. Panic sets in as he looks around for the cabin but can't find it. 'I must be in the wrong place,' he worries. 'But, my clothes are here.' Heaving himself out of the water, he stands alone on the rocks.

"Where is the cabin?" he calls out to his companion. Hoping she's still around.

"It's gone, Tom. They are all gone. It's time to move on. Time to decide what you really want. You're safe," she says as she gently touches his arm.

Feeling a rush of calm and peace wash over him, Tom gets dressed and follows his companion back over the rocks, along the shoreline of the beach and climbs back into bed.

Waking early the next morning, certain he's had some kind of dream but the memory fails to settle in his brain. He feels different. Calmer, somehow. More at peace. *Maybe it was all that writing.* He muses as he pushes himself up and climbs out of bed, a slight spring in his step.

Staring at his reflection in the bathroom mirror, *wow, you look good today.* He says to himself. Raring to go to work, knowing he has so much to do. He feels a renewed sense of vigour for life. One he hopes he will keep.

Tom Visits Jack
Friday 20th December

The past week or so has flown by for Tom. Putting in place the actions from his new client plan, ensuring his customers are happy. Long days and even longer nights to make sure as much is in place as there can be in the run-up to Christmas.

Friday lunchtime, Tom calls a team meeting. He thanks all his employees for their hard work also making sure they are all ready for the new contract and employees in the new year. The whole team is excited by the prospects and opportunities opening up for them. His secretary has laid a few nibbles and drinks on in Tom's office to start the celebrations.

"Right, you lot," Tom shouts over the raised voices. "I've said my thank yous, and I'm so privileged to have such wonderful people working for me. I want to give you the rest of the day off."

The cheers explode all around him, all the staff in turn hugging and thanking him. His secretary the most shocked and pleased of them all. So out of character for him, but she likes the new Tom.

Overwhelmed by their reactions, Tom taps his glass and shouts again. "As we are going to be so unbelievably busy in the new year, and you've all worked so hard to complete the outstanding jobs, I don't want to see you until 2nd January. Go home, relax and have a fabulous Christmas and New Year."

Astounded by his generosity, all the staff give him a final hug on the way out, each one of the hugs, in turn, helping him to relax a little more. Little knowing that just this small act of kindness has induced even more loyalty in his employees, ensuring their future success.

Helping his secretary lock the factory up for the shutdown and ensuring all the machines are switched off, Tom bids her a Merry Christmas and heads for his car. Wrapping his large overcoat tightly around him, the wind swirls around his legs, almost knocking him over, the first flurries of snow gently fall. Tom laughs as one of them lands on the end of his nose. *At least the snow won't stick.* He thinks to himself as he locks the gates of the car park and heads to the pub to see his father.

***

"Thought you might like a progress report, Dad," Tom says as he settles himself at the bar in *The Black Dog*.

Busier than usual for a Friday lunchtime, Tom senses he's in for a long wait, but craving being able to curl up in the warmth of his nice open fire, he jumps at the first chance he gets to fill Jack in on the situation.

Clapping him on his back, Jack says, "I'm proud of you, Son. You've done so well. No wonder you look so tired."

"I've been working twelve-hour days to set everything up. It's been worth it, though. And the overwhelming feeling of gratitude I got when I told the team I was closing until after Christmas was electric."

"Contract all signed, Tom?" Jack asks, hoping against hope he hasn't made the same mistakes as him in the past.

"Yes, Dad, new starters all sorted.

"That's fabulous, Tom."

"Ooh, more customers, Dad." Tom nods at the couple who have just entered, bringing the winter chill in with them. Catching a glimpse of the snow, Tom jumps down from his stool and bids his father goodbye.

Brr, Jack Frost would have a field day out here. Tom muses to himself as he climbs into his car. Starting the engine, he waits a few minutes until it's warmed up, even though he's only driving up the hill. He sits and listens to the purr of the engine, reminiscing on how far he's come. How much further he has to go to, but proud of himself.

A sharp tap at the window startles him, and he looks up to see Kay. Her nose is the only thing sticking out between her scarf and a woolly Santa hat. Winding the window down, Tom laughs, "Hey, Rudolph, how are you doing?"

"Not great, to be honest. Can you give me a lift, please?"

"Sure, hop in."

As she closes the door, Tom puts the car in gear and gently reverses out of the space and drives off the car park.

"Thanks, Tom, you're a star."

"What happened to your car?"

"It won't start. I only came into the village for some last-minute presents. Popped in here for a drink and left the lights on."

"Oh, dear, flat battery then?" Tom asks.

"Yeah, I guess so. I'll have to get the garage to have a look on Monday. I'm sure it will be fine. So, what are you doing over Christmas, Tom?"

"*The Black Dog* on Christmas day. There are a few of us having Christmas lunch there. The pub's closed, so it will be a small gathering. How about you?"

"Well, I was going to my parents but, what with the weather and the car, I doubt that will happen now."

"That's a shame; why don't you come to the pub?" Before Tom can stop the words tumbling out, Kay has accepted.

That's not going to get you any closer to asking Katie out on a date. Is it, you numptee? Cursing himself for his loose tongue and stupidity, Tom drives the rest of the way in silence.

"Thank you, Tom, shall I come to yours on Christmas morning? We can walk down together then as your place is closer."

Knowing he will be lonely on Christmas Eve and there is no chance he will get to speak to Katie before Christmas, "why don't you come to mine on Christmas eve, about 5 pm, and we can have dinner?"

"That would be lovely, thank you." Bracing herself for the walk and the weather, but she dare not ask him to pick her up. Kay bids him farewell.

Cursing himself again, *oh, well, there's always the new year, and Kay is good no strings attached company.*

Christmas Day
Wednesday, 25th December

"Mmm, wakey, wakey, Tom," Kay nuzzles into his back as she reaches around to stroke his belly, her fingers circling his navel and slowly making their way through his pubic hair. Gently tugging, she rolls some around her finger. Tom barely stirs and rolls onto his stomach. The intense twitching sensation confuses him in his early morning daze.

"Tom," she whispers into his ear, "Tom." She runs her finger down his spine, attempting to wake him. Shuddering, he lets out a low groan and rolls onto his side towards her. As he turns over, she gently kisses him, teasing her tongue between his lips to kiss him fully. Probing deeper with her tongue, she pushes her body against his.

Trying his best to ignore his throbbing penis, Tom pulls away from her to look at the alarm clock on the bedside table behind her. 6 am. *What the hell is wrong with her. Twice last night, now again.*

Tom attempts to roll away from her, but Kay is having none of it. She's horny, and she isn't taking no for an answer. Locking her legs around his, she gently teases his ear, purring like a kitten. Tom realises resistance is futile. He may as well enjoy it. Not wanting to be as rough with her as he once was with Cassie, his thoughts drift back to his time in her tiny bed in her small flat. Kay stroking his stomach brings his thoughts back to the present day. He gently strokes her right breast, teasing the nipple between his fingers. Flipping onto his knees, he expertly positions himself between her legs and pushes them apart, teasing her. He rubs his now erect member up and down her thigh as he takes her breast in his mouth and begins gently sucking. Flicking her nipple with his tongue, she arches her back, searching for his penis, gagging for him to enter her. Groaning loudly, Kay wriggles beneath him, the pressure within her body electrified, her skin growing ever more sensitive to his touch. Tom straddles her and kneels above her, just out of her reach. Slowly moving his tongue down her body, he gently licks and kisses each of her breasts, her tummy, both of her thighs. Kay is almost squealing with pleasure. *Just do it, man. Just... do...it!*

Tom, turned on by her squirming, gently licks her pubic bone, flicking his tongue around her labia, pinning her legs down with his so he can feel her excitement. Becoming more and more aroused, he inserts his tongue even further and licks her clitoris, sending her into a frenzy. Trying her hardest not to climax, Kay begins panting. Pulling away, Tom kneels between her legs, leans over the bedside table and pulls a condom out of the packet. Not taking any chances. Ripping the wrapper off with his teeth, he deftly places it over his throbbing penis.

Kay opens her legs wider, allowing Tom to enter her. Positioning himself gently inside her, he slowly teases and withdraws, building her frenzy even more, taking her breath away. Thrusting into her again, Tom is shocked when she flips him onto his back. Straddling him, she pins him down by his shoulders and squeezes her knees around his sides. She rides him. Fast. Only caring about her climax, she rides faster and faster, attempting to make herself come.

Shocked at the sudden change in position and the roughness of her moves, Tom attempts to keep pace with her, realising this was what he used to be like with other women and how uncomfortable it now feels.

Slowing her down, he gently rolls her onto her back and penetrates her again. She wraps her legs around him. As he thrusts into her, she manoeuvres to take him deeper and deeper inside. Her need to orgasm becomes so intense she feels like she is about to burst. On the edge, she closes her eyes, ready to lose herself completely in their orgasm when Tom suddenly stops.

"I'm sorry, Kay, I can't do this. It's too rough for me."

"I thought you liked it rough." She pants.

"I did, I do, I... don't know. I'm changing, and I want to make love, not bang away for all I'm worth. I'm sorry."

Pushing himself up and withdrawing from her, his once erect penis now hangs limp against his thigh. He goes to the bathroom to buy himself time to think.

This won't bode well for the day. I just hope she doesn't spoil it.

***

The blizzard is worsening, Tom shouts to Kay, "we'd best get going. With this storm, we may not make it."

"I hope we do; I'm looking forward to Christmas lunch. Who's cooking it, by the way?"

"We all did a bit. Well, Mrs Dainty did my bit."

Still reeling from earlier, Kay isn't saying much as they battle the storm down the hill.

Finally making it to the pub, they take their coats, hats and scarves off and settle in for Christmas lunch. Kay listens to White Christmas playing in the background and suddenly feels very sad. Going over this morning in her mind, wondering what she had done wrong, she barely touches the delicious plate of food in front of her.

Tom sits next to Kay but pays her little attention. He is too distracted watching Katie. *She looks stunning. She*

283

seems different. He muses to himself. Watching her, chatting with his mother, laughing and smiling. *Well, I guess that's half the battle. She already knows the parents.*

Jack's voice breaks his reverie as he asks everyone to raise a toast to Katie, without whom this day wouldn't have happened.

Tom raises his glass, watching Katie intently. Desperately wanting to go over to her, take her in his arms and kiss her.

What are you waiting for? Do it!

Tom places his glass back on the table and wanders off to the gents. Talking to himself in the mirror. *Time to do it. It's easy. Katie, will you go out with me?* Seven little words. That's all.

Taking a breath and making his way back to the bar, he arrives just in time to see the door shut as Katie's coat floats through, and Jack closes the door behind her when it misses the latch.

About to shoot forward to follow her, the gentle tug on his arm from Kay stops him in his tracks.

"Tom, can I stay with you tonight?" she asks as she grabs their coats and prepares to leave.

New Year's Eve
Tuesday 31st December

Knowing everyone in the village does have its uses, at times. Tom muses to himself as he bangs on Katie's door. Hiding behind a huge bouquet of flowers. Twice the flowers for half the price, the shop closed tomorrow for the bank holiday.

Using the excuse that he missed her birthday, Tom hands Katie the flowers, reminding her not to be late for the party at *The Black Dog* later that evening. Heartened that she's looking forward to it but running out of excuses to stay, he bids her farewell.

Hesitating as he turns back towards her once he's stepped back outside, *Katie, will you go out with me?* Too late as she waves him goodbye and closes the door.

What is wrong with you, man? He chides himself. Another perfect opportunity wasted.

Slowly walking back up the hill, Tom decides to write his letter to Katie when he gets back, always assuming Kay leaves him alone for more than five minutes. *Some no strings attached this is turning out to be.*

Letting himself back into his house quietly. He creeps into his study and closes the door. Still cross with himself for missing his opportunity. He sits down and pours his heart out again. No beating about the bush, he writes to Katie as if he's talking to her.

Dearest Katie,
As soon as I caught the first glimpse of you near my favourite bench all those months ago, I've wanted to ask you out. I must have given you such a fright, dressed as I

was and dozing off. It's been a tough few years for me, and that day just topped it off. If I'm honest, I didn't want to go on. I know you can relate to that too. Seeing you standing there, shouting to ask if I was OK, somehow gave me a boost. You sounded like you actually cared, and I just knew I had to pull myself together. You almost felt like a guardian angel. I bet this doesn't make any sense to you at all, does it?

I know you've had your troubles, but you've helped me so much. Listened to me when I needed you. You're helping me kick my gambling habit: you and Monica, of course. I'm not quite there yet, but I'm so much further forward, thanks to you. And so much better off too.

I want to tell you about the huge contract I've taken on at work which starts in two days. I'm scared and excited in equal measure. Pray, I get it right this time, Katie. It could be the making of the business. I'll be working long hours for the foreseeable future. I had hoped to get to know you properly, maybe even... become a couple. I just don't know how to ask you out. I guess now there's not much point if I won't have time to see you.

I was so pleased when you agreed to move in with me, albeit for a short time, and let me look after you. Well, Mrs D did all the looking after, but it was so good to have you around. I managed to screw that up, too, didn't I? Will I ever learn?

You looked so different when I brought you the flowers today. I wanted to ask you out, but the words just wouldn't come. I flunked it again and made out the flowers were for your birthday and Christmas.

I can't believe I'll be coming to The Black Dog tonight with another woman again when all I want is to be with you. Why do I find it so hard to ask you such a simple question? Will you go out with me? Fear of rejection, maybe?

"Tom, Tom, are you here?"

Cross that Kay's voice has disturbed his flow, Tom swears under his breath, folds the piece of paper up and stashes it away in the top drawer of his desk. Promising himself, he'll finish it later.

Slamming the drawer shut, he leaves his study and bumps straight into Kay.

"Where were you? I was looking for you?"

"Here." Was Tom's sharp response. "Why were you looking for me?"

"You seem to have been gone hours. Did you go out?"

"Why would I go out? It's New Year's Eve, and I'm going out tonight."

"Don't you mean we are going out tonight?" Kay demands, stroking Tom's chest, hoping he'll make love to her before they go out.

"Kay, what's this we? You only want casual no strings, now all of a sudden it's we this, we that." Close to losing his temper now, more at himself than her, he removes her hand from his chest. "I'm going out. It's up to you what you do." Storming off, he heads for the shower in the hope it will cool his temper and her sexual appetite down.

Kay wonders along the hall to the main living room and flops down on the sofa. Contemplating Tom's words. *Why did I have to fall for you? That wasn't part of the plan.* Determined not to let her emotions get the better of her, she makes her way upstairs to repair the makeup it's taken her half the day to do, now the tears have trickled down her face.

287

Showered and dressed, Tom leaves his bedroom just as Kay enters it.

"I'll meet you downstairs, Tom, if that's OK? I'd like to come to the party."

Tom grunts his acknowledgement and waits for her by the back door.

Thankfully, the weather is a bit better now, the blizzard has passed, and the wind has dropped significantly.

"I'm sorry, Tom, I've spoiled your Christmas break. I should have gone home when the weather changed."

Tom's anger is still bubbling away, and he shouts to her, "yes, you should."

"Why are you shouting, Tom? I've said I'm sorry." Kay finds herself shouting too.

Tom spots Katie walking down the last part of the hill in front of them. Her pace quickens, almost as if she wants to get away from them.

I hope she enjoys herself; she's been through so much.

Entering *The Black Dog*, a few moments after Katie, Tom is shocked by how busy it is. He can no longer see Katie's long black winter coat. Disappointed, his eyes scan the room for her, but she seems to have vanished into thin air.

After fetching a couple of drinks for himself and Kay, they settle down at Tom's favourite table at the opposite end of the room to the Christmas tree.

Tom scans the room again and finally spots Katie on the dance floor. Mesmerised by the complete change in her. Her now slim figure perfectly shapely under a pale blue sequined dress. Tom fidgets in his chair; the twitching in his underpants makes him feel uncomfortable.

Still, he can't take his eyes off her. Almost forgetting Kay is there, he jumps when her hand touches his knee.

"Do you want to dance, Tom?" Kay asks, leaning close to him to make him hear over the music.

"No, you go ahead. I'm fine here, thank you."

Disappointed, Kay makes her way to the dance floor.

Tom can't take his eyes off Katie. He watches her as she leaves the dance floor. She seems to be in pain. As she sits in a seat near the Christmas tree, Tom catches her eye, gently nods at her and raises his glass, clocking a look of confusion on Katie's face. He wonders what she's thinking.

Not realising that Kay has come back from the dance floor, Tom is suddenly soaking wet and freezing cold, taking a moment to realise what's happening. He sees Kay replace the glass on the table, the contents now dripping from his hair to his nose and down his clothes.

Anger and humiliation bubble up inside him. Tom grabs his coat from the back of the chair and follows Kay through the crowded bar and out into the street. Furious he catches up with her, vaguely hearing his dad announce that it's almost midnight, the whole pub follows them out for the firework display.

Grabbing Kay's arm as they break away from the crowd, the flash of anger apparent in Tom's eyes, "what the hell was that for? What is wrong with you?"

"I saw you. I saw you. S… st... staring at that… that... girl on the dance floor.

"So, what if I was staring? You made it plain more than once that you don't want anything serious. No strings, you always said. And besides, there were a lot of people on that dance floor."

"I saw the way you looked at her, Tom. Like you were in love with her. The way I look at you, but you never notice."

Looking at her for the first time since they left the house, Tom can see tears in her eyes. "It's OK, Tom. I know when I'm not wanted. I broke my own rule and fell for you. Something I promised myself I wouldn't do. Your reputation has preceded you."

Almost losing his patience, Tom shouts, "what do you mean, my reputation has preceded me?"

Laughing, Kay retorts, "so the only thing you picked up on from that whole conversation was about your reputation. What an absolute joke. I'm clearly wasting my time here. I'm off, Tom. I can't stay somewhere I'm not wanted."

His mouth opens to respond but Tom is left shouting at himself as Kay hurries off into the night.

Gobsmacked but somewhat relieved, Tom walks slowly home, watching the fireworks as he ascends the hill. Relief washes over him now he's saved the added aggravation of telling Kay he's doesn't want to see her again.

The chill of the midnight air mixed with the soaking he received earlier forces Tom to quicken his pace. Once home, he locks the door behind him, grabs a towel to dry his hair and throws his clothes into the washing basket. Heading to the bedroom to grab his dressing gown, he finishes his letter to Katie before retiring to bed.

Oh, my word, Katie. You looked stunning tonight. I couldn't take my eyes off you. I'm speechless. I fell for your laugh, smile, and gorgeous personality, but tonight I wanted you in my arms. I want to make love to you and never stop. Oh, Katie, how do I ask you out?

A little voice inside his head asks, *why didn't you go back to the pub?*

1992

Tom Invites Katie to Breakfast
Saturday 28th March – Afternoon

Feeling utterly exhausted, Tom has taken his first Saturday off since the start of the new year. Whilst being very lucrative and increasing the area's job opportunities, the new contract is proving difficult to manage. The whole team are pulling together, and Tom is grateful to his staff for all their hard work and support. Having eaten a light lunch Mrs D had left for him, he takes a walk in the woods to clear his head and shake off some of his exhaustion. Walking slowly through the trees, Tom can sense someone near him, walking along the path. Heading slowly for the clearing, he spots Katie wandering along. Quickening his pace, he catches up with her. He's been so busy he's barely had time to think about eating and sleeping, let alone, Katie and damn it, he misses her.

Drawing up alongside her on the path, he calls her name not to startle her.

Chatting away, teasing each other, Tom can't help but think how much better she looks now. How confident. Embarrassing her again. *Oh, I love it when you blush; it makes you look so incredibly beautiful.* Tom finds himself admonishing her. She is forever telling him off or jumping to the wrong conclusions. The final straw is when she assumes there are a string of women in his wake once he confesses to being single again. Feeling the need to explain himself, he admits that he hides behind women. All because he was hurt all those years ago.

Apologising to each other for their misunderstandings, Tom invites Katie for breakfast in the morning, asking her to walk Charlie as she confessed how much she'd missed him. With Tom going away on business, again, it suits them both. Even better if she'll do it daily while he's away. Thrilled when she agrees to breakfast but gobsmacked when she arranges to be there for 7 am. *No lie-in for me tomorrow, then.*

Bidding Katie goodbye after the arrangements have been made, Tom stands staring at her as she walks down the hill. Unable to tear his eyes away from her, he finally continues his walk once she's disappeared out of sight. Shaking his head to himself, *what it is about this girl?*

I need to ring Mrs D; someone needs to help me cook breakfast in the morning. Continuing his walk through the woods, determined not to go near George's, Tom turns off and heads towards Malthaven. Walking the extended route, Tom exits the woods from the alleyway opposite *The Red Lion.* Clocking the time, surprised he's been walking for so long, he wanders into the pub.

"Hey, Ben, how's business?"

"Tom, good to see you. It's been a while. Business is good. You?"

"Yeah, good too, but I'm knackered."

"Having your usual, Tom?"

"Please, I'll have a basket of scampi and chips too, if you're cooking yet?"

"For you, mate, anything. I'll go and start your food; the chef will be here soon anyway."

"Thank you. I'll be in my usual seat."

Having taken to carrying a pen and small notebook everywhere with him, Tom takes it out of his jeans pocket and starts to write down his thoughts from his walk. Seeing Katie again has awakened something in him. Something he has put to sleep to stop the hurt. Throwing himself into work. It begins to dawn on him that he's been avoiding intimacy, proper intimacy, for far too long. Never having found the intimacy and love he truly desires.

"You writing your memoirs there, Tom?" Ben laughs as he places Tom's basket meal on the table.

Returning the laugh, Tom shakes his head. "Nah, mate, just some ideas I'm having for work, that's all."

Partly true, Tom finishes his last scribble of ideas for the factory, leaving a mental note to speak to his father about it as soon as possible.

A Shock
Sunday 29th March

Being a domestic god isn't exactly Tom's thing; grateful to Mrs Dainty for changing her day off to help him, Tom rather enjoys cooking breakfast for himself and Katie. Full English with all the trimmings, peppermint tea for her, coffee for him and copious amounts of toast. Looking at the spread on the dining table, *there's enough here to feed an Army,* he thinks to himself. *I hope she's hungry.*

Having been up since 6 am cooking in his scruffs, Tom leaves Mrs Dainty to let Katie in while he goes to change.

Not used to eating breakfast this early, if ever, Tom surprises himself by having second helpings. Katie's presence has given him an appetite.

Wishing he was walking Charlie with her, Tom explains to Mrs Dainty that Katie will be taking the dog and may walk him while he's away too.

Once the meal is finished, they both sit back and let their food go down. Katie startles him by grabbing his hand. Letting him know that's she's there for him if he needs her. Embarrassed, Tom collects the plates, hiding the emotion bubbling behind his eyelids.

Grateful that Katie changes the subject, Tom begins washing up, answering Katie's questions regarding Mrs Dainty. She's always been there. As far back as he can remember. His grandmother died just after giving birth to his father, and Maurice took on a cleaner come nanny, Mrs Dainty's mother. When she passed away, Mrs Dainty naturally took over her duties and has been there ever since.

With Katie ready to leave, Tom calls for Charlie and grabs the bag of treats from the table. Some for her, some for Charlie. Courtesy of Mrs D. Watching them out of the window, Tom is heartened to see them wandering down the drive, in amicable silence, a spring in both of their steps.

***

Once Tom has finished packing ready for yet another business trip and a meeting with his largest client, he settles down at the dining table to read the papers. Yesterdays and todays have been sitting idle on the table. Turning straight to the sports pages, Tom checks today's paper first for the results of yesterday's races. Smiling to himself, *I'm so glad I didn't place any bets yesterday. None of the horses I would have bet on have even placed. No point going in today either. George won't be there by the time I arrive.* Pleased with himself having made a good decision, Tom continues to read the rest of the news until he is disturbed by what sounds like Charlie barking his head off.

Bit early for them to be back yet.

Even more disconcerting is the sallow-faced short gentleman in a brown suit standing on his doorstep. Tom recognises a plain-clothed police officer when he sees one. Panic threatens to take over, but Tom realises, *now is not the time to sit with my head between my legs.* Taking a deep breath, Tom invites the gentleman in. He introduces himself as Detective Giles. Tom's thoughts run riot, he's concerned about Katie, and the fact that Charlie is here, but she isn't. Sinking into his chair at the detective's request, Tom is stunned to learn that his father has been found in Pebble Woods.

Nothing Detective Giles is saying to Tom makes any sense. Found him in a burnt-out car. Badly hurt. Weak pulse. On his way to the hospital. Tom had always expected the knock on the door from his father's past, but he never expected this. Completing the formalities with Detective Giles's colleague, utter shock takes over Tom, and as he bids goodbye to the officers, he feels rather than sees Katie take the detective's vacated seat.

Making them both a strong cup of tea, Tom asks Katie to tell him everything. Her voice wavers slightly; Tom remains silent as Katie relays her morning to him.

"Oh, Tom, I don't want to upset you, but it was Charlie who found him. He was barking incessantly; I couldn't stop him. I knew something was wrong, so I quickened my pace. When I rounded the corner, all I could see was a burnt-out car. I kept calling Charlie, but he wouldn't come. He just sat there, barking for all he was worth. I ran over to him. All I could think was, Tom will kill me if he's hurt his paw again."

Taking a sip of her drink, she gathers her thoughts; a shudder passes down her spine. Unsure whether it's the awful tasting tea or the flashback to the sight she saw, she shakes her head, takes a breath and carries on.

"I thought I could smell something cooking, but as I got closer, I realised there was someone in there. I had to put my hand over my mouth to stop me from throwing up. I only realised it was Jack when I saw the birthmark on his neck. Oh, Tom, I thought he was dead."

Staring up at Tom's face, the tears gently roll down hers. A look of bewilderment on his. Tom didn't speak. He couldn't. Waiting for her to continue, he takes a sip of his drink.

"One of the neighbours opened the window and shouted to shut him up," I remember thinking, she was

301

louder than the dog. I didn't know what to do. I checked Jack's pulse. It was weak and thready, but I had to go and get help."

Fighting back the tears for Tom's sake, Katie carries on.

"I didn't want to leave him, but I had no choice. I raced back to the woman leaning out of her window and told her to call an ambulance. I've never prayed so hard in my life that she actually called them, and they could save him."

Taking another sip of tea, Katie carries on, still holding on to Tom's hand.

"I got back to him and kept shouting his name. Nothing. No response."

Thinking back to his twisted blood-soaked hand protruding out of the top of the car. Not wishing to upset Tom, she omits the gory details, "I shouted to him to squeeze my hand if he could hear me."

Looking at her expectantly, praying himself now, Tom is relieved when Katie tells him she felt what she thought was a tiny squeeze. Enough to give them both hope.

"Charlie was licking Jack's other hand while I kept asking him to squeeze my finger. A few minutes later, I heard the sirens in the background and prayed the woman who called them would direct them to us. I needn't have worried, though. Charlie went to fetch them."

Putting her face in her hands for a few moments, trying to forget the scene she had witnessed.

"I don't remember much else, I'm afraid. I moved out of the way so the paramedics could get to him, and I had to sit down because I was feeling dizzy. They spoke to me and asked me questions, but I couldn't tell them much, except his name and where you live."

Not wishing to upset Tom anymore, she refrains from telling him half the village were out staring at the car. Luckily the police cordoned off the area so no one could see what was happening.

"I wanted to come back here and tell you myself, but Detective Giles wouldn't let me. I'm sorry, Tom." Katie says as she looks up at him. A mixture of shock, horror and bewilderment on his face.

Katie sits still, waiting for Tom to speak. His voice cracking slightly, he finally asks her what she thinks happened.

Uncertain how to answer, she is loath to say it, but she thinks it was deliberate. She couldn't make him out except for his birthmark, and according to rumour, he hadn't been home for a few days.

Watching Tom's face, Katie is shocked at the vehemence in his words when he spits out that Jack had probably been up to his old tricks.

Snatching his hand from under Katie's faster than he intended, Tom gets up from his seat, informing Katie he's going to the hospital. At a loss for something to say. Katie bids him goodbye, leaving Tom staring. On her way out, she hears him say he's glad it was her who found him and not a stranger. Oddly, Katie feels the same.

Tom Visits Jack in hospital
Sunday 29th March – Evening

"Oh, my God," Tom exclaims as he enters the room where his dad is lying. "From Katie's description, I knew it was bad, but I never expected this."

"Would you like to sit down, Sir? You've had a nasty shock." The kindly doctor, as tall as he is round, asks Tom as he walks with him to his father's bedside.

"No, no, thank you, I'm fine." Swaying gently on his feet, Tom falls backwards. Luckily the doctor, his reflexes on high alert, catches Tom and guides him onto the chair behind him. Shocked at seeing his father in such a bad way, Tom feels all the past resentment, hurt and pain flow away.

Please don't leave me, Dad. Things are just starting to look up for us.

Leaning forward in his chair, Tom takes his father's hand in his, gently, the cuts and bruises on his hands and knuckles protruding like arthritic demons. "Dad, can you hear me?"

Tom feels a gentle squeeze.

Phew, thank goodness, you taught him well, Katie. Tom smiles to himself.

Sensing the doctor hovering behind him, Tom turns toward him, "what's the prognosis, doctor?"

"It was touch and go, but we are hopeful he will make a full recovery. He was badly beaten and has suffered several burns; we are still running tests, so we are unsure of the extent of the damage at present."

Tom thinks he can see Jack's face swelling as he is sitting there, barely recognisable. *Now I know what Katie meant about his birthmark.*

Shaking his head, Tom is at a loss for what to do. Hearing a strange gurgling sound brings Tom back to his senses.

Looking around for the doctor, he releases his father's hand and shouts for help. The doctor rushes in and asks Tom to leave for a moment. Praying his father will be OK, Tom walks along the corridor to what he believes must be the relative's room. Entering, he helps himself to a drink from the coffee pot on the table in the corner and collapses into the chair.

Unsure how long he's been sitting there, lost in his tumultuous thoughts. *Just when everything was going so well. I can't let this set me back. Dad will be fine.*

Tom keeps repeating. *Dad will be fine.* Over and over. Finishing the last of his now cold coffee, Tom makes his way back to his father's ward, only making it as far as the door he collides with his mother on her way out.

"Mom, you've seen him then?" Judging by the ghostly paleness of her face, it now seems like a stupid question.

Sylvie can only nod when she looks up and pulls her son into her arms; Tom reels at the stench of the alcohol on her breath. "Mother, I thought you'd stopped all that."

"All what?"

"The drinking."

"Tom, please. Don't. Not now. Your father is lucky to be alive."

"Yes, I know."

"They say if it hadn't been for the young girl who found him…"

Choking back tears, Sylvie takes a minute to gather herself again. "Do you know who that was, Son? I'd really like to thank her. Send her something… I don't know. Do something…"

"You already know her, Mom. It was Katie."

306

"Really? The poor girl must have had an awful fright. I'm somehow glad it was her, though. Not a stranger."

"Yes, I'm glad too."

"Have you already seen him, Son?"

"Yes, I have. He was making a funny sound, so the doctors had to come in to him."

"Oh, yes, they said that was just the position he was lying in. The tube in his mouth moved slightly. He tried to cough, but… anyway, he's OK now. They've made him more comfortable."

Heaving a sigh of relief, Tom places his hand on his mother's shoulder, "come on; there's nothing we can do here. We need to go home and get some rest—Doctor's orders."

Nodding her head in agreement, they make their way to Tom's car, Sylvie having arrived in a police car.

Climbing into the car, Sylvie puts her hand on Tom's arm, "I'm so sorry, Son. I can't believe it's taken something like this to make me realise how bad a mother… and wife I've been."

"Now isn't the time for a guilt trip, mother, but now you mention it, it hasn't been easy. The bullying at school was enough, but getting home and finding you drunk, that was the pits."

"I know, Son. I am doing something about it."

Not believing her, Tom responds, "so you say."

"I am. I've been reading loads of books. I'm getting better. I've been to church too; I even took Katie with me."

Shocked, Tom asks, "which one?" *Katie never said.*

"The one in Malthaven."

"Oh," was all Tom could think of to say. Realising he hasn't been for a while, he wonders whether he should go back. *Maybe I'll get some answers about Dad's attack?*

Although, it doesn't take a genius to work out that it's connected to his past.

"I am trying, Son," Sylvie says again, sure that Tom doesn't believe a word she says.

"Why do you smell like a brewery then?"

Not wishing to discuss where she's been or who she's been with, especially not with her son, she makes up an excuse, "oh, it was a friend's birthday yesterday. We were out celebrating."

Just from the look on her face, Tom knows she's lying. *Why does she keep doing this?*

Both of them fall silent for a while. Tom breaks the tension and starts the engine, "let's get out of here. This place is depressing."

Taking her back to his house, he makes them both a strong cup of tea. Brandy in his. Extra sugar in hers. They sit opposite one another at the kitchen table. For want of something to say, Tom asks, "did you get a grilling off the police?"

"Yes, they made me feel like I was guilty."
Were you?

"Did you?" Sylvie asks.

"No, it wasn't as bad as I expected. I guess that's still to come."

"They asked all sorts of questions, Tom. I haven't seen him for a few days, though, so I was at a loss with most of them. Apparently, he's been back to his old drinking haunts in Hopland. They found a train ticket in his belongings."

"Why on earth did he go there. He knows they have long memories, and anyway, I thought that was all behind you now."

"So did I, Son. So did I."

Taking a sip of her still piping hot tea, the sweetness contorts her face as she swallows.

"We haven't been getting on lately. I know it's not your concern, but I think he's seeing another woman."

There I said it out loud.

"What?!" Tom almost chokes on his tea. "Don't be stupid mother. He hasn't got time."

"Seriously, Son, he says he's going to business meetings. I know he isn't."

"And how do you know?"

"Call it... women's intuition."

"Well, your intuition is off the radar then. He's been coming to meetings with me, Mom. He's helping me with the business."

"He never said."

"You never listen."

Feelings of shock and confusion engulf Sylvie's already clouded brain. *Oh my, what have I done?*

"Let's not worry about any of this now, Mom, he's going to be in hospital for a while, and he'll need a lot of looking after when he comes out. The doc thinks he'll be in for a couple of months at least.

"Mmm," Sylvie has drifted off into a dream world and barely registers what Tom is saying.

"Mom, did you hear me?"

"Yes, Son. Who did this to him? Why was he so stupid as to go back to his old haunts?"

"I don't know, Mom, but it couldn't have been anyone from there, he only went for a couple of days, and he'd only just got back when it happened. I assume. Has he been down before?"

"I don't know, Son. I don't know what to do. I have to go to the police station tomorrow to meet with Detective Giles."

"They haven't said they're going to interview me yet."

"They will, Son."

"There's nothing I can tell them. We've not long started speaking again."

"I know, Tom, that was all my fault too. I can't believe he stood by me all these years."

Talking to herself more than Tom, Sylvie pushes herself up from her seat at the table, "I'm going to sort myself out. I'm going home to throw all the booze away."

"You can't go home in that state, Mom." As loath as he is to do anything for her, he knows this situation will bring them closer, and he feels he has to try and rebuild the bridges. He was no innocent, after all.

"The spare room is made up, Mom. Stay here, even if it's only for tonight."

Nodding in agreement, both of them utterly exhausted, Tom makes them both a mug of Horlicks, and they slowly make their way upstairs. The enormity of the situation suddenly impacts them like a ten-tonne train.

Tom sleeps fitfully and wakes early, heading into the office. Most of the workers will have undoubtedly heard by now, it is a small town, after all. *I'm going to need all the help I can get.*

Calling a meeting and explaining the situation, the workers, who will never forget Tom's kindness last Christmas, rally around to support him. Assuring him, they will look after the business as if it were their own.

Tom loses himself in his thoughts as he makes his way to his office. *This was no random attack. Someone is out to get Jack. Could they be after me too?*

Jack Discharges Himself
Sunday 12th April

After two weeks in the hospital, Jack is looking much better. He demands to be discharged to recover at home.

"Jack, we can't look after you properly at home," Sylvie sighs, shocked that he is packed and ready to leave when she visits. "What are you thinking?"

"I'm coming home, Sylv. I'm not staying here a minute longer. I'm stronger than I was when I first came in."

Well, that's not hard, is it?

"You can barely walk," Sylvie screams at him, "what's wrong with you." Just as she tries to coax him back into bed, Tom appears in the doorway,

"Dad, what are you doing?"

"Don't you start, Son. I'm going home. No arguments."

Jack raises his hand as they both attempt to protest.

"Can't you do something, doctor?" Sylvie asks in desperation."

"I'm sorry, Mrs Gold, we can't force your husband to stay. He's already signed the discharge papers."

Shaking their heads in disbelief, they struggle with him out to the car park.

Tom has a sudden brainwave. "Why don't you ask Mrs D to help? I'm sure she could use the extra money, and she would probably enjoy it."

Before Jack can protest, Sylvie has agreed.

"Jack, don't even think it. I can't cope with you on my own, so it's that, or you can pay for careers. Or stay here. Your choice." Sylvie commands, brooking no argument.

As Sylvie shuts the car door behind her husband, she walks Tom towards his car. "What are you doing, Mom?"

Looking around to make sure Jack hasn't wound the window down and he can't hear them, she replies, "Did you know they've arrested John?"

"John. Who's John?"

"Katie's ex-boyfriend."

Stopping short in his tracks, "you're joking. What the hell has he got to do with it?"

"No idea, but I know he didn't do it, Son. I went to see him in prison." Tom looks down at his mother, his eyes questioning her as if to say, and how would you know.

"He didn't do it, Tom."

"How can you be so sure? Look at the mess he made of Katie. He almost killed her. Don't bloody tell me, you have a soft spot for him." With disgust in his eyes, Tom turns away from her and opens his car door.

"I'm telling you, he didn't do it, and we need to find out who did."

Staring at her in disbelief, "Leave it to the police, Mom." Knowing his mother once she gets the bit between her teeth, he feels the need to reinforce his opinion. "I mean it, Mom, leave it. If his past caught up with him, they'll find out. We have enough to deal with."

They don't know the half of it. Nobody does. Sylvie whispers to herself.

Holding her hands up in the air, "OK, Son, OK." She prays the police will investigate further but has her doubts. Detective Giles is sure he has the right man.

312

Tom Visits The Black Dog
Saturday 20th June

The next couple of months flash by for Tom. He barely has a moment to worry about Jack. Knowing he's in safe hands with Mrs D, who grudgingly agrees to work for them for three months until he's back on his feet. Work is going well, he's gambling less, and with business trips galore and new clients coming on almost daily, he's rather pleased with himself.

Jack has asked Tom and Sylvie to keep their eyes on the pub, and knowing Katie will probably be working this evening, Tom dresses in his favourite tight jeans with a turn-up, printed vest and doc martin boots and has a slow walk to *The Black Dog*. Being a gorgeous evening, he takes time to smell the greenery. Taking a slight detour so that he can walk through his favourite part of the woods, he stops and listens to the birds, laughing as he spots two squirrels chasing each other up and down the branches of the trees. Losing each other in amongst the leaves.

That's the life, eh. I'm coming back as a squirrel. Tom decides. Enjoying the evening breeze on his face, Tom glances at his watch and hoping to be able to have a nice long chat with Katie, he hurries on to the pub.

Wow, this place is busier than ever. Dad was right. Katie is doing a good job. Impressed, Tom heads to the bar. He knows his dad has been in today, and seeing the accounts, Tom isn't worried about the pub in the slightest. Grateful for that. He tries to catch Katie's attention, but she's deep in conversation with a couple and scribbling away furiously. *Ooh, I wonder what that is then. Entertainment booking, maybe?*

The young lad who's been working with her since, what was his name… Michael, that's it, since he left, is all of a sudden in front of him, waiting to take his order.

"You're usual, Mr Gold?"

"Yes, please, a pint of snakebite."

Pouring his drink and taking his money, he leaves Tom pondering over Katie.

Doesn't look like I'm going to be able to speak with her tonight.

Tom is disappointed, glad the pub is thriving but disappointed Katie hasn't even noticed him. He watches her work for a short while. Realising how much he misses her company. Happy that the pub is so busy and she looks so… content.

Wanting, no needing an early night, Tom takes a piece of paper from his ever-faithful notebook and scribbles a note to let Katie know he'll see her next Sunday if not before. Catching the attention of the young man behind the bar, he passes him the note then leaves. Half smiling at the busyness of the pub but half sad that he yet again didn't get a chance to speak to Katie.

Katie Shocks Tom
Sunday 28th June

Tom, up early for a Sunday, hopes Katie has received his note.

Sitting on his favourite bench, he stares at the stunning views of bright green fields intermingled with houses and country estates. He waits patiently for Katie. Checking his watch every few minutes. He's very early to ensure he doesn't miss her. Again.

Shielding his eyes from the early morning sun, low in the sky, he sees Katie's head bobbing up and down as she makes her way to the top of the hill.

He gets up from the bench and walks towards her, falling into step with her. As she reaches the top of the hill, she stops a moment to regulate her breathing. Tom is first to speak, but he is shocked at the turn of events the conversation takes. Pondering on them later that evening, Tom is ashamed to say he feels quite jealous of Katie. Her life is moving on. She's booked a holiday. A holiday abroad at that. The girl who's never been more than 10 miles from home. And even more surprising is, she's going on her own.

In his mind's eye, Tom can see the beautiful golden sandy beach, the deep blue ocean and himself and Katie swimming with the turtles.

Shaking himself out of his reverie. How he wishes he was going with her.
So many questions run through his mind. Where? When? Why? He remembers gushing them all out on one go, making Katie laugh. *Why didn't she answer me? And why didn't I offer to go with her?*

She's changed so much, and she seems so happy.
Maybe I should take a leaf out of her book.

Katie
Saturday 29th August

Watching Katie as she walks towards him, staring at her feet, shielding her eyes from the sun. He knows she'll bump into him if he doesn't move. Tom leans against the wall outside Vera's. *She seems to be in a hurry. Wonder where she's going?*

Not moving, Tom waits for Katie to stumble into him, asking her where she's going. Katie tells him she's shopping for last-minute holiday items. Unbelievably, Tom had been so busy again, he'd forgotten all about Katie and her holiday.

She looks amazing. He thinks to himself; I wish I were going with her. Complimenting her and pleased, she seems so happy. Before he can stop himself, Tom has instructed her to cancel the taxi she has booked for the airport. Promising he will take her, despite the fact that they have to be there by 4 am. Staring down at Katie's face, full of concern for him. He assures her he's OK. Before he leaves, he confirms he will take her to the airport.

Why am I torturing myself? I need to ask her out or keep away. Now I'm taking her to the bloody airport.

Tom Takes Katie to the Airport
Monday 7th September

It is with mixed emotions that Tom knocks on Katie's door shortly before 4 am. He almost didn't turn up. Picking the phone up several times in the past hour in an attempt to call a taxi for her.

Why am I so scared of my feelings for this woman?

Tom notes how badly Katie's hands are shaking as she answers his knock.

Grabbing her suitcase, incredulous at the weight of it, Tom drags it up the path and loads it in his car.

Tom isn't sure why he feels so strange this morning. Something seems to have shifted in their relationship just at that moment, as he catches her eye, but he can't quite pinpoint what it is. Tom starts the car while he waits for Katie to lock up, hoping the journey won't be uncomfortable.

Katie has barely closed the car door before she asks Tom if he's OK. His only response is that he's worrying about his parents and work. Chatting away, Tom drops the bombshell that her ex, John, has been arrested for Jack's attack. More bombshells for Katie as he tells her Sylvie had visited him in prison. Neither of them believing he was responsible.

"Jesus Christ, Tom, I had no idea. I should have expected it when Charlie found the ring, but…"

Tom turns to face her, intending to ask her what she means… what ring, but all he can see is the contents of her handbag being strewn all over his car?

Before Tom can question what on earth she's doing, she forces a note into Tom's hand, which she'd found in the zipper of her bag. Katie apologies profusely; she'd forgotten it was there.

Quickly she explains how she came to have it.

"Oh, God, Tom, it must have been a year or so ago when Michael worked at the pub. Do you remember him?" Not pausing for a breath long enough for Tom to respond, Katie continues. "He called me into the kitchen just as my shift was about to finish. I was watching you walk past the window, and he asked me to look at something. It was this." Katie says, pointing at the note. "I questioned him on it. He says he found it if I remember correctly." Katie's brows furrow as she tries to recall the conversation. How could she have forgotten about this?

Tom, not daring to breathe, waits for her to continue.

"I'm sure he said he found it with the crisp boxes when he was cleaning the kitchen.

Staring at her, Tom can only listen in disbelief.

Was she protecting someone? No, she can't be. She's my friend.

"I asked again if he knew anything, but he denied it. He seemed to be telling the truth, but I never trusted him. Not fully. I wasn't sure what to do with it, so I stuffed it in here. I rarely use this bag now and completely forgot about it. I'm so sorry."

Grabbing her things off the floor of Tom's car, she turns back to him, "he kept asking about John. They knew each other, somehow."

Tom squints at the note, "but what the hell does it mean. 'leav the ney in he burn ou ca'?"

Rushing to get into the airport, Katie takes her case from Tom and dashes away, shouting something

320

incoherent after her. Leaving Tom staring at the note, trying to make sense of it all.

Short Stop at the Police Station

Monday 7th September

Barely able to think straight, Tom climbs back into his car and heads straight to the police station, even though it's only just turned 5 am.

Thankfully the station is quiet; Tom approaches the officer at the desk.

"Is Detective Giles around, please?"

The young curly-haired probationary officer, whose name on the desk defines him as Gavin James Nicholls, looks up from his paperwork, "just a minute, Sir, I'll check. I haven't seen him yet, though, so I doubt it."

"OK, thank you."

Moving away from the desk while he makes the call up to the CID office, Tom looks around the station, gripping the note firmly in his hand.

"Excuse me, Sir," the young officer calls to Tom.

Walking back to the desk, Tom asks, "is he here?"

"No, Sir, I'm afraid not. He's not due in until 8.30 am for a briefing. Can I take a message, or would you like to come back later?"

"Erm, could you give this to him, please?" Tom asks as he almost grudgingly shows the officer the note.

"Can I ask what it is, please, Sir?"

"I'm not sure, it may be evidence in a brutal attack on my father, but I don't know."

Although the young officer is new to the force, just by glancing at the piece of paper, he knows it's important.

"Could you hang on just a while, please, Sir? I need to check with my sergeant to make sure."

"Yes, of course."

At least he's being thorough.

Picking up the telephone again, he explains the situation to his sergeant. "Yes, Sir."

Listening intently and taking notes to make sure he hasn't missed anything, "yes, Sir, I understand, I'll do that now. No, I checked. There isn't a detective available at present. Will do. Thank you, Sir."

Replacing the receiver and grabbing an empty clear evidence bag from the filing cabinet next to his desk, he turns back to Tom.

Opening the bag, he asks, "could you please place it flat in here so that the note can be read?"

Tom does as he's bid. Gavin seals the packet. Taking his notebook out, he asks Tom for a few details regarding the incident in question, takes his name, address and telephone number and passes the notebook to Tom for his signature. Assigning the note as exhibit GJN1. Adding these details to the evidence bag too, he returns his attention to Tom.

"Could you just wait for a few moments, please? My sergeant would like to have a quick chat with you before you leave?"

"Yes, of course, no problem," Tom responds, wondering if he's done the right thing, bringing the note in.

The duty sergeant, pleased with the work young Gavin has done, asks Tom a couple of questions. Satisfied that he has nothing to hide, he allows him to leave. Letting him know that one of the detectives from CID will be in touch with him shortly.

Thanking them both, Tom leaves the station, feeling a strange sense of relief.

Maybe we'll finally get some answers now.

Tom's Visit to Jack
Monday 7th September – Evening

Letting himself in the backdoor of his parents' house, Tom calls out, "Dad, are you here?"

"Ah, yes, Son, in the living room."

Tom wanders into the living room. His father is sitting at the table, his face buried in a pile of paperwork. Without looking up, Jack speaks, "I'm glad you're here, Son. I was going to come and see you tonight. I want to talk to you about the pub." Waving the paperwork, he's been reading at Tom, "sit down, Son. Sit down."

Met with a wall of silence, Jack looks up, "What's up?" he asks, seeing the strange look on Tom's face.

Slowly lowering himself onto the sofa directly in Jack's view. "There's been a… development."

"What kind of development?"

Tom explains the bizarre happenings from this morning as Jack listens, open-mouthed.

"Why did you take the note to the station, Son?"

"Why would I not, Dad?"

"I would have thought it best to bring it here."

"Whatever for? Surely this means they can investigate properly. Maybe release an innocent man from prison? I know John's no angel, but…"

Even more certain of his course of action now, Jack changes the subject. "Oh well, what's done is done. Let's talk about the pub."

Confused at his father's conversation change, Tom listens intently to his ideas for the pub.

His decision already made, Jack tells Tom, "I'm giving the pub to Katie. Unless you have any objections, of course."

Why the hell.

"Tom, you've gone quiet. Would you rather I didn't?"

"No, no, not at all, I have no objections. I just don't understand why."

"I have my reasons, Son, and she did save my life, after all."

Knowing his dad won't say what they are, no matter how much he pushes, Tom asks, "what does Mom say?"

"She thinks it's a great idea. I've no use for it anymore, and I want to retire."

"What are you going to do for money?"

"I have enough, Son, let's leave it at that. It's time for the younger generation to take over, and you don't need it. You have your legacy with the factory."

Still reeling and having had enough shocks for one day, Tom bids his father a good evening and drives home.

Family Gathering
Saturday 26th September

Things are going well for Tom, but he's feeling apprehensive as he dresses for an evening with his parents. The first time they've all been together since his grandfather's funeral.

Tom drives the couple of miles to his parent's house. Using the car as an excuse not to drink. He needs to keep a clear head to have any chance of building a proper relationship with them. He hopes his mother does the same.

Sitting down to their evening meal, Sylvie has cooked Tom's favourite again. Her idea of a peace offering.

"Did you know Katie is buying the cottage on Dolphin Brook Lane?" Sylvie asks Tom in an effort to get the conversation flowing.

Tom almost chokes on his chips, "No, I didn't. When did that happen?"

"Today. She came in *The Cave* all flustered and on edge. Apparently, she looked at it when she was with John, but…"

Without needing to say more, Sylvie continues her meal. Tom still has the day he found Katie lying on the floor like a frightened animal imprinted on his memory. "She never said anything last time I saw her. I wonder why?"

"Didn't know I would think," Sylvie says between mouthfuls. "It sounded like it was a last-minute call, and Shaun is helping to make sure she gets it."

At the mention of the name Shaun, Tom skin prickles, and a shudder runs down his spine. "Shaun, who's Shaun?"

"The estate agent. Tom, what's wrong? You look pale."

"Oh, nothing. I'm fine." To take his mind of the memories now niggling in his head, Tom turns the conversation back round to Katie.

"That's all I know, Son. I'm surprised you don't know more than me. About time you two got together, isn't it?"

Tom finishes the last bite of his meal before he looks at his mother, who is gazing at him expectantly.

"I wish, Mom. I wish."

"Well, do something about it then."

Jack, having kept quiet so far, savouring his meal too much to get involved with idle gossip, suddenly speaks, "Tom, we have a few things we need to go through with you."

Clearing the plates away, Jack brings out piles of paperwork.

"I know about you giving the pub to Katie. What else can there be?"

Trying hard to find the right words, Jack picks up his glasses, more for something to do than because he needs them, when Sylvie responds, "we're getting divorced, Son."

Having mentioned it to Katie earlier today, Jack thinks it's only fair they tell Tom too. Not wanting him to hear from elsewhere.

Not in the least surprised or, if the truth be told, the least bit bothered, Tom shrugs his shoulders nonchalantly. "Whatever makes you happy."

"You don't seem bothered, Son," Jack states.

"It's nothing to do with me, is it? You're old enough to make your own decisions. I'm just surprised it hasn't happened before."

Nodding in agreement, Sylvie and Jack both breathe a sigh of relief. The evening is going better than either of them expected.

"Any news from the police?" Tom blurts out, not wishing to discuss his parents sham of a marriage any further.

"Couple of visits, but not much. So far, anyway." Jack answers. "I just hope they don't do too much digging."

Not wishing to know any more for fear he will be implicated in something dodgy, Tom attempts to take his leave.

"Just a minute, Son, aren't you going to give us your news?"

"My news. I don't have any."

"No new contracts then?"

"Oh, that, yes, Dad, I have won another new contract, so the business is going well. I should be able to give you the rest of the loan back next month."

"Don't worry about it, Son. It will only be included in the divorce settlement, and neither of us is bothered about it, are we Sylv?"

"No."

For the first time since he arrived, Tom notices how relaxed everything feels. *Strange, considering the news.*

"Are you both happy?" Tom suddenly asks, surprising himself as much as them.

Glancing at each other, they both state in unison,

"Yes," Sylvie continues, "we are happier than we've been in a long time. We agreed to do everything amicably and remain friends."

An old bond from years gone by ensures that will always be the case. They both know too much.

A companionable silence falls over the room, but Tom, not wishing to stay any longer than necessary, thanks his parents and bids them goodnight.

Pleased with how the evening went, Tom drives with a clear head for the first time in a long time. Life is looking good for him. Although he knows he still has quite a way to go.

Tom Helps Katie Move
Saturday 5th December

Tom is astounded that half the town is blocked off with vehicles, all helping Katie to move house. Filing along in convoy from Katie's tiny old flat to her new cottage.

The first to arrive, Tom is overwhelmed by a sense that he's been here before. The figure of eight door knocker is the first thing to attract his attention, a sense of calm washes over him as he carries the first of the boxes down the path from his car. He can see Katie slowly ambling along the road, no room in any of the vehicles to accommodate her. Placing the box gently on the wall near the front door, Tom pulls his thick winter coat around him and blows on his hands to relieve the numbness. Glancing around him, he can't shake the feeling that he's been here before, but he is absolutely certain he hasn't been. Stamping his feet to warm himself, *why didn't I just wait in the car!*

Tom shouts to Katie to let them in. Hurrying her pace, she opens the door, standing back to let Tom enter.

With everyone rallying around, the heavy items are placed where Katie wants them, and the boxes are stacked in her new living room.

One by one, all the helpers leave, but Tom holds back, wanting desperately to speak to her. Katie disappears into the kitchen to make herself a cup of tea. Tom watches from the living room.

Now's your chance. Ask her.

"Katie," Tom calls softly from the living room. Not hearing him over the sound of the boiling kettle, Tom makes a move to walk towards the kitchen.

She needs to settle in. Maybe next time.

331

Quietly Tom turns on his heel and lets himself out of the front door, careful not to let the door bang behind him, and heads home.

The End

Acknowledgements & Contacts

Thank you for reading. I'd love to hear from you. Feel free to share your thoughts with me about my book. I would be very grateful if you would leave a review on my page.

https://www.goodreads.com/author/show/20889351.Lisa_M_Billingham

You can contact me at lisa@lisambillingham.com or via my website:
www.lisambillingham.com

Charitable organisations
https://www.veteransfoundation.org.uk/
https://www.samaritans.org/
https://www.mind.org.uk/

Professional business contacts:

Book editor, Kathy De Cicco
www.daggerandkill.com

Cover design by Bill Bishop
https://www.arcanumdesign.net/

Author headshot photograph by Andy Neale
https://whizzyfingers.weebly.com/

Social media content and copywriter, Sarah Mullaney
https://www.shesawriter.co.uk/

Spiritual coach and mentor (all round good egg)
Nigel Tinsdale
ntinsdale@gmail.com

Website designer & IT Support - Lee Baker
https://it-techno-phobes.co.uk/

Marketing support – Arup Biswas
https://www.absolutelywrite.co.uk/

Contacts for support if you have been affected by anything contained in this novel.

Steve 'Lobby' Thornton
https://www.trojanwellbeing.com/

Lisa Tighe
https://www.lisatighetherapyandcoaching.co.uk/

Marie Jenkins
https://www.advanceyourwellbeing.co.uk/

Andrew Mullaney
https://www.andrewjmullaney.co.uk/

Gareth Keyte
https://www.oxygencoachingcompany.com/

If you enjoyed this book, you might like to read previous work by Lisa M Billingham.

Katie – A New Chapter

PREFACE

Katie lets her book fall into the white sand as she gazes out across the vast blue ocean, watching the waves curl their way up and down the beach. Rocks and boulders, their edges worn smooth by the endless movement of the waves break the surface to her right. At this time of day, the sun is just perfect and she is enjoying the feel of it on her naked skin. A little smile touches her lips at that thought. Whoever would have thought that frumpy Katie Chester would be lying naked on a beach? The same Katie who always wears black trousers and grey high-necked jumpers. That particular memory pushes at a corner of her mind taunting her, reminding her that her body isn't good enough to be seen naked, let alone on a beach. Taking a gentle breath, she pushes that thought away. She is now a slim size ten and she feels a world away from that frumpy, overdressed girl she once was. Life has been far too stressful lately and she closes her eyes letting the warmth of the sun kiss every part of her naked body until she wants to purr like a contented cat. This is a world away from the dull, grey, and damp days back home.

Something catches her attention and she opens her eyes, frowning, she looks along the beach. Her gaze is immediately drawn to the muscular figure of a handsome stranger standing a few feet away. Using her hand to shield her eyes from the bright sun she can't help but notice that he too is naked. Attempting to avert her eyes from his freely swinging member, she looks away, embarrassed, hoping he hasn't noticed, then she spots a large knife strapped to his calf. 'How odd,' she muses. His piercing blue eyes demand her attention. As she takes it all in, he waves her over. There was no hesitation on her part as she swings her feet off the sunbed and into the sand, warm between her toes. Standing up, she walks over to him. She knows that he is watching her and she revels in the feeling of being admired. As she approaches him, he holds out his hand, taking it, she feels his firm grip as his strong fingers wrap around hers.

"Swim with me, Katie," his voice sends little tingles down her spine as they walk together to the sea. The waves feel cool as they curl over her hot skin, sending goose bumps down her body as they wade into deeper water.

Katie gently kicks off as they paddle slowly through the clear water heading towards the rock that she had seen earlier. The waves gently push at her as she gracefully moves through the water still feeling the warmth of the sun on her back. As they reach the rocks, he is first out of the water, turning to offer his help to Katie who grasps his hand. She notes the strength in his body as he pulls her from the powerful grip of the ocean. He holds her hand as they make their way across the rugged rock formation, the promise of a little piece of heaven on the other side.

"Wait!" Katie sees something moving at the edge of the water.

'Help me...' the words whisper through her mind.

As she gets nearer, she sees, the beautiful brown and mahogany colours of a turtle's shell peeping through the water. It looks straight at her, its black eyes begging her for help. She could swear tears were forming there. Without a care for her safety, she dives straight back into the water only vaguely aware that her handsome stranger is close behind.

"Look!" she tugs at an old orange fishing net that is wrapped in endless knots trapping this beautiful creature.

He joins her in the water and somehow, between them, they manage to get the turtle out of the water and onto the rocks. Katie sits holding it on her bare legs where it remains still.

"How could anyone do something like this?" she whispers. The net is sharp and hard on her fingers as she tries to work it free from where it is wrapped around the turtle's shell and flippers. There was no way that it would have been able to swim. It almost breaks Katie's heart to think that this gentle creature would probably have died if they hadn't come along. It still might unless they can somehow get it free. With tears burning in her eyes and barely able to see, she pulls angrily at the stubborn net.

"Here, let me."

Again, she looks into blue eyes that seem to see into her soul. His sharp knife easily cuts through the net as they work together in a comfortable silence.

Katie holds her breath as his long fingers pull away the last of the net before he gently checks the turtle for any injuries. She has no idea what they were going to do if it needs any treatment – she doesn't even know if there are any vets out here…

"All clear."

Finally, she can breathe and the turtle, as if it knows that it is now free, turns to the sea. It is almost as if it were asking to go free.

"Let's get you back where you belong," he lifts the turtle easily off Katie's legs, returning it home. Katie stands

337

alongside him, as he places the turtle in the water. For several long seconds, it lets the waves wash over it and then heads for deeper waters.

Katie was only vaguely aware that her handsome stranger had his arm around her but then she rests her head on his shoulder. Suddenly the turtle breaks the surface of the water, and Katie could have sworn it looked straight at her as if to say thank you.

"Beautiful," Katie whispers feeling that today, they have both achieved something rather special.

"Ready for another swim?" he asks smiling down at her.

Katie nods thinking that maybe they would see their turtle friend. This time the cool of the water is welcoming after sitting out in the hot sun. Together they calmly swim until they reach another outcrop of rocks where they get out. Feeling weary, Katie finds a large, smooth rock and stretches out letting the sun warm her body. She can hear the sounds of the waves lapping as her breathing falls into the same rhythm. She is only vaguely aware of her handsome stranger lying down next to her, cocooning her in the warmth of his aura.

Tension that she didn't know she had, slowly slips away as she gazes up into the sky. A huge cloud in the shape of a teddy bear catches her attention as suddenly she rises to meet it, the cloud wrapping itself around her. It feels safe here. Nothing matters on the cloud.

Lying back, she can see the setting of the sun as beautiful pinks, reds, and oranges are painted across the sky. Turning, she is surprised to feel the warmth of the man's body as he lies next to her. He turns to face her as he takes her hand and gently places something in it, closing her fingers over it. Puzzled, she opens her hand to see a large silver key lying on her palm. She quickly closes her eyes against the burn of the tears...

338